Praise for *The Witch of Belladonna Bay*

"Murder, mystery, and magic meld in a novel of absolute enchantment. . . . Palmieri's book is a stunner."
— Caroline Leavitt, *New York Times* bestselling author of *Pictures of You* and *Is This Tomorrow*

"If you're a lover of Southern fiction, magic in its many forms, and the kind of storytelling that keeps you turning the pages, you've come to the right place, y'all."
— Lesley Kagen, *New York Times* bestselling author of *Whistling in the Dark*

"Palmieri delivers a rich and magical story about the two most powerful forces in life: family and love."
— Elin Hilderbrand, author of *Beautiful Day*

Praise for *The Witch of Little Italy*

"Enthralling . . . It'll keep you on the edge of your seat until the end."
— *RT Book Reviews*

"A magical story of family, secrets, loss, and rediscovery written in beautiful prose and sprinkled with effervescent characters you won't soon forget."
— Karen White, *New York Times* bestselling author of *The Beach Trees*

Also by Suzanne Palmieri

The Witch of Little Italy
The Witch of Belladonna Bay
I'll Be Seeing You (as Suzanne Hayes)
Empire Girls (as Suzanne Hayes)

The Witch of

Bourbon Street

Suzanne Palmieri

ST. MARTIN'S GRIFFIN

NEW YORK

THE WITCH OF BOURBON STREET. Copyright © 2015 by Suzanne Palmieri. All rights reserved. Printed in the United States of America. For information, address St. Martin's Press, 175 Fifth Avenue, New York, N.Y. 10010.

www.stmartins.com

Library of Congress Cataloging-in-Publication Data

Palmieri, Suzanne.
    The witch of Bourbon Street : a novel / Suzanne Palmieri.—First edition.
    pages cm
  ISBN 978-1-250-05619-1 (trade paperback)
  ISBN 978-1-4668-7773-3 (e-book)
  1. Young women—Louisiana—Fiction. 2. Families—Louisiana—
Fiction. 3. Witches—Fiction. 4. Domestic fiction. I. Title.
  PS3616.A353W58 2015
  813'.6—dc23
                                                             2015013349

St. Martin's Griffin books may be purchased for educational, business, or promotional use. For information on bulk purchases, please contact the Macmillan Corporate and Premium Sales Department at 1-800-221-7945, extension 5442, or write to specialmarkets@macmillan.com.

FIRST EDITION: JULY 2015

10 9 8 7 6 5 4 3 2 1

To my mother, Theresa Anne Germanese Cooper. Mama, you never liked your name, but to me . . . it's the most beautiful name in the world.

Acknowledgments

Dear Readers, this book could not have been written (trust me) without the constant and soothing waves of love you all gave the first two "witch" books. There were times I felt I simply couldn't give this story what it deserved, but there you were, all of you, sending me messages about the previous books and how much they meant to you. It gave me the courage to press on, and produce a novel (this very novel!) that I believe may have the most "me" laced throughout its pages. I hope you enjoy its odd ways.

"Thank you" is simply not enough when it comes to the readers/writers who read almost every draft of this book. Erica Olivier (as always, your brutal ways burn away my nonsense). Nicki Duncan, a reader and now a true friend. Three up-and-coming authors to watch: Leigh Hewitt, Gina Miel Heron, and Kasey Corbit. Damn, ladies . . . I mean, wow. I could not have gotten through that crazy Halloween deadline without you. There I was, trick-or-treating, while you guys were parceling out chapters. To my friends who are always willing to read: Casey Heyer Schwing, and Julia Nadeau, who over that fall pause descended on my house and left behind a plot fix that I thought could never be fixed. "Stupid Witch . . ." I mean, how simple!

To my brilliant elegant agent, Anne Bohner. You've become so dear to me, a true friend and champion. And my editor, Vicki Lame, HEY GLITTER, it's baby number THREE, you bored yet? I'm not! Bringing a book from a thought to the shelves these days takes a village, and I'm so lucky I got a good one. To the entire team at St. Martin's Press, I am always in your debt. Dear Marie Estrada, you are the best kind of taskmaster, holding me to high standards that, when I meet them, surprise and fill me with confidence. It's been the finest gift.

To my student India Miller who gave me Sippie. I love you.

To Alice Hoffman, who was kind enough to return my midsummer frantic messages of "OH MY GOD I'M NEVER GOING TO GET THIS RIGHT!" with calming beautiful words of logic and perseverance. I was crying in the barn in early August at about 5 A.M. (add that to the list of sentences I never thought I'd say . . .) when she sent a message that read "Don't forget that you are one of the few people who even gets to have this type of worry." And bam. I was back on track. Her steady hand on my back. Sometimes there are no words.

To the people of Nola and the bayou and barrier islands throughout the Gulf Coast: The rest of us could learn a thing or two about community, respect, and perseverance from you. I know I did. My father, James Cooper, told me endless stories of shrimping those waters and living among the "realest people in the world." Amen to that.

To my brother, Talmadge James, for being the Jack to my Sippie.

Deep affection and gratitude to Robert L. Mele, my godfather extraordinaire. You pick it all up when things fall apart. You always rescue me, and I'm forever grateful even if I don't say it enough. The worst part of this amazing dream is the fact that when I'm writing, I don't do enough with those daughters of mine. You quietly notice and pick up that slack without ever demanding anything but love in return. And you have that. Trust me. So much love.

And speaking of them, hey . . . little witches . . . Rosy, Tess, Grace Louise, I'm so in love with you. Thanks for putting up with my crazy ways. And don't ever forget, YOU are the loves of my life. Writing makes me happy, and I couldn't do it if I didn't KNOW you were all on the same . . . ahem . . . page.

And last but never last: Dear Bill (spouse of my life), you didn't marry a writer. And here we are. Just know that no matter where I go (in my mind or on the road) you are always there. You are my home.

Entrances and Exits

Crow

When Serafina came across the sea
A casket girl of only 10 and 3
She conjured for herself a life of dreams
And captured all the hearts in New Orleans.
Serafina purchased land from Spain
A bayou to the south that bears her name
With money earned from clever conjure magic
She'd planned it as she crossed the wide Atlantic
She built a town for lost souls needing solace
A new society both just and lawless.
Her plot worked well, as generations prospered
The trouble came when lies and secrets festered
And Sorrows started painting pasts untrue
Until young Jack went missing in the bayou.

Redemption hides in vines that blossom sweet
On the gates of 13 Bourbon Street.

I

Sister Vesta

Grace's Confession

Serafina's Bayou, Tivoli Parish, Louisiana
August 14, 1901

To: The Law Office of A. A. Monroe
13 Bourbon Street
New Orleans, Louisiana

It must be late in the evening now, the sky is mercilessly dark. It has been a season of storms, has it not? The people here who wish me dead believe that not only did I kill the Sorrow family, but that I brought these wicked storms to our shores as well. I almost think it to be true, which proves how altered I am by these circumstances. I feel as if something vast has shifted inside my soul. I lost my way, didn't I, dear Albert? Drank too greedily from the well of this enchanted world, and now I will be punished for my sins. I warrant I would be terribly upset if I still believed in sin. However, I no longer care about evil or seeking redemption. I'm as bent on vengeance as those who have spent the last month surrounding Sorrow Hall. They want to see me hanging from a cypress tree as much as I wish to see each of them burn in hell for what they allowed to occur to this fine family that both you and I adored.

Do I sound harsh, Albert? I fitfully tried to pray tonight. The sky raced from gray to black so quickly, it is as if I am a creature lost in time. When I first arrived, that voodoo witch, Rosella, told me this was a sacred place, this Sorrow land. One of the few places on earth where geography and mysticism collide. I did not trust in it then, but now, after all that has happened, I know it to be true.

I sit here, alone in the cottage Madame Helene provided me, in the shadow of Sorrow Hall, writing this letter by the flickering light of the last candle I could find. I know you told me that if I chose to ride out this storm, you wished for me to close myself up inside the stronger confines of that grand house, whose walls could hold off the wind and the tides. Only, those same walls still echo with the laughter of the children, haunting me. Perhaps they have come back to escort me to the other side. I would gladly go with them, I miss them so.

Please know I did not take your warning about the "mob" lightly. I know they will come for me and mete out their justice. You were right when you said they believed me to be a demon, a rougarou, or at the very least a murderer of children. And I have done nothing to calm their hysteria, thus I am convicted in the court of popular opin-. ion. So, when you asked me to come with you, I wanted to run to the safety you offered. But who would I be if I ran toward the very thing that was ripped out from under this beautiful family, be it my fault or not, the very day I arrived? No, I deserve to be alone with these dangers.

I realize that my previous silence has frustrated you. You have spent weeks patiently interviewing me, taking your copious notes. Asking me repeatedly to summarize my tenure with our beloved Sorrow family in the hope that I would give you some proof that I was not guilty. The zeal with which you have tried to clear my name is admirable. I did not mean to cause you pain. I never meant to cause pain to anyone. After all, I was brought here to ease suffering.

When you walked away from me (was that only yesterday?), pausing before closing the iron gates behind you (I adore that you called them Edmond's Folly, you were quite right about that), urging me one last time to accept the refuge you so graciously offered in New Orleans, I saw you pause before you disappeared into the damp mist of the leafy canopies that line the path to the docks. I saw you look back, Albert. Don't ever look back. You must always only look forward.

Be it the storm, or the mob, I'm not long for this world . . . and though I struggle with the fear of what is to come, it is no worse than the weight of what is already lost. As one of the people aside from myself whom the Sorrow family allowed to be part of their magnificent world, I feel it only right that you should be the one to hear my confession, such as it is. Do you see now why I could not give you what you wanted? I could not state that I had nothing to do with their deaths, because I did.

Though a mere two years have passed, it seems a lifetime since I arrived to begin a new life in this savage paradise. I remember the day it all began in perfect detail. And, Albert, as it began with you, it seems fitting it should end with you as well. When Edmond and Helene decided to find a sister-nurse, it was left up to you, their solicitor, to make the proper inquiries. Oh sir! You must have felt discouraged from the start. What they were looking for was entirely too detailed. They needed a nurse to live with them, to care for darling Edmond Jr. (poor Egg, for whom there was no cure) and the rest of the children, SuzyNell, Edwina, Mae, the twins . . . Lavinia and Grace, and little wild Belinda B'Lovely. The act of writing down *their names is disconcerting to me, Albert. Like casting a spell, or saying a prayer (which I have come to believe might be very similar things).*

I was to be a governess, healer, and religious adviser. Tasks that would prove to be nearly impossible in this strange, wet wilderness. But I fought back any fears I had, and came.

Perhaps it is that same lingering fear, deep inside, urging me to tell you here the very information you needed to clear my name. It is such a puzzle, Albert, that instead I will tell you what I did not do in the hopes that you will see the bones of truth spanning the blankness in between. I did not go from room to room killing them. That should be clear from the indictment itself. I am, as you know, accused of the following: instigating fits of insanity resulting in the suicides of Edmond and Helene. I am also accused of purposefully poisoning Edmond Jr. and the twins. It is believed I drowned beautiful Mae in the bayou, and lest we forget, delivered a fatal blow to Edwina's head with a metal croquet ball. SuzyNell, of course, had escaped the madness before it began, running away to France with her beau.

That leaves but one Sorrow child, Belinda B'Lovely, who is still missing. And though her body has not been found, I am presumed responsible for her death as well. Do not think me wicked if I tell you that I hope her soul is resting with her family, for that would be a finer fate than dying all alone in Meager Swamp, that desolate, tidal plane fed by the magical Sorrow Bay. We couldn't keep her away from it, remember? She'd come home dragging mud from her skirts. But I digress. Here is what you have been asking for.

I say this with the honesty that comes from the threat of imminent death: Albert, I did not do the things I am accused of.

So, why didn't I profess my innocence when the blame was cast my way?

Complicity. I was complicit in the demise of the Sorrow family, and one does not have to start a fire, or even watch it burn, to be guilty of arson; you need only be the one who fanned the flames.

I understand this may not appease your curiosity as much as you may have hoped.

Only the Virgin Mary, my confessor, will know the entire truth. Once this storm has passed, if you should decide to return from the safety of 13 Bourbon Street to find me, I will no longer be on this earth. I am sealing this letter well, casing it in wax, and placing it on a high shelf. I pray that you will find it and its contents will convince you to let this community continue to believe I am at fault. That is the only way it will heal. Let it be known that I died taking full responsibility, and though I go to God now with a clear mind, I have a stained conscience. That should be enough to keep the feux follets from stealing my soul. Or if that not be true, and you see lights over the bayou, run.

With deep affection,
Sister Vesta Grace

2

Frances the Great

Tivoli Parish: Present

I grew up the way the water moves, in twists and turns with temperamental, amorphous boundaries. And I danced, lightly, over precarious situations and a thousand half-submerged ideas as they tried to surface above the waters of my bayou, reaching out their pale limbs and beautiful, lost faces from under the dark waters. If I looked carefully, I could see the reflections of Sorrows past, my ancestors, peering up at me from the world beneath. I liked to imagine the Sorrow sisters with their hands intertwined, long hair flowing, and white dresses billowing around them like sunken clouds. They'd be smiling slyly, teasingly, about a shared secret.

"You keep smiling like that," I'd threaten, standing barefoot on the maze of rotting wood that wound itself around the length of the Sorrow property. "I'm Frances the Great, and when I'm grown I'll know all your sorry truths!"

I thought I knew everything back then, but I was dead wrong about those ghosts. They weren't hiding any secrets, they were trying to tell me things about myself I didn't want to know.

My name is Frances Green Sorrow. I'm thirty-two years old. I have one blue eye, one green. My grandmother Dida Sorrow says it's the reason I grew up all confused and stubborn. But Dida's like that. She's got a reason for *everything*. She walks this earth believing she's the product of a dark fairy tale come to life. That she fell into a deep sleep for one hundred years and then somehow woke up, still just a child, wandering the bayou. We try not to upset that applecart of hers. After all, I used to think just like her until I grew up too fast and began doubting every single thing I ever thought true.

I was brought up to believe that I was a witch. Just like freckles, or hair color, or dimpled chins, my family has a collection of tiny . . . *quirks*. Talents or "strange ways" or whatever it is people call those things. For us Sorrow women, it was called magic. So we all became Witches with a capital "W." After generations of exaggerations and folklore, it's hard to separate what's real from what's fake anymore. The same thing happens with religion, or politics, or any other sort of thing a person is brought up with. It all begins beautiful and pure, and then year by year, everyone forgets what it meant in the first place, twisting it up into something it wasn't ever supposed to be.

We burn bonfires on the water to celebrate solstice. Summer and winter. But, is it winter solstice? Or is it Christmas? Is it St. John's Day? Or is it summer solstice? No one even cares to remember that the word *bonfire* comes from burning bones. We never burned bones, we burn willow, but still . . .

There *are* a few "absolutes" in my life, though. I am without a doubt Daniel Amore's ex-wife and Jack's absentee mama. And for all the terrible things I found out carrying secrets can do—like rot a whole family to its core—I carry my own deep inside.

When I was little, though, it was all true. The legends were my lineage; the curses were as real to me as the cane fields. I believed there wasn't anything we Sorrows couldn't do.

I've never been good at that thing called a "middle ground."

Two weeks before the summer solstice of my thirty-third year, I woke up to the sound of music floating through the air. Dida and my mother, Claudette, had wound up that cranky antique gramophone and had those old blues albums playing. The notes whimsically traveled the short (but still achingly long) distance from Sorrow Hall to my little shack. And somehow, instead of feeling the terrible burden of facing another day, I woke up happily wanting, *needing,* to go see my mama and spend time with Dida, maybe even help them prepare for the upcoming festivities.

When I was fully awake, I almost got dizzy with the lightness inside. *They conjured up a spell to make me happy, those witches. . . .* Except, even thinking that way was all upside down. It was the way I used to think before I made a mess out of my life.

I'm good at that, making messes.

Later that morning, Millie Bliss came by on her boat. I'd shut out the world, but I could never really shut out Millie. We were brought up together, side by side, not blood kin. But closer, somehow.

"Hey, Frankie," she said, smiling.

"Hey, you beautiful creature!" I called, beaming at her. Millie pulled her boat up to my dock, a frown creasing her delicate features. My upbeat attitude was apparently a shock to her system. (Not that I can blame her.)

"You feelin' okay, Frankie?" she asked skeptically.

"I'm feeling downright strange, Millie. I almost feel . . . *alive*."

"What happened? You eat something funny?" She frowned again.

"Shut up. I'm just . . . hell, I don't know. I woke up less . . . hateful."

For sixteen years I'd been working as hard as I could at being cold and shut off from everyone. I guess even Millie had grown used to my sour, sarcastic ways.

"How about we go back to the Voodoo together and have a drink? We can sort out who or what put the sunshine back in your step."

"Isn't it a little early for a drink?" I asked, crossing my arms playfully, an eyebrow raised.

"Or a little late!" we both burst out at the same time, laughing. While most of the shared jokes had disappeared—along with the laughter—some remained.

"Get in this damn boat, girl. And Danny called. Don't you think it's time for you Sorrows to get a phone line?" she asked while I got in and she tied off.

"Hell, no," I said. "What'd Danny want?"

"Said something about a good haul out there in the Gulf with Old Jim. I think he was just checking in. Asked me to look in on Jack."

We both grew silent, staring out at the water. Of course he'd asked her to look in on him. It was the first time Danny left him to fend for himself, and everyone knew I didn't leave the bayou. That morning, it hurt more than usual, because everything was turned on its head inside my heart. See, to Jack, Millie was the mama I was supposed to be. She went to town and cheered for him at his baseball games, then took him out for ice cream after. I only saw my son when he came down to the bayou. My self-imposed exile made sense while I was deep inside of it, but in moments where my thoughts were clear, I just felt foolish, especially when I considered what I was missing with Jack.

We stayed quiet as we wound our way through the bayou. No matter how much faith I lost in myself or what those batty witches used to call "my destiny," I never lost my faith in the land and water I lived on. Serafina's Bayou is my safe haven, a warm, private place layered with magic and held together by tangled vines of crazy. It's soft like the quilts we sew and sour like the pickled things we put away for the off-seasons. It echoes sweetly with shouts and screams of strange that make it the most wonderful place on earth.

The Voodoo is our local juke joint and part of that comforting "strange." A gathering place for wayward souls since the founding of Tivoli Parish. Some even believe it used to be a drinking den for pirates. Whatever its origin, the Voodoo is the source of so many pivotal changes in my life. A gateway from dark to light and back again, and, the only place in Serafina's Bayou with running water, electricity, and a phone line. Millie was the current owner and lived in a small room off the kitchen.

"Why you gonna live there?" I'd asked her, years back.

"You think you're the only one who can run away without really runnin' away? If you're moving out of Sorrow Hall, so am I. And since there's no room for me in your little 'Killer Nun' shack, I'll just park myself close to the bourbon."

And there we'd stayed, for too long, separate but together. Quiet and loud.

I hooked my arm inside hers as we walked up the bank to the Voodoo and let my head rest on her shoulder.

"Everything's gonna be fine, Frances," she said. "I'll keep you safe, if you let me."

We sat at the bar, listening to JuneBug haul in a shipment of bottles while he yelled at the band scheduled to play that night. "I told you, none of that newfangled modern noise. We like swamp blues here. Now get it straight or get out, *ça va*?"

"He don't never change," I said.

"He's been sober for a good week now, that's something," said Millie. "Want some whiskey?"

"Always."

"Now tell me, what's goin' on with you, Little Bit?"

Little Bit was a nickname Old Jim gave me, and when Millie used it, I missed him with a fierce ache.

When I was just a little girl, he'd take me on his pirogue to go exploring and tell me stories about up north where he came from, where people understood how to use those talents everyone said the Sorrows had. He said, "You women are just like this bayou, wild and untamable. Up north, those women who got the magic, they know how to use it. But then I guess you sacrifice all the fun, don'tcha? All I know, Little Bit, is on the day you were born, with a head full a' hair darker than the bottom of Meager Swamp, the hopes and dreams of too goddamned many generations were pinned on you. And it worries me. Just know your grandpa loves you very much."

Whiskey cradled in one hand, a rolled cigarette dangling from the other, I felt tears prick my eyes, then begin to fall, as the memory of my grandpa's comforting voice blotted out the noise of the band and JuneBug's yelling. And I needed some comfort, much as I hate to admit it.

"Now I'm really worried, Frankie, tell me, honey," said Millie, breaking through my fog.

So I sat there, slowly spinning the whiskey in my glass, and told her about how I was starting to warm up inside, how it was making me think about all the time I'd lost. Time with Jack, time with my family, time with her.

"Because, Millie . . . if I can admit we have magic in us, the kind that goes beyond those little tricks of the mind, then that means I was wrong. And if I was wrong about that . . ." I paused, taking a long sip, then whispered, "I might have been wrong about . . . everything."

Millie sat there, the sunshine pouring through the windows changing the hue of her green eyes. Everyone always said we looked like twins. Even though she's older than me. And right then, I wished I looked exactly like her, because her wild hair and glistening skin were all the lunchtime rush could see. Bayou folk, young and old alike, who came together at the Voodoo on weekends, crowded in and fell over themselves when they saw her.

"Losing faith in something you held true is a terrible thing," she said, pretending not to notice the stares. "But losing faith in everything you ever thought was good and right and safe . . . well, that's a bigger problem. It all goes back to whatever happened when you ran off to New Orleans. We all know you came back different. Hell, you demanded we knew how different you were. Maybe it's time you talk about it?" she prodded gently.

"Millie, I just this very day decided to rethink this whole thing. If I let myself go back there, to that time . . . It won't work. I can't do it."

"You got to take baby steps, is all. Like one of them addiction programs or what have you," she said, looking serious and silly at the same time. Something I loved about her.

I was a little tipsy, so I laughed hard at that. She was *so* right, in all the *wrong* ways.

"So, if your first step is trying to weed through all this witchy stuff, let me remind you that you can't deny there are some pretty important differences between us Serafina witches and regular people. Not everyone can see spirits, or learn things so easily, or age a little slower. Not to mention the root work and healing skills that were handed down to you, and then to me when Old Jim brought me down here from up north all those years ago."

"You got a black thumb, Millie, you can't do root work for shit," I said.

She raised an eyebrow. "You've been letting your magic wear down thin for all these years, and I've been letting mine flourish. How do you know what I can and cannot do?"

"When the lady is right, the lady is right," I said. "But, Millie, a stain is a stain, and when I start doubting one thing, that doubt casts its long shadow over everything."

"Look, cha, I'm just trying to be supportive. Truth is we been dancin' around the whats and the whys of everything that either happened or did not happen to you when you ran off to Bourbon Street for ages. Sixteen years is a long time . . . so long I'm not even curious anymore! Besides, I already knew the whys." she said, holding up her glass and looking at me all playful through its amber contents. "You can't keep secrets from me. I know you too well."

My breath caught, trapped underneath the relief, the almost blissful terror, of being exposed.

"And you changed before anyone else saw it. Before *you* even saw it. It was that summer, you were fifteen, I was seventeen . . . we went down to Saint Sabine Isle hoping we'd find a couple of pirate ghosts to fall in love with. Only you didn't find a pirate ghost, did you? You found Danny Amore. Then he left for college, broke your heart, and you ran off. Simple."

"The worst things always are," I finally breathed out, wondering if she knew more than she was saying. And wanting, after so many years, to tell her the whole twisted truth. I took another sip of whiskey, changing the subject slightly. "You remember how he made fun of us when we were little? Hell, everyone he ran with did. I could always tell you cared, that it hurt you. But I never let it bother me. He told us we were the dirty daughters of demons. Would practically spit in our direction. I see some of them from time to time, all fat and unhappy. You ever notice that? Everybody always gets what they deserve, don't they?"

"Not all the time," she said quietly.

I finished my whiskey and rested my head on her shoulder. I was a little drunk. "I want to call Jack, Millie." I needed him to help me set a new course for myself. Just talking about it wasn't helping. But Jack, he could help me by answering one simple question.

"You gonna call him from out of the blue?" asked Millie.

"It's not like I *never* see him. Danny brought him by Sorrow Hall before him and Old Jim went offshore last week. Asked if I thought it was okay to let Jack stay on his own at the house. And you know, with Jack about to turn thirteen I thought . . . it'd be good for him to be on his own for a bit, show him how much we trust him."

Truthfully, Danny had come by to ask if Jack could stay with me, and I was gearing up for a whole summer with the boy, custody agreements and all that real-world dark magic. And I said no. Not because I didn't want Jack two weeks early, but because I couldn't stand the way Danny was looking at me or the way I wanted to look back. Our chemistry was toxic. We had two switches, on and off. When we were "on," we made such a mess of things. And now that we'd been off for about two years, I liked not feeling my heart beat so hard in my ears. So I said no, because I knew Danny was really asking if he could come back to my bed when he got home from shrimping the Gulf.

Maybe I shouldn't call. . . .

JuneBug pulled the phone out from under the register. "Here you go, Frankie."

Damn JuneBug. Always payin' attention when you least expect it.

I dialed slowly, my fingers tingling as the rotary phone clicked back over the numbers.

Jack picked up quick. "Hello?" Just hearing that boy's voice, free and clear from the cement heart I'd somehow shed, was heaven.

"Jack!"

"Hey, Mama! How you doin'? When you learn to use a phone?" He started laughing.

"Shut that sass mouth . . . I got an *important* question. And the way you answer will help me out with a lot of new things I'm thinking of."

"Okay, shoot."

"Now, Wonder Woman, from those comics we read together . . . she's all powerful, right? Like, the most powerful one?"

"Yeah, I guess so. For a lady superhero. What about her?"

"Well, she flies an invisible jet, right?"

"Right."

"So if her plane is invisible . . . why can we still see Wonder Woman flying it? I mean, if she's supposed to have all that power, why can't she just . . . poof, make herself invisible, too? It makes me doubt she has any power at all. But I need *your* opinion, Jack, so what do you think?"

Jack was quiet for a while. I could picture him scrunching up his face just like his daddy when he was thinking something over.

"Maybe she wants to be seen, Mama. And if you're that strong, you can do whatever you want. Seems to me, if someone like that doesn't want to be seen, or have anything to do with life at all, they can disappear better than anyone. And, I guess, they make that decision themselves. Those are the lucky ones, right?"

It was the perfect answer. It was the answer I needed. It confirmed what I was already reasoning out, that I could choose different. Things could be different. That they could be better.

"I love you, Jack. You be safe now. I'll see you next week," I said, and hung up the phone.

"Millie, will you take me home?"

"Ain't you got your own boat tied out there by Trinity Bridge?"

"I do, but that whiskey made me lazy. And you invited me. So get your butt movin'!" I said.

On our way back to my house, Millie looked out at the water and frowned. "Do me one favor, Frankie? In all this soul-searching you're about to do, leave Danny out of it."

"Where did that come from?" I asked. "We haven't played the 'maybe we should be together' game in two years. And I don't intend to try again, that last time was brutal."

"Good. It's just that, I feel like this is a really great change you're trying to make, and I don't want to see him come home and ruin it."

"That's a load of shit, Millie. You like me better evil, and you know it."

"Well, that might be true, but if you're gonna go through with this change of heart, maybe you'll come back and help run Thirteen Bourbon? It's a bear to run alone. And after all these years I still got tourists asking after Frances the Great." She smiled at me.

"Maybe," I said, letting my fingers trickle in the water. Then my mouth found a little piece of courage and the most unexpected thing popped out. I swear I need to keep it under lock and key sometimes. "Millie? You ever hear anything about Eight Track?"

Though she'd spent most of her life on Sorrow soil, Millie never did learn the art of being dead honest. She had a way of lying that I almost admired. She lied in a circular way, almost like she wanted to make it as interesting as possible while she was doing it. Some kind of self-entertainment or something.

"Eight Track! Damn, that's a name straight out the bad old, sad past." She sighed heavily.

"What do you mean?" I asked, trying to get my voice steady.

"Well . . . Simone died. You remember how beautiful her voice was? Like silk. Well, that was about ten years ago now. After that, Abe said Eight Track's drinking picked up something terrible. Sometimes I see him panhandling down on St. Mark's, but he don't talk to me. He just looks away. I tried a few times."

"Why didn't any of you tell me that happened—" My voice broke. *Simone died?*

"Have you lost your whole mind in one day?" she asked, giving me a weird look. "You knew Abe took over as bar manager, you could have asked about Eight Track back then. Besides, you told us never to speak of any of that. You go for weeks, months, not talking to any of us. And we were supposed to come on over here to your gypsy kingdom and talk to the deaf? Shit. Go on back to your sour self, Frankie. You were right; I don't like this side of you."

"I wasn't criticizing you, Millie. Really." Millie never liked to be criticized. She glared at me as we reached my dock. I leaned out of the boat to pull in closer before climbing out.

Millie could be mean when she felt cornered or neglected. Like, if Dida payed too much attention to me when we were growing up, Millie'd find ways to remind me that my mama was blind. It never really bothered me. I just knew it was her way, trying to hurt someone to take away a little of her own hurt. We always understood the worst in each other. It's why we were so close. And that's exactly what she was doing now as a grown woman. Trying to take away some of her pain by telling me about Simone like that. But *why* is what I didn't understand.

The only "why" I could conjure up was that she knew . . . she *had* to know my secret.

"Anyone know what happened to her little girl?" I asked, meeting her eyes. Daring her to tell me she *knew*.

"I don't recall them having a child," she said sharply, pushing off back down the dark waters.

"You come back when you want to tell me the truth, Millie Bliss!" I shouted after her.

"Ain't *my* truth! That one is yours to tell, Frankie . . . ," she yelled back.

"Crazy witch," I grumbled, making my way back to my porch. Then I smiled, because at least *someone* knew. It made everything easier. And, like Dida always said, "Everything happens for a reason. All the bad, *mostly the bad,* happens to teach us things we got to know. Like directions from here to there." Millie's mean little moment helped me understand my shift in heart and chart my course.

It was the blues . . . the music Simone used to sing, that woke me that morning. Those notes must have strung themselves inside me as I slept, like stars waking up my instincts. Maybe even the very same stars I stitched on my baby's quilt before I wrapped her—my beautiful little secret—up and gave her to Eight Track to raise. Whatever it was, luck, magic, maybe both, I didn't care. My course was clear.

I had to find my daughter.

3

Simone Sings the Blues

New Orleans: Before

"Life," said Simone St. James, her breath magnified, echoing out from the small stage at 13 Bourbon Street, "is stitched together from a series of mistakes, some little, some big, like the patches on the clothes we wore growin' up, you know?"

The shadow people who filled the smoky bar nodded, laughing. She stood there, chin tilted, confidently gearing up to sing her set of Billie Holiday covers. A salmon-pink chiffon dress clung to her body yet seemed to swirl around her in a blur of feathers. It accentuated her dark, marblelike skin and showed off the only thing of real value she owned, an opal brooch she inherited from her mama.

"But those mistakes . . . ," she continued, glancing behind her, cuing the small band to start playing the first song, soft and low under her words. "Well?" She laughed, deep and sultry, shrugging her thin shoulders. "They can also be lessons. I picked up a little of that . . . fi-loss-oh-fee from them drunken, half-assed conversations, you know the ones. . . ." The music got a little louder. "Only, we can't have the blues if you think that way, noooo, sir." She tossed her head. "You got to know a mistake is a *mistake.* And then, when those old blues come along, we get to sing 'em away . . . just like this . . . a one, a two, a one two three . . . 'All of me, why not take all . . . of me . . .'"

As the notes unfurled from her lips, she gazed out under the lights into the crowd and saw her little Sippie sitting with the bartender, Abe, at the back. Simone tried not to let the tears fall looking at her girl. No amount of singing, or drinking, or pills, could dull her pain when she thought about the sorry years she'd given that lost child.

As she sang, she thought about her own mistakes. The first, marrying Eight Track. The second, letting him bring that baby to her in the middle of the night. And the third, letting herself love either of them. To Simone, love was the worst kind of mistake a woman could make. "The dream killer," she called it.

But tonight she was going to fix as many of those as she could. She'd brought Sippie along to give the girl back to the people who gave her away to begin with. Eight Track would be mad as all hell at her, but she didn't care. She was going to fix that *other* mistake, too: Simone was leaving. She was going to finish her set to the thunderous applause she deserved, do that other nasty work she'd taken up to put food on the table since Eight Track started drinking hard, and buy a bus ticket straight to Hollywood.

She was a star.

Something magic filled her voice that night; it was stronger and freer than ever. Released from its mistake-gilded cage, it flew out of her with wings all its own. The crowd broke out clapping and whistling as she glided off the stage. Sippie ran to her, jumping into her arms.

"No one sings prettier than you, Mama," she said, hugging her tightly.

"Hush, girl, you go sit back with Abe. I got to talk to the woman who runs the place."

"Who?"

"That lady over there, the pretty one. You see her? She looks a bit like you. Got your bright eyes with all that gold and green, only yours are better. And got that untamed hair of yours. And Sippie . . . she knows some people who can do the most wonderful things."

"I see her." Sippie watched her curiously.

Simone buried her face in Sippie's tangled curls, holding her close with an honesty she'd never fully let show.

"Sippie, you listen here. No matter what happens from tonight on, you got to *survive*. You gonna do what you're told. But at the same time, don't trust nobody but yourself. You hear me, girl? And if anything bad *ever* happens to you, you remember . . . the first time, it's not your fault. But the second? The third? When you keep letting the same thing happen over and over again . . . that's on you. And only you can make it stop. *Only you.* Don't let yourself get fooled by love, Sippie."

Simone put down the child, who looked confused but also sad, like she knew something bad was about to happen.

"Now, git back there and let me finish my business."

"Yes, ma'am," Sippie responded quietly, walking back toward Abe too slow and looking back over her shoulder with that pout face of hers. *Them heart-shaped lips.*

"You sounded better than ever, Simone," Millie said through smoke rings, looking awestruck.

"Millie, I got to speak wit you."

"Of course . . . come in the office." Millie walked through the crowd and beckoned her to follow.

Simone closed the door carefully behind them, resting her head for a moment against the glass panel before turning and forcing the words out. "I know something I'm not supposed to know, Millie. And it's time to share it. But I can't just come right out and say it. So I'm hoping you can put two and two together. I've known you for a long time, Millie. You and Frances ran around here like wild, little heathens when you were just Sippie's age. And I know Dida and Claudette. I know the family and the history. And when Frances came on down here, just a child herself, and tried to live like a grown-up . . . something changed her. We all know that. But, because she ain't never been back, I got to give you this burden I've been carryin'. I can't carry it no more."

"What are you talking about, Simone?"

Millie was still smiling, but her knuckles had gone white from gripping the large wooden desk in front of her a little too tight.

"You got to take her back, Miss Millie. Take her back to her own kind," Simone pleaded, hating herself for begging anyone for anything.

She figured she'd have to explain the whole situation. Only she didn't have to, because it seemed Millie already knew everything. And that's when that witch lost her temper. Her eyes flared with a dangerous sparkle, her cheeks flushing. Fear coursed up Simone's spine. It was as though a power surge ran through the room, through the building, down the whole goddamned street.

"You must be crazy." Millie's voice took on an edge. "I'm not doing any damn thing. You think I'm gonna bring that child back so she can break my best friend's heart into smaller pieces? People got *reasons* for doing the things they do. You don't have the right to change anyone's future but your own, Simone. Now, I seem to remember, about a year ago you came here practically begging for a job. And when the singing didn't pay enough, you had to beg me to look the other way when you started taking men into that room upstairs. In fact, I remember telling you I could get you other kinds of work, and you didn't want it. You know what I think? I think you're *weak*."

Her eyes wild with desperation, Simone tried another strategy—the truth.

"Fine, Millie. You right. I'm weak. I've always taken the easy way out. But this time, this *one* time, I'm not. I swear it. I'm begging you, take her. I ain't got nothing to offer her here. She's like you. She's got the shine. She needs her mother."

Millie laughed. But it was a callous sort of sound, with the roughness of sandpaper, not like the way Simone remembered Frances laughing. Frances sounded like wind chimes.

"Let me tell you a little something about that child's 'mother,' " Millie scoffed. "Her *mother* got married, had another baby, and in the end, left that one too. And right now, she's all shut up inside herself. And there's no room for anyone else in there."

Millie calmly lit two cigarettes and gave one to Simone.

"Can I at least ask if you can keep an eye on her till I'm finished tonight?" Simone asked, taking it.

"Of course I will. Or Abe will. Someone will. We always do. Even though you never pay us for watching her. Think this whole world is free for you to cry all over. Think we enjoy your tears. We don't."

"Here," said Simone, finding a sliver of bravery and using it to unclasp her opal brooch and offered it to Millie. "If there's one thing I know, it's that nothin' in this world is free. Maybe this will cover it. And if it don't, or maybe someday if you find a heart in that empty soul of yours, you could give it to her."

Millie took it and tossed it on a desk cluttered with papers and receipts. "I can do that, I guess."

Simone had the oddest feeling that Millie was disappointed. As if she wanted a better fight, or to lose the fight, or to win a bigger prize. "Millie?"

"Yes."

"How did you know about Sippie?"

"Now, Simone, I'm a witch, remember? There's not much I don't know just by looking at you. And you know what I see when I look at you?"

Simone walked out the door before she could finish, only hearing the steely hush of Millie's voice add, "Nothing."

That's when Simone knew she was beat. But then she thought she'd probably known all along that this was the way it would end. And that maybe, just maybe, the reason her voice had soared out so easily that night was that something inside of her knew it was her last time singing. Maybe it was her soul flying out of her, and now she just had to make her body follow.

Resigned, she went to the third floor. And she did her job. She let one man after another climb on top of her. Sweat on her. Use her. Then she rolled up the cash and put a note on it that said, "For Sippie."

Afterward, she pulled a bottle of pills from her purse. The pills she took to make those nights she worked late go by a little easier, the ones that freed her mind from her body. She opened the bottle and took them all.

And somewhere, lingering between the life she was leaving and whatever was waiting for her on the other side, she heard a knocking on the door and the voice of a little girl crying, pleading, the little girl she'd tried so hard not to love but loved harder than she thought she could ever love anyone, "Don't leave me, Mama! Please don't leave me. . . ."

The Waxing Moon

The waxing moon casts more inner light than external. It is the moon of attraction, and will bring forth all the things you desire.
But be warned, you must notice when they come your way.

—Serafina's Book of Sorrows

4

Jack's Great Idea

Tivoli Parish: Present

Jack Amore Sorrow, twelve years old, woke up smiling to the
sweet sound of silence. Today was *the day*.

He loved being alone, far away from the noise of his fractured
family. It wasn't a big family, only his dad, Danny, and his great-
uncle Pete on the Amore side, who lived in Tivoli Proper. The
other side of his family, the Sorrow side, they lived in Serafina's
Bayou in what Jack considered the most interesting place in the
world: Sorrow Hall. Still on the list of "the Grandest Estates in
Louisiana," it had fallen into disrepair—some might even say
despair—over the years and was now a rambling, treasure-filled secret. Dida and Old Jim, his grandma Claudette, and his mama,
Frances Green Sorrow, all lived there together. Well, his mama
lived in a little shack out of sight on the property, pretending to
live a world apart. But, small family or not, they could yell large.
(Especially when they got over being all quiet and tense with one

another all the darn time.) They yelled in voices and feelings and all the spaces between, and Jack didn't like it one bit. He was determined to patch up everything that was broken, even if he had to do it all himself. He'd given the grown-ups more than enough time to figure it out on their own. And man, grown-ups liked to take forever to figure things out.

"Today is the day," he said to his quiet, sparse little room. His dad wasn't much on decorating, and the whole little "ticky-tacky" house, as his mama put it, had no character at all. It always seemed exhausted, almost unhappy with itself, like it could have been more in life . . . kind of like his daddy, now that he thought about it. "Ha!" he cried out into the silence. Jack liked it when he woke up clever, and today was the perfect day to be on top of his game. He'd been planning his "Great Idea" for over six months, carefully going over all the details so he wouldn't make any mistakes.

The "Great Idea" started to grow at the beginning of seventh grade, when he read *Adventures of Huckleberry Finn*. He knew if he ran away, making it look like he'd been abducted, his family would be forced to come together to handle it. Jack liked to see the world like video game levels. Sometimes when you're stuck at one score, you got to take risks in order to figure out the exact moves you need to win. Just thinking about how clever the whole thing was made his stomach ache from laughing so hard. He knew he'd be in trouble when he showed up unharmed, knew that the people he loved most would be worried and terrified. But he was willing to try anything to bring them together again, to be a real family.

He wanted to keep his plan a secret but figured he needed at least one person he trusted to know the truth in case anything went wrong. Jack, born with Sorrow blood, was no fool. So he went to the one person he had some control over, Millie. The kind of control only a child can have.

Millie was Jack's aunt, sort of. His mother's family was all sorts of strange. Old Jim said Millie and Frances grew up "attached at the hip." And they continued to be "attached at the hip" until some kind of craziness made his mama run away to New Orleans, saying *she wasn't no witch and wasn't gonna be no part of any of that nonsense NO MORE."*

Of course, eventually his mama ran right back home again, only to pretend she wasn't and hide out from the world in that little shack. And she still claimed to not be part of that *nonsense*.

His mama sure was stubborn.

Millie had stepped right in and filled her shoes in all their lives. And when he was smaller, he liked it. She almost even smelled like his mama and was around a lot more. And she believed in the magic. All the Sorrows and those who wandered in and out of Serafina's Bayou looking for themselves, they had what Dida called "talents." His mama did, too, even though she didn't want to admit it. Anymore, that is.

"Why doesn't Mama believe, Maw Maw?" he'd ask Claudette. But he never got a full answer.

"Your mama went away to take over the whole world. And when she came back? She was broken in too many places. That's all I know, cha. And call me Claudie, I don't know how many times I got to tell you. I'm too young to be anyone's grandma."

Claudie sometimes let him touch the film that covered her eyes. While snuggling him on the porches of Sorrow Hall, she would tell him the story of when she was little and the lye blinded her. She was good at snuggling. He just couldn't understand why all the people he loved so much couldn't see their way to loving one another. When he was little, he couldn't help asking about it.

"Why don't you and Mama get along, Claudie?" he'd ask.

"Oh, Jackie boy, I get along fine with her, she just decided one day she wasn't havin' any part of this family. And I still don't know why. Maybe *you* should ask her, honey cha. She don't mind talkin' to you."

Jack knew better than to do that. His mama'd get all cold and send him off to do chores. He hated when Frances shut down. Being with Frances was his favorite thing in the entire world. Almost thirteen or not, he wasn't ashamed of how much he loved his parents. Jack was a confident, complicated boy who shone from the inside. And everyone saw it. The kids didn't make fun of him, and the adults—the same ones who bullied his mama when she was growing up—wished their kids could be like "that Jack Sorrow." No one even cared that his name was all turned around. His daddy's last name was in the middle, Amore. And his mama's last name was the one he was given—Sorrow. That's just "the way of the Sorrows" and one of the only things Danny ever agreed to. Probably because he was afraid Dida would curse him but good if he didn't agree. His daddy had a weakness when it came to unexplainable things.

The reason Jack decided to tell Millie about his plan was that she was part of why he was running away to begin with. About two years ago, Danny and Millie had started seeing each other, which just plain old made Jack angry.

"You're gettin' worked up over nothing and for no good reason," Danny had told him, burning a minute steak in their dark little kitchen.

"I'm just trying to tell you how I feel, Daddy. Mama says it's important to always say how you feel."

"Mama says? Mama? Nice. Maybe *she* should take some of her own advice."

Later, when Jack got quiet and picked at his burned dinner,

Danny grabbed Jack's hand. "Look, do me a favor, son, don't tell Mama about this," he implored. "It might hurt her. And I don't want to hurt her. 'Sides, I'm a grown man, Jack, and I'll do what I want. It's not like I'm going to marry Millie, so don't you worry."

But Jack *was* worried. And when he told Millie what he was planning, he made it clear that if she spoke a word of it, he'd tell his mama that she'd been messing around with his daddy. He knew Millie wanted to keep that a secret, too. Everyone around him was scared of making Frances mad, sad, and everything in between, which made everything impossible. But it gave Jack a reason to trust Millie. "That's what I call *leverage*," he said aloud, looking at the clock on his night table. It was still early, six A.M. He pulled his notebook out of the bag he'd packed the night before and went over his list. Jack liked lists.

The first list was titled:

WHY AM I DOING THIS?

His mama always said it was important to understand your *motivation* before you made a big decision. Frances was good at giving out life advice; she just couldn't seem to follow it for herself. But he forgave her for it. Danny always said Jack was "blind" when it came to his mama, but Jack didn't care.

He looked back down at his notes.

MOTIVATION FOR RUNNING AWAY:
1. *Mama and Daddy get together.*
2. *Everyone forgives each other.*
3. *I get to use magic.*
4. *Give those long-ago Sorrows a redo or something.*

Jack was obsessed with the history of the Sorrow family. He'd listened to stories and spent more than a healthy amount of time at the Tivoli Parish Historical Society poring over whatever they had. He especially liked reading about what happened to the Sorrows in 1901. "The Lost Generation," was what Mr. Craven, the curator (and the only other person Jack knew who shared his passion for all things Sorrow), called it. Mr. Craven reminded Jack of a cross between Mark Twain and Edgar Allan Poe (which amused both of them) and was, as Craven said, "right on the money."

"Murdered by a crazed nun! Can you even believe it, boy?! The family was never the same again. Some say they're *cursed*. It's all just so . . . *compelling*," Mr. Craven would say, fluttering about.

Jack agreed.

Mr. Craven had helped him put together a Sorrow scrapbook. Jack kept it in his bedside drawer. He reached over and took it out, then opened its wide, too-full, satisfying pages. It started with a copy of the original letter that Edmond and Helene Sorrow had their lawyer, Albert Monroe, send out. "It was the beginning of the end for all of them, Jack," Mr. Craven had said.

To the Sisters of The Bon Secure Ministry
RE: Private Home Care

I write to you on behalf of the Sorrow family of Tivoli Parish. I am their Solicitor, Albert Monroe of A. A. Monroe, LLP. The family is in need of a Sister-Nurse willing to live on their bayou estate and be the sole care provider for the household. There are seven children: six girls ranging in age from sixteen to eleven, SuzyNell, Mae, Edwina, Lavinia, Grace, and Belinda. There is one boy, Edmond Jr., who is six years of age and suffers from a chronic, debilitating illness. The chosen Sister-Nurse will also help take care of their mother, Helene Dupuis Sorrow, and their father, Edmond Senior. There is a small staff that works with the family on the grounds, but let it be duly noted that those who work there seek their religious and physical care elsewhere, be it Tivoli Proper, Sweet Meadow, or Saint Sabine Isle. None of the staff live on the estate. Your candidate will be the first to live among the Sorrows in many years. The family requests that the Sister you choose be fluent in English and French. She should be educated so as to help in the capacity of a Governess as well. She ought to have a stellar record when it comes to healing illnesses, a heart that belongs to God alone, and a peaceful temperament. The most important quality we are looking for, however, is a Sister who knows the value of privacy. The Sorrow family is one of the oldest and most influential in southern Louisiana, and they will not tolerate gossip of any sort, neither kind nor malignant.

We will expect her on the first of June. And we trust you will choose wisely.

Sincerely,
Albert Monroe

Then there were faded family photographs amid things they left behind: patches of the original Sorrow Hall wallpaper, pressed flowers (the twins had a collection), notes between SuzyNell and her boyfriend. His newest prized acquisition was the newspaper clipping from Paris when SuzyNell and her own family finally decided to come back to Serafina's Bayou in 1910. That whole generation fascinated Jack for many reasons.

Mostly because he knew them.

Since as early as he could remember, he'd spent his days at Sorrow Hall running in and out of forgotten corridors and musty rooms playing hide-and-seek with the Sorrow sisters. Baby Egg, too (who was pale, even for a ghost).

"You count, then we'll look together. I don't like it when they pop out at me," baby Egg would whisper. *Who knew ghosts could be scared?* They always played on the east side of the house that his family didn't use. When he told Dida about it, she was delighted.

"Oh, cha! You see those pretty babies!" she exclaimed, clapping her hands. "You ask what happened to them. And you tell them I miss them so much. You know, I can see them, too, and Millie, and even your mama when she cares to admit she has magic. But we mostly see shadows, echoes of them. But they talk to you? You scared when they do?"

"No, Dida, I ain't scared."

He was the opposite of scared. Sometimes during the long stretches of time during the school year he spent with his daddy, he missed the ghosts most of all. When he got older, he wrote down their names and tried talking to them. Edwina was so grown up and bossy. Mae, she was the prettiest. (Jack had a crush on her.) The twins liked to hide in closets. When he found them, they'd always lean out from the darkness, put their fingers to their lips, "Shhhhh!" before giggling and disappearing again. The only ones he never saw were SuzyNell (he figured she just passed on happily and never got stuck inside the "curse"), and Belinda B'Lovely. And he wouldn't have been able to see her, because his Dida *was* Belinda. Lost little Belinda B'Lovely Sorrow. It didn't seem possible, because that would make his great-grandma over one hundred years old. Some believed her, some didn't. Others just let it go. But Jack wanted to believe. Mr. Craven tried to tell him otherwise, but Jack wouldn't listen. He liked the idea of being tied so closely to his Sorrow ghosts.

He leaned over his bed, making sure he'd packed *The Legend of the Sorrow Women,* the book he'd borrowed to read during his "kidnapping." It was there. He went back to his notebook to go over his checklist one more time.

Book: CHECK
Clothes: CHECK
First-Aid Kit: CHECK
Supplies: CHECK

The day before, he'd gone over to Uncle Pete's gas station, Pete's Gas and Imports, which sat right on the border between Tivoli Proper and Serafina's Bayou. Jack liked to think of it as a portal that ushered you from one world into another.

"Where you goin', son?" Uncle Pete asked, bagging up a few bags of jerky and bottles of Mountain Dew.

"Fishin'," Jack said, shoving the bag into his knapsack.

"When you plannin' on coming back? I know your dad let you stay alone this time, but I'm supposed to be checking in on you."

"Aw, Uncle Pete. You worried? I cleared it with Dad before he left. But if you want to act like a hen, I can try to send you smoke signals all day from the bayou. Besides, I'll be back tonight. I'll stop in, okay?"

Uncle Pete was one of those men who had a lot of thoughts about what it meant to be a man. And Jack knew Pete would get all flustered when he called him a "hen" (manly man that he was).

"I ain't worried, you got a good head on yer shoulders," Pete said. "Have fun."

"I will!" said Jack.

He'd stopped in that night as promised, but Jack hadn't gone fishing. He grabbed some bottles of water while he was there. And some fudge rounds, for luck.

"Catch anything?"

"Nah, Daddy and Old Jim must've cleared out everything before they set off. You hear anything from 'em? They still on schedule?"

"Heard from them just today. They've had a good haul and are coming back on time. Next week, right when you're supposed to leave for your mama's. Danny told me to tell you he wants to see you before you leave, okay?"

"Sure thing, Uncle Pete."

"Now, what do you have planned for the rest of your week of freedom, son?"

"Not much. I'm fixin' on beating some levels on that game you got me for Christmas last year."

"Okay. Just call or stop by if you need anything."

"Should I start calling you Aunt Pete?"

"Oh, go on, git outta here, you smart-ass."

Between both well-planned stops at his uncle's, Jack was able to collect the provisions he needed without arousing suspicion. *I should join the FBI,* he thought, and decided it was time to get out of bed.

Jack washed his face and looked in the bathroom mirror, wondering if turning thirteen would make him feel more like a man. *I need a haircut,* he thought, pushing his hair up from his forehead until it stuck up like his dad's did during his college football days. He opened the medicine cabinet and took out the pomade his dad used when he was goin' "out on the town" at the Voodoo and smoothed some in his hair, smiling at his reflection.

"Damn!" he suddenly exclaimed, remembering he'd forgotten to pack something important. He went to his room quickly. "Where is it, where is it . . . Come on!" He shoved aside the contents on the top of his dresser and found the conjure bag dangling from a Little League trophy that had fallen over. Dida made it for him when he was a baby. A tiny canvas bag, dyed red and dipped in wax so it was waterproof. Inside were things supposed to keep him safe. Salt. Rue, a silver dime, a lock of his mother's hair. And other items he didn't yet understand. He fixed it around his neck, tucking the bag under his T-shirt. "That was close," he said, relieved, then finally grabbed his knapsack and headed out.

Out in the hot morning sun, Jack picked up a basketball off the cracked driveway and threw it behind him. It swooshed into the hoop nailed to the garage. "Yessss!" A good omen. He jumped on his bike, rode fast and free down his block, avoiding the school yard where the mean boys, AKA "Tivoli Trash" hung out (they were always bothering him to get his mama to read their futures), then up main street, whirring by Pete's Gas and Imports with extra speed as he rode out of town.

He headed for Trinity Bridge. *Look, Mama, no hands!* When the bridge was in sight, Jack felt happier than he had in a very long time. He was almost home with the Sorrows. *A week from now,* he thought, *everything will be different. Everything will finally be right.*

But what Jack didn't know was that there was a storm coming, one he hadn't planned on or prepared for, one that would test everyone he loved in ways he couldn't have imagined and never would have wanted.

5

As the Crow Flies

Sippie Wallace

While Jack was reading through his list one last time in his ordinary room, about to embark on an extraordinary adventure, sixteen-year-old, wiser-than-her-years Sippie Wallace woke up in a dingy rented room in New Orleans with Crow standing on her head, hopping from one foot to another.

"Go away, Crow," Sippie grumbled, trying to swat him off with her hand. "I'm tired. Let me sleep a little more." He cawed, pecking her hand hard. "Ow!" she cried out, sitting up quickly as Crow flew around the room, leaving feathers in his wake.

"You like my new place?" she asked, knowing he'd hide his head under a wing. Sippie had to agree.

The little bedroom she'd leased was nothing spectacular, unless you wanted to put it into the spectacularly *bad* category. But Sippie liked real things. And this place wasn't pretending to be anything other than what it was. You had to respect that.

Crow perched on the wide windowsill, preening. She knew

that old crow. Her whole life, every time something was about to shift, that crow showed up and put in his two cents.

"Well now, lookit you, Crow. I hope your visit means I'm about done with this dreary portion of my life. You got news?" she asked, stretching. She smiled. It was good to see him. He always made her curious, which was her favorite way to feel.

He sat there, too calm for a bird, serious in a way Sippie hadn't seen before.

"You gotta wake up before you say somethin'? Want a cuppa coffee? You never this quiet, old man. It's makin' me nervous."

She sat up against her pillow, staring the bird down as some bees buzzed around her. There wasn't a screen in the window, and Sippie was just fine with that.

She kept the window open all the time. She didn't like the smell of burnt sugar and decayed dreams that emanated from the rest of the apartment. And she felt better knowing there was a quick escape route. She'd had to escape from more dark places than she cared to count.

Sippie had memories of Crow here and there while she grew up deep in the ninth ward with her parents, Simone and Freddie St. James. Only they weren't her real parents. They'd adopted her or somethin', her father hadn't been real clear on the details when she'd asked. Simone and Freddie (whom everyone called Eight Track) didn't have much, and when Sippie was six, Simone died, thinkin' she'd be the next Billie Holiday. That's when Eight Track started drinking for real. She didn't like to think about those early days; thinking about Simone was like sinking into quicksand made of darkness. After Simone died, Sippie took care of Eight Track. But when she was thirteen, the state found out she was pretty much taking care of herself. That's when her life began to get interesting. Crow started making more frequent visits. But before it got interesting, it had to get sad again, equal parts light and dark. See, Eight Track loved his girl, and Sippie loved her Eight Track, and neither of them wanted to say good-bye. Sippie entered the foster care system, going through five good-for-nothing foster homes, and when she was fifteen, she made a life for herself. No one ever even noticed she was missing.

Sippie wasn't like any of the other girls she'd ever met. It wasn't that she defied categorization—not black, not white, light eyes, freckles, not white-girl hair, not black-girl hair—though it didn't help. It was more how those girls let all the badness in the world eat them up from the inside. Becoming these mean girls with no respect for anything, especially themselves. Though she didn't finish high school, she'd done enough to grab the attention of one of the counselors. "Why these girls got to act like that? Don't even know that the more they yell, the weaker they are. I can't take it," she'd said. The used-up man with dandruff on his shoulders just removed his glasses, looked at her like she was his last hope at saving the world and he was too damn tired, and said, "That is precisely right, Sippie. The problem is, they just don't know any better. But you do."

So she dropped out, becoming invisible, and found herself, at the beginning of her sixteenth year, all alone in the world. Only the world was scarier, dirtier, harsher, than any foster home could ever be. Which was why she could always breathe easier knowing exactly where the closest exit was. But at least she was free. And she had the good sense to hide her shine away for when she really needed it, rather than giving it up to the dark like those other girls. She'd never just hand herself over to this world.

Meanwhile, Eight Track spent his nights in homeless shelters but could be found wandering the French Quarter daily to listen to the blues drifting out through open windows. Sippie visited him almost every day.

They'd talk for hours in Jackson Square while he panhandled and she read tarot cards for tourists. She made sure to make them feel hopeful so that she could direct their smiles straight into Eight Track's pockets.

"You be feelin' the air change right before someone's even gonna decide to mess wit you, Sippie. Don't ignore that. You always had a shine to you. I guarantee if you listen close, and look for them exits, you gonna keep youself safe, cha."

"I love you, Eight Track," she'd say.

"I love you too, Sippie Girl. And I love you 'cause you beautiful, and you smart, and 'cause you *always* been different. You kin see what other folks can't. Hear what dey can't hear. And in a right-side-up world, those abilities a yours should keep you safe, only people . . . they don't seem to appreciate it much when someone shines a little *too* bright. It makes them feel worse than they already be feelin'. So they try and steal that light, or put it out. And if that happens, you come see old Eight Track. Or listen to that old Crow. Fly with him, see through his eyes. That bird be a fine teacher. And he know all the secrets. Shoot, Sippie, he know *your* secrets."

"What secrets, Eight Track? I need to know," she'd say, the lost little girl inside gazing out from her eyes. She'd carried the ache of not knowing her own truth for too long.

"You follow that old Crow. He'll tell you in his own way. You stay safe, Sippie girl."

Each time she walked away from him, she wanted to run back and beg him to take her to a time when they were happy. To get well, sober, clean. To make her feel safe. But Sippie couldn't bear to burden him with her fear. It would just make him drink a little more, die a little more. So she'd smile her good-byes, letting the hot tears fall only after she had turned her head to leave.

And now, that "fine teacher," Crow, was perched on her windowsill, his gaze steady in a way she hadn't seen from him before. This time she would discover the secret she'd been waiting for. She could feel it, and it made her scared, excited, and, beyond all reason, tremendously sad.

"I had the dream again last night. About that strange little house surrounded by water and wildness. The one with those beautiful colored glass bottles hangin' from the trees outside. And candles and flowers all mixed up between odds and ends of pretty dyed fabrics. Like someone's makin' all sorts of things. Quilts, jewelry, paintings. But, this time there was something different."

Crow moved closer. He was happy.

"This time, the barefoot woman turned and looked right at me. And she looked so sad, Crow. She looked like the blues. She was wearing a plain ol' white men's tank, the kind you buy nine to a package. Her long, gypsy skirt was tied up on one side, and her ankles and wrists chimed with bangles. Black curls fell down her back with bits of leaves and moss braided right in. And she looked up at me from under those curls and said, 'Come home, cha, come home.'"

Crow stood, unblinking, on Sippie's chest.

"That's her, ain't it, Crow. Is it time?"

The bird nodded.

"Let's fly, then . . . old bird. Let's fly." She closed her eyes, smiling.

Sippie was never quite sure if she was really flying with Crow or dreaming or both, but she knew everything he'd ever shown her had been true. And they were things she couldn't have known any other way. Sippie learned long ago not to question the unex-

plainable. Sometimes there were questions that simply had no answers.

Crow swooped low and high, soaring over the rooftops of New
Orleans until the canvas of the earth below changed from clustered homes to a thick, dense green sliced with narrow blue wa-
terways and tan dirt roads. Then Crow coasted down as they almost
clipped a sign that read: ENTERING TIVOLI PARISH.

*Look close, Sippie. . . . The ruins of the Sorrow golden age stretch wide
across this bayou and back again all the way to Bourbon Street.*

He darted and ducked under low-lying branches and lazy
clusters of hanging silver Spanish moss. Then they met the sky
again, circling above a long strip of land.

*See that there? That's Saint Sabine Isle. Used to be the finest resort in
all the world. Gone now. All of it gone.*

The Gulf of Mexico lay endlessly before them, breaking free
from the land, its small waves lapping at the shores. He circled back
around and soon they were homing in on a small group of build-
ings along the bayou, where he landed softly atop a tin roof next
to the narrow metal chimney of a two-story house on stilts with
peeling paint and a sign that read: THE VOODOO.

Three women sat on the lower, creaky open porch while a man
banged a hammer on the upper porch, trying to win a losing battle
against some patch or another.

*That's JuneBug Lafourch. His family runs the fish house. They
moved out of the bayou a long time ago, but Junie, he stays and struggles
with the drink,* Crow said, moving down to the railing so Sippie
could better see the women. *And these, minus one, are my witches.*

His witches sat there in mismatched chairs positioned not too close, but not too far apart. Next to them, a vintage fortune-telling machine leaned against a cracked front window. It was the kind where you put in a coin and a plastic gypsy inside lit up, vibrated, then spoke to you before spitting out a ticketed fortune.

Of course, it doesn't work anymore. Everything and everyone living in Serafina's Bayou is broken or used up in some way or another, Sippie. I think you can help fix some of that, Crow said, fussing. These witches, the Serafinas, they call themselves, they gettin' lazier each year. That pretty one with the dark curls and perfect features, she's Millie Bliss, but don't be fooled. She's both charming and charmed, but unhappy down to her core. When that hurt she has inside comes out, the whole earth shakes. And the old hunched one? That's Dida. Most people, including Dida, believe she's the lost Sorrow child, and if that's true, she doesn't look too bad for her age. She always wears that red bandanna in her hair. And her eyes, they still shine so blue and pretty. Claudette, her daughter, the one next to her . . . she had the same kind of eyes, before she got into the laundry soap when she was four. Got blinded by lye. There she is, one hand on the whiskey, the other on her tarot cards. Most think she's hiding from her blindness, but in fact she's letting her blindness hide her.

Sippie looked at Claudette. Her eyes were cast over with a film, gazing out unseeing, like the opals in a brooch Simone used to wear. It was damn eerie. And she looked so breakably thin, with stringy blond hair pulled back into a severe bun at the nape of her neck.

"Crow!" Millie yelled suddenly. "Where you been, cha?"

Crow flew down, perching on Millie's outstretched arm, then moved up to her shoulder and then back down again, pacing. Sippie could smell her. She smelled like a vintage dress.

"That damn crow better be bringin' good news this mornin', not bad," Claudette said.

"The crow bring what the crow bring," said Dida, rocking in her chair. She lit up a pipe.

He cawed loudly.

"What's wrong with you, Crow?" asked Millie.

"There you go again, askin' questions you already know the answers to," said Dida. "That damn crow is here to warn us about somethin'. And we been talkin' all morning about how we all feel something just ain't right."

"Is that so, Crow?" asked Millie. "You puzzle out our mystery? Wish you could spit it out. We been sittin' here arguin' over what kinda bad is on its way."

Crow cawed again. Louder this time.

It was Dida who stood first, arched her bent back, and placed the quilt she'd been sewing on her chair, before roughly pulling at Claudette to get her inside the juke joint.

"Let's check the cards. We been chattin' all this time but never thought to use any of the magic we know we got. Millie, put on a kettle for the herbs, I'll get *The Book of Sorrows*."

"You gonna go get in the boat, find JuneBug, and ask him to take you into New Orleans on such short notice?" asked Millie, frowning.

"Ain't got to. Frances has it."

"What do you mean, 'Frances has it'? I thought we all agreed it stays at Thirteen Bourbon!" Millie said angrily. "That book is too damn important to risk exposure to storms or damp. Why on earth did you let her take it?"

"*Let* her take it? You're funny! No one lets or stops that girl from doin' anything," said Dida. "Claudette told me just yesterday."

"She tell you she was takin' it, or did you 'see' she was takin' it?" asked Millie.

"Neither, Abe brought it to her. Why do you care so much? And she don't need our permission to take that book for a spell. It's as much hers as ours," said Claudette.

"And besides," said Dida, "you should be glad she wants it. I swear there's a glow comin' off her all soft lately, you notice?"

"Be that as it may, we know that a big storm is coming! That book should be safe on higher ground."

"Seems you be a little *too* upset about this, Millie, what you hidin'?" Dida asked sharply.

Millie didn't answer. She turned her attention to Crow.

"Go now," said Millie, shaking him off her arm. "Go tell Frances we want that book back right now. I don't like that it's here in the bayou, but we know you're trying to tell us somethin' and the book might help. Go'n, shoo. You bothered us enough for one day."

Crow hopped off but didn't fly away. Instead, he peered inside the window at them.

See them, Sippie. Listen to them. Learn. . . .

Claudette slowly weaved her way around the carelessly arranged tables, eventually reaching out to hold on to the long bar that ran the length of the room. Dida switched on sets of mismatched lamps that made the whole place light up like a colorful paper lantern. Beads and crystals decorated every surface imaginable, and a strand of Christmas lights shaped like moons and stars draped across the stage at the back, glowing like candles.

Dida helped Claudette find a seat at the bar. "Maybe Crow's just worried over the hurricane on its way, honey, you think that's it?"

"No, Mama. I think it's more than that," Claudette responded quietly.

"JuneBug!" yelled Dida while Millie disappeared into a back room. "Stop all that bangin'!"

The banging stopped.

"So what do you think it is, child?" asked Dida.

"Don't you think I would have told you if I knew?"

"Why not look a little harder, cha?" asked Millie, reemerging and preening in the mirror behind the bar. "We all know your sight can be limited when it comes to things you don't want to see. Which makes us money with tourists, but isn't very helpful in times like these."

Hold on to your hat, Sippie girl, said Crow. *This is why I brought you here. To see how they treat each other.*

"Frances will be better prepared than any of us for whatever it is that's going to happen. Crow will get her, she'll bring the book, and she'll sit with us. Together we'll be able to figure it out," Dida assured them. "Things will go back to the way they used to be. The way they were supposed to be."

The kettle started to scream, and Dida rushed to the kitchen to quiet it.

"She's not going to pay him no mind. And she's not comin', she's not goin' to bring the book, and she's not the damn savior of this family" said Millie. "I know her better than you do. She may be reconsidering some things, but she's never coming all the way back. Trust me."

"I'm not in the mood to argue with you," snapped Claudette. "But you should know when to hold your tongue, Millie Bliss. You're always tryin' to pretend you know her best, like you were a child raisin' a child. But, you listen here, once and for all. She and I might have our differences, but she's *my* daughter. You don't hold no rights over her. And you ain't been such a good *friend* lately, if you know what I mean."

Millie swung around from her reflection with a glare to face Claudette.

It never takes much to set Millie Bliss on fire, especially when she's been caught doing something she shouldn't.

"You only want to lay claim on her when it suits you, Claudette. That's not what a mother does. A mother is supposed to be there for her child. When was the last time either of you even checked in on her? Never mind. I already know the answer. Too long ago, that's when."

"Ain't my fault she took down the ropes that lead me to her place."

"Excuses. Always excuses. You're a cold woman, Claudette. Alligators could've raised her better."

"Shut up! You just shut your filthy mouth, girl." Claudette's voice came out hurt and full of broken glass. "You have no idea, no idea what it was like havin' a baby and bein' blind! I was good to her, I was—"

Dida came back in with a pot full of boiling water and set it down. "Not now, ladies. Not now."

"Tell her, Mama," Claudette whispered. "Tell her I was good at bein' a mama when Frankie was first born, tell her."

"You know you were, you don't have to prove it to nobody," said Dida.

"We gotta hash all this out again? Really?" asked Millie. "Frances was four, I'd just come to live with you. Only six at the time. And you were supposed to be watching us. And Frankie was swimming in the bay by the lighthouse, and she got caught in that current. And you couldn't see her, *so I had to save her.*"

"I don't need remindin', Millie. I think about it every damn day. And besides, I meant the time before *you* came, when it was all warm and quiet," said Claudette.

"Millie," said Dida, "You take too much to heart. You belong to us as if you were our own. That's why we argue. Aint that right, Claudette."

Claudette shrugged and Millie looked as if she were almost sorry.

"Look, Claudette, you know how I get when I'm mad. I've had a really bad couple of weeks. Don't pay no attention to me."

"I hope Frankie never finds out you been with Danny." Claudette spat out like a slap.

"I swear to god I might lose my mind, Dida! Hold me back. If she weren't already blind I'd put a fork in her eye." shouted Millie.

Suddenly Dida shouted out, "No one gonna listen to their matriarch? I told you now was not the time! Claudette, we bettah leave this for today. We'll try again tomorrow."

Crow flew away fast, not wanting an angry Millie to see him still hovering. Sippie had a million questions, but there were only two repeating over and over in her mind. Looping like his wings in the sky. *Is Frances my mother? Are these my people?*

You already know, Sippie. You known for a long time. You dream of her. And your instincts keep drawing you to 13 Bourbon Street. You got to go to her, Sippie. Tell her I sent you, and you give her a message. You tell her I said to find Jack, find Jack, find Jack. . . .

"Who in the hell is Jack?"

"*You know that too. He's just like you.*"

As they flew back to her apartment, Sippie saw shadows everywhere. Omens, perhaps ghosts. Then they were in her bedroom again. Usually she'd wake right up, but now she watched herself sleep through Crow's eyes. He didn't want to leave her, and that's when she knew why she'd felt sad before their flight.

This it, Crow? The end of the line for you and me?

You don't need me anymore, Sippie. You find Frances, help each other. Maybe we'll fly together again someday. But everything has an end. You get the choice on makin' it happy or sad. Endings are just doorways, Sippie. Endings are just doorways, doorways. . . .

And just like that, she was sleeping inside herself again. She was barefoot in a hallway, banging on a door, searching, with an ache in her heart, for something she knew she'd never be able to find. But that was just a dream, and part of her knew that when she woke up, she'd find the door she was always trying to open. The door home. Crow had given her everything she needed.

And not one thing he gave her would help once she arrived on Sorrow soil.

6

Frances Tells Her Secret

The morning Jack disappeared, I stood on my little porch, blissfully unaware of his plans, wrapped in a quilt to fend off the damp. I held *The Book of Sorrows* to my chest and looked up into the blue sky. The fig trees near Sorrow Hall were heavy with fruit, and I inhaled deeply the clingy sweet scent of the ones ripe for picking. That's when I saw that strange, fine bird, Crow, swooping down and around, taking in what I'd grown up thinking of as "Crow's World." He only showed himself when things were about to change—a Sorrow sort of weather vane—for better or worse. "You bringin' change, Crow? Because, if so, you're late to the party!" I shouted at the sky, twirling, but he wasn't paying me any mind. "Fine," I grumbled. "I don't need you to tell me things are changing anymore, I feel it buzzing all up inside me like a million honeybees."

I took a deep breath, opening the book with intention. I wanted to make my way back to those I loved. And the summer solstice ceremony that was held on Solstice Eve at Sorrow Hall every year seemed a fitting time to start. I'd been at the center of the celebration until I was fifteen and then never went to another one again. By the end of that summer I was in New Orleans masking my broken heart with the grown-up task of running our family business at Thirteen Bourbon. Then, when I came crawling home the following summer, bent and broken from my year spent in an upside-down world, part of me was afraid that on the off chance the magic was real, I'd set my family on fire with my mind. Millie took over my responsibilities, both here and in New Orleans . . . and I was just *fine* with that.

But that was a lifetime ago, and dammit, I was trying. I'd prepare the teas and ointments for the ceremony, and that way, they'd just *know* I was ready to start living again and we didn't need to have some sort of dramatic sit-down discussing it half to death.

We Sorrows don't like going soft.

I turned to the chapter on celebrating the summer solstice. I used to know every last word by heart, but I hadn't held that book in my hands since I decided to hide all up inside myself. "Okay, what do I need?" I scribbled down the list of herbs and took a basket with me into the garden.

I glanced at Sorrow Hall in the distance and thought about telling—more like *warning*—them that I was fixin' on forgiving everyone. But then I figured it'd be best to take the one-step-at-a-time approach. Those women could make me angry so quick, I might end up reconsidering my reconsideration.

I picked through the herbs before deciding I needed some red phlox. It wasn't in the recipe, but I could feel it would be important. It grew wild and tall along the dirt roads of the bayou running in and out of Tivoli Proper. If I was going to reclaim my talents, I should be as creative as I could be right off the bat. I went down to the river, pushed my pirogue out from the tall grasses, and poled down to Trinity Bridge, muttering to myself the whole way. "Red phlox . . . uniting souls, thinking alike . . . working together for a common goal . . . can help foster courage inside of people too afraid to love. Place the flowers in salads or teas, safe for ingestion. *Perfect!*"

Just then I damn near fell out my boat when I saw Mama and Dida making their way back from what must have been a morning powwow with Millie at the Voodoo. They looked so solemn, like they came straight out a history book. If they were a painting, it would have been titled *The Absurd History of the Bayou Witch Queens* or something more impressive and equally ridiculous.

"Mornin'," I greeted them as I glided by.

Dida almost tipped over their boat in surprise.

"Millie wants the book back," said Dida, blinking curiously.

"She'll get it back." I shrugged.

That was easy enough, I thought, securing my boat. Wading onto dry land, I looked down the road, over Trinity Bridge, toward the tall red flowers blossoming in huge clusters. I hadn't been over that bridge for almost nine years, since I walked away from Jack and Danny. And I couldn't deny that anymore. Sure, Danny fought me for custody, but I was the one who walked away. Feeling a chill wash over me, I knew I couldn't cross that bridge, not just yet. I turned around and faced the dirt road. If I went south, I'd hit Saint Sabine Isle, which wasn't much of anything anymore thanks to storms. It was where Danny and I—no, I wasn't going to think about him. If I went left, I'd hit the Voodoo and loop back around to the other side of Meager Swamp. But if I turned right, well, I'd eventually hit another bridge just outside of Tivoli Parish, but it would take hours. A lot of poachers and Cajuns lived inside the woods off that road. But it seemed the best bet for avoiding too many memories too soon. The phlox grew there, too, thank the Lord.

It felt good, surprisingly good, to escape the limited confines I'd set for myself. The soft crunch of dirt under my bare feet, the damp bottom of my skirt drying against my ankles while I picked wildflowers. *It's a good day.*

When I'd collected enough and turned to head back, it was as if my mood had turned right around with my body like it used to. All pride and sadness and hope for some real magic to happen that would heal me. I stopped thinking my way forward and found myself thinking my way back.

I wish I hadn't walked so far, because all I wanted now was to be safe at my little house. I didn't want to think about the time I couldn't get back. No amount of red phlox in the world could turn back time.

If I could make a pie chart, like we made in ninth-grade math, mine would read: REASONS I LEFT DANNY AND JACK.

Twenty percent would be red, with a label: "Unable to live a normal life without losing her mind." Sixty percent would be purple (like the dresses I used to wear around New Orleans when I thought I was queen of the world) and labeled "Her deep, dark secret." And the last twenty percent would be some kind of sick, sour yellow, labeled "Cursed." . . .

Leaving behind things you love is the worst kind of drug. It makes you feel brave and solid. Love makes you crazy and leaving makes you sane, so why would leaving be anything but heroic? See how that works . . . it gets all turned around, and then the second you feel like your heart may fly untethered again, you take another dose of "leaving" and get yourself gone.

When I left for New Orleans (intent on handling the business and becoming the witch everyone said I was supposed to be) I didn't feel like I was leaving at all, I felt like I had *arrived*.

"If I'm the queen of this Sorrow clan, then I'm gonna run it proper," I'd said. And I packed up my things and left.

I *thought* I was happy, that I knew everything, holding some kind of absurd court and loving every second of it. I'd always loved it, Millie and I grew up like wild things inside a traveling circus that didn't travel. And the people, they came to us. "Come one, come all," we'd sing out from the corner. "Come all you magic-less, lost, searching souls. Come see the sorrows your fortunes they hold. Explore life's surprises before they unfold . . . right this way, right this way . . ." We'd dance to the tap-tap-tapping of steel-toed shoes and the shining moans of the brass bands echoing through the streets. And that old building full of crazy, with its stucco peeling back one hundred years of Sorrow memories captured behind its iron gates blooming with trumpet vines.

And I loved our apartment on the third floor. How that hallway curved dramatically and the atrium that rounded out the back of the apartment had windows in surprising places that let light into all the dark corners. The golden lamplight that fell on the once red-painted walls now faded to coral, the lanterns with colored paper shades, and all our mismatched china. And those double French doors that opened into our secret greenhouse garden, its space filled with the scent of the bayou from the plants we needed to do our work.

At night I always wore the gypsy clothes people expect to see when they come to get their fortunes told by a Sorrow witch.

Especially Frances the Great. I was also quite the alchemist, concocting all the tinctures and oils for the shop downstairs.

Every night, people came—by appointment only, which I found very fancy—and Eight Track would stand guard while I gave those people what they wanted—stories of love and happiness tinged by sadness so they felt true—and they gave me money for it. There was a little buzzer under the reading table in the parlor, so if someone got angry or drunk, I simply pressed it, and Eight Track came in and took care of the problem right quick.

Everything seemed like it was okay. More than okay. Until that night I lounged in a booth with Jazz Man, and I'd had a little too much to drink. Eight Track was behind the bar, and he'd called out, "Frankie girl, look see who just walked in. Lookin' all lost." Eight Track always had a way of sucking the awkward out of any situation by saying the very thing that could make it even more awkward. I used to be able to wield my humor like that. I lost that somewhere down the line. That's one thing Danny said during an angry fit a year into our marriage: "You used to be funny, you used to smile, now you walk around lookin' dead inside."

I looked up that night and there he was. Danny. He'd come in from Tivoli only to find me all cuddled up with Jazz Man.

He was so young. So was I. Sometimes, when I think on it, I get mad I ever expected him to act any differently.

"What you want, Danny?"

"I'm on my way . . . I mean, I'm leavin'. You know, for college. And I wanted to say that last month was, well, I just wanted to know if I could write to you or somethin'."

I didn't mean to laugh. And it was a cruel little laugh that escaped my lips. Jazz Man laughed, too. I felt like an older woman that night. Sultry, without a care in the world. Besides, Danny was leaving. And he'd already had his chance. His feeling torn up about it wasn't bothering me. Not. At. All.

"Move along now, little man. I don't know what this fine woman saw in your skinny ass anyways." Jazz Man smirked, taking a long drag of his cigarette.

"Look, mister, I'm a quarterback. Gonna be all-American. Frankie, this guy is a grown man. Does he even know how old you are? She's fifteen, did you know that?"

Jazz Man left right quick after that, muttering, "It just ain't right," the whole way out the door. I never did find out if Danny did that on purpose. Not that it mattered.

Danny reached for my hand. "Come on, Frankie, come outside. Let's say good-bye the right way. I didn't mean to ruin your date."

"My date? Danny, I've been here for a whole month now. You didn't ruin my date, you just broke up an entire relationship! I'm not yours anymore." My voice trembled more than I wanted.

"If he really loves you, it won't matter."

"What are you talking about? That man is out there now thinking he's a damn pedophile and never knew it! And what are you talking love for? You think there's always got to be love?" I said harshly, and pulled nervously at my necklace, a chain with a key shaped like a mermaid tail inscribed with the words, "She came from the sea." He'd found it while we combed the beaches of Saint Sabine Isle. *That was love, not this, this is life.*

"You still wear that?"

"Of course! Why wouldn't I? I loved you once, didn't I? You sure you still got your senses? Good luck at college, Danny. Seems to me your dumb self is gonna need it. I swear." I gave him a quick shove and ran upstairs. And that damn fool ran right after me.

We made all kinds of magic that night, but he still left. And I acted like I didn't care.

"They always leave," said Simone at the bar the next day. "Chin up, girl. You your own strength."

I never saw Jazz Man again. A month later I found out my own body betrayed me, carrying a child I couldn't fathom meeting. I went to bed each night staring into that mirror, the one that dates back to Serafina. Sometimes I'd even place my hands on it and beg her to let me inside, to fix everything that was broken, to talk to me the way my family told me she would. But all she gave me, month after month, was a growing belly. Danny wrote a few letters, called a few times. Maybe even more than a few . . . but letters and phone calls are easy. Staying is hard.

And all I could think of was Dida, Mama, Millie, and Old Jim. Heck, I even wanted JuneBug. I wanted everything I had always known through and through. All I wanted was to go home to Sorrow Hall. But something held me back. A stubbornness, sure. I'm stubborn as all heck. But it was bigger than that. How does the queen of the world, Frances the Great, get knocked up and not know if the father was a fool boy or a second-rate musician, and either way, neither of them loved her enough to stick around? How does that even happen? Witches ought to be able to see those kinds of things coming. Turns out I wasn't anything special at all. Just a lovesick, stupid girl dressing up like a freak and spinning lies for money. Would Dida, Claudette, and Millie still love me if they knew I wasn't powerful after all? And that's when it hit me: None of us knew what love was. Because we were all so damn in love with that ridiculous Sorrow legend. It eclipsed everything. But so what if I wasn't a witch? Choke, gasp, horror of my life . . . I had more pressing issues. I had a baby on the way. And I was gonna have it. It'd be fine.

It had to be fine.

"You'd think we could conjure some more money, right, Eight Track?" I had laughed uneasily after glancing at the books.

He'd smiled at me. "I heard tell that Serafina did that very thing. That true, Frances?"

"If you'd asked me last week, I'd have said yes and started trying it myself. But I've *seen the light,* and now all I can say is, raise the prices on that whiskey, will you?"

"You a fine businesswoman for someone so young, Frankie." Then his face grew serious. "I'm sorry I let Danny tell that good-for-nothin' Jazz Man how young you are. But if he really loved you, he wouldn't have taken off all scared of a law we both know you could have fought."

"Don't worry, Eight Track. It'll all work out."

"Or it won't," he'd said. "But either way it still works out, right? 'Cause we can't control what happens to us, just how we react. Either way I'll help you. You know I'll always be here for you. I have been since you were little and came in like a ray of sunshine. Ain't nothin' gonna change that."

"I know." I'd hugged him.

It'd be fine. It had to be fine.

It *would* be fine. No one would be angry with me. Heck, I came from a family that would have celebrated such a disastrous thing. Unwed teenage motherhood was a right of passage or something. The odder the better . . . I walked out into the bright sunshine of Bourbon Street with my heart almost light.

But then I saw them, a *family.*

The little boy rode on his father's shoulders, and the mother held a little girl's hand. And the shared smiles that kept breaking out over their faces were more magical than anything I'd ever seen. Entranced, I found myself following after them.

I watched them for a whole day.

I watched how the mother always seemed to have whatever any of them needed, right there in her bag. Abracadabra, a Band-Aid. Poof! A tissue. A bottle of water, a box of crayons. A sweater.

I watched how the father gently disciplined them. "Don't touch, too hot . . . ow!" he'd say as their eyes grew wide.

I watched how they did a graceful dance of safety, always making sure the kids were on the inside of the sidewalk instead of walking by the curb. Even as they grew tired and the kids started to cry, those parents still smiled at each other and shared secret eye language that promised warm bodies pressed against the tide of chaos when they were safely back in their hotel and those little monsters, *their* beloved monsters, were asleep.

Then, as twilight hit the French Quarter, the parents— knowing it would soon be a den of iniquity and no place for their darlings—got into a cab. I was sad to see them go. Then I was just sad.

When I returned to 13 Bourbon Street, I saw the place already packed with the usual crowd. Drunken tourists, regulars, and just plain old lost souls searching for cures that would never help, looking for the hopeful lies I'd tell them about their futures.

I couldn't bring myself to go in. Instead I wandered off toward the Old Ursuline Convent. There's a marble tomb there, raised up to keep it safe from the waters that rise without warning sometimes, and when I was a child I loved sitting on it and talking to that little girl, the Lost Girl of August. The memorial carved into that stone meant more to me that night than it ever had before:

HERE LIES THE BODY OF THE LOST GIRL OF AUGUST.
BORN—UNKNOWN. DIED—AUGUST 1901.
A REMINDER TO ALL THOSE STORM-TOSSED SOULS: CHILDREN ARE
GOD'S CREATURES FIRST.
LET NO OTHER CHILD DIE ALONE.

Alone. I'd felt loved yet alone my whole life. Between that family I'd watched all throughout the French Quarter and the Lost Girl of August, I'd made up my mind.

The baby deserved what I'd never had. Something I'd made fun of, turned away from. Something I'd been taught to disdain. The baby deserved a normal life. Uncomplicated. Free. *Safe.*

Eight months later, I gave that beautiful secret to Eight Track. And even though we'd worked the whole thing out, he was still trying to give me grief. I'd just pushed a baby out all by myself at sixteen years old, and that man was trying to father me, a wild girl who wanted nothing but a father but didn't know how to listen to one.

"You bein' too hard on yourself, Frances. You just a child, you can't throw the baby out with the bathwater. . . ."

"I know, but this is better for her. Just take her. You and Simone raise her like your own. But don't tell nobody. I'll die, I swear it. Nobody can know."

"Ain't you gonna miss her? Want her back?"

"She deserves better than me. I'm a lie from a long line of other lies. Make her true, Eight Track. Make her strong. Not false like they made me. Don't lie to her. Make her like Simone's voice and your strong arms. Fill her up with your goodness. Okay?"

"When she gets big, you want me to tell her who her real family is?"

"An honest person knows when to tell a lie, Eight Track.

That's from *The Book of Sorrows*. I never knew what that meant until just now. It's better if she doesn't know. Tell her I died. Because, I did. I did die. I'll never be the same person again."

By then I was crying, and Eight Track was sitting on the bed holding that quiet baby, who was already watching her world fall apart. Already soaking up tears that weren't hers.

"You ain't no lie, Frankie. And you still magic, you hear? Even if you don't want that to be the case, it is. You can't change that. You can't be someone you ain't. Just 'cause something ain't the way you thought it would be, don't mean there ain't no truth to it. Sometimes . . . sometimes the true thing is even better."

He was making some sort of sense, and I didn't want any doubts. "Get out!" I screamed. And kept screaming long after he'd taken my baby away and hidden her inside what I believed would be a better life.

And with my body aching for her, my crumbling faith fell apart completely. I knew that no one on earth had ever been more wrong about anything.

I wasn't the queen of anything. I wasn't magic. My family wasn't magic. I was nothing but a poor, backwoods girl with a foul mouth and a fistful of mud.

The day after I had her, I returned to the bayou. My body sore, my heart sorer.

"She's lost her mind," I heard them whisper my first night home. I'd walked up the stairs slowly, almost falling through the rotting ones I used to avoid with ease. I was silent but screaming inside.

The next day, I found my mama in her usual spot in the back gallery, turning over cards. The whipping sound soothed her. I wanted to talk to her because I hoped she knew my secret. She was supposed to be the mind reader.

See it. Prove me wrong. Make me believe. See what I've done. Oh, Mama, see it. I've made a terrible mistake. One I can't take back. I can't speak of it, Mama, you have to see it.

I held my breath, hoping against hope.

"What's the matter with you, girl?" she said, sensing me standing there. "Someone break your heart? If so, you just tell Old Jim and he'll make sure whoever it was makes a nice meal for the alligators. You know there ain't nothin' he won't do for you, Little Bit."

"He can't tell me the truth," I said.

"What does that mean? Your granddaddy ain't never told a lie."

"He doesn't know he's lying. You're all lying. We're nothin' but fakes. . . ." My voice came out sharp and unforgiving as those hateful words that covered the truth I couldn't tell came pouring out.

She listened, I'll give her that, and when I finished my tirade, she pushed back a stray wisp of her thin blond hair and asked, "But what about the facts, Frances? What about those people who come to New Orleans just to see us and have us read their fortunes? We even have a place in that book, *The Top Ten Most Psychic Families*, or whatever it's called."

As if that were all we needed to make it true.

"So what if we can do a little more than most when it comes to being strange?" I argued. "What makes that magic? Some families, they have generations of people who are athletes, or entertainers, or politicians. Talents, that's all it is. Something one of us decided we were good at a long time ago, and then we made up a bunch of silly fairy tales around it. Blew it up in our minds. All I see is a freak show, Mama. A carnival act. All those people who make fun of us, who steer clear and snicker when we go into town? They're right. How about that? We've been making fools of ourselves for a hundred years, and you all can keep right on doing that. But I'm done."

Dida had snuck in and was waiting in the doorway. "You can't be done," she piped up. "You're the best of us. You're the shining hope, honey. You're the one Serafina will speak to. Whatever happened to you, you'll get over it. It just takes some time, sugar."

"Why don't you know?" I whispered.

"Know what?" they both asked.

"Why don't you know why I've changed? If you're all so full of the power, why don't you whip up some truth tea? Your cards ain't tellin' you nothin'? And while you're trying to explain why you can't 'see' what made me lose my mind, why not try and explain how any of you, if you love me so damned much, let me move to New Orleans by myself to run a bar! I was only fifteen years old. Who does that? You never even asked why I was leaving, because you didn't want to know. All stoic and proudly wearing your lies."

"You've always had a mind of your own, Frances. We trust you. You've been grown since you were born. Besides, can you imagine if we'd tried to stop you?" asked Claudette.

"But you didn't try. And now I can't fix it, I can't fix it!" I yelled, slamming my way out into the back gardens so they wouldn't see the tears fall.

"Where are you going?" Claudette called after me.

From the shadows, I watched her grip the side of the table and stand up shakily in that way that used to make me want to run to her and help, to feel her soft skin against my cheek, and then move away so she'd have to try to find my face with her hands. I loved how she would run her hands over my features. But now even her shaking seemed like an act. She'd walked this house and property her whole life, she must have memorized it by now. She was just pretending not to know. They all pretended not to know, like it was too much trouble to try to fix what had been broken in me. I hated her in that moment. I hated everything.

"I'm going to the Voodoo. And I'm going to drink. And you should stop me, because that's what I hear mothers are supposed to do. But you won't!"

She sat back down. She didn't call after me. She just sat down, head cocked to one side, and started turning over those cards of hers again, listening longer to whatever she thought those raised braille numbers were telling her than she did to my silent cries for help.

I never lived there again. After a few nights with Millie at the Voodoo, I decided to move into the little shack down by the docks. Still on Sorrow soil, but tucked out of view in an area even more overgrown than that big house. If you can imagine.

Mama came to find me once, right when I was fixin' the place up. She used those ropes Old Jim had strung up all over the property after she went blind and raised, year after year, as she grew. Now they're overgrown with vines and flowers so you can't see the rope at all. I sort of love them.

"Come home," she said. "I need you."

"That's exactly the problem, Mama. Children need their parents. You're not supposed to need me. It's backwards. Like everything else in this family. Besides, if you need me so much, why did you let me go away in the first place? You only need me now because I'm *convenient*."

She left, angrily calling out after her, "Ingrate!" And so I cut the ropes. And the next day when I saw Old Jim trying to repair them, I yelled, "Don't you dare, old man! I cut it on purpose."

He stopped and looked at me with that heavy sort of disappointment he covers up his anger with. "You just let me know when you get on with the forgive and forget part of this tantrum, and I'll put it back up, okay, Little Bit?"

I don't remember what I said, but it must've been something mean because he smiled and said, "See? You ain't *that* different."

A few years later, I was back with Danny. And things were more rocky than before because there was a lie of omission inside each exhale. In the end, I always came home to that little shack, the silence of hiding becoming my norm. No one ever questioned it. But the whole while, I couldn't help wondering what would have happened if I had kept my baby. . . .

I had to stop all this remembering. I had to move on, move forward. Things were changing. Red phlox in hand, I shook myself from my reverie, got in my boat, and pushed along, my eyes catching on something in the distance.

Jack.

He was deep in the cypress trees where Millie and I used to play when we were little, heading toward the lean-to hidden on the right banks of Sorrow Bay. He didn't see me. I smiled to myself. "What you up to, boy? An adventure?"

I left him there. Confident that he'd be safe, that all boys about to turn thirteen should feel wild and free.

And when I got back home, ready to settle in, that's when I saw the boat full of trouble heading my way. I put down my basket of phlox and picked up my gun.

7

Sippie and the Meat Boys

Sippie opened her eyes. Just like all the other times she "flew" with Crow, she felt queasy. But this time, it was a bigger sort of feeling. She was close this time, so close to what she always wanted, she could almost reach out and touch it. Like the brass ring on the merry-go-round Simone took her to once when she was little and they were happy and safe.

She slowly packed up her few belongings. "I have to tell Eight Track where I'm going. And maybe . . . maybe he'll finally get his act together if he knows that *I know*." She dumped a box of costume jewelry into a bag; stuffed in some of her short, second dresses and torn leggings. She found the other red Chuck, even though she didn't really want to look under the bed. After all, how could she face her real mother without wearing her red sneakers? She had standards.

She threw the bag over her shoulder and went to find Eight Track. But when she got to St. Mark's Square, he wasn't there—which worried her more than she cared to think on. He'd been looking thinner lately, weaker. It had been a solid two months since she'd seen him, and last time he had said, "The liver can take only so much."

It was so hot out, the air felt like it was burning holes in her eyes. She took the back streets to 13 Bourbon, so she could get herself a little piece of luck from the Lost Girl of August. She'd loved that tomb by the Ursuline Convent since she was a little girl and Eight Track had first told her the story, what there was of it. "We lost girls together," she'd whisper, and tap the cool marble twice, for luck.

She'd been to 13 Bourbon before. Too many times to count. She had always felt like a spy, peering in through the windows, pretending to be fascinated by the faded posters inside, advertising tours. Swamp tours, ghost tours, haunted New Orleans tours, voo-doo tours, even "Authentic Witch" tours. That was the one that caught her eye. The illustration of the woman reading tarot cards—of Frances reading tarot cards. "Meet the cursed Sorrow witches and have your fortune told LIVE right here on 13 Bourbon Street! But be warned! These ladies don't lie!" Then, in fine print across the bottom: "By appointment only." Just looking at Frances was like looking in a mirror. But even though she'd known, she'd still needed Crow to spell it out for her.

These are my people, she thought to herself, trying to find a little courage in her deep well of sarcasm. "Beggars can't be choosers," she said, standing in front of the big green doors, staring at the gold "13" right above the mermaid-tail knocker. Everything was different now. The times she'd been here before, she was only guessing she belonged here, to this building, to these people. But now she knew. All of this was part of her. Every part of her wanted to run away. But she couldn't run anymore.

She opened the door and walked in. She was one step closer to Frances.

Inside, it was cool and dark. A flight of old stairs rose in front of her to a second-floor hallway lined with doors. To her left was a tourist trap magic shop. People milled about, bumping into round wire postcard holders and shelves of fake voodoo doll kits. No one was behind the counter. There was a torn sign taped up: RING FOR SERVICE. She grabbed a map that read, BAYOU TOURS: TIVOLI PARISH, and walked back to the foyer where it opened upon a cozy lobby. She continued through the large archway that led to the bar. She hoped Abe was there. She could go for some gumbo and a root beer. It was still fairly empty. Just the bartender and a few loud twenty-something boys drinking too much, too early.

All of me . . . why not take all of me . . . , she heard from some far-off memory. She shook the sound out of her head.

"Hey there, Sippie! Haven't seen you in a dog's age. What brings you round today? You need something?" asked Abe. He always reminded her of a younger, happier Eight Track.

"Hey, Abe." She smiled, walked up to the bar, and sat on a stool, spinning a little as she did.

"If you've finally gotten up the courage to meet with one of the Serafinas, you're out of luck. They're all back in the bayou getting ready for their big celebration."

"That's just it, Abe. It's not about courage anymore. Now I got no choice. I got to go where they are."

"Why you got to go there, little lady?"

"This one here, this one's Frances, right?" asked Sippie, pointing to the laminated poster fixed to the side of the big, gold, old-fashioned cash register. For some reason, it always reminded Sippie of an organ grinder.

"Dat's right," Abe confirmed, picking up a glass and drying it with a perfectly white towel. "But you never asked for her before. And she don't come here. Gave up on all this hoodoo years ago, before I took over this bar. Your daddy knows her, though. Knew her real good when she was growin' up. How's Eight Track doin', anyway?"

Sippie tried to answer but couldn't.

"Still can't find him?"

"I'm scared he might have gone and died, Abe," she whispered.

"I kept tryin' to tell him to come back and work here with me. But he just wouldn't. Strange. And if he's gone, Sippie, maybe he's better off. All those years I watched him, that big strong man, get smaller and smaller."

Sippie didn't think it was strange. She already knew part of why he couldn't bring himself to go anywhere near 13 Bourbon. And why he'd always forbidden her to go as well. It was where Simone made her final mistake.

She shivered.

"Okay, sugar, let's change this sorry subject. Now, I know Frances pretty well, Sippie. She's hard. A hard woman with a name that suits her. Full of Sorrow, that one. I'm not sure surprising her would be the best idea."

"Come on, Abe. Just take me. None of these maps you have in this tourist trap even have Serafina's Bayou listed."

"The Sorrows like it that way, cha."

"Abe, I got to go. I got some news about Jack."

Abe put the glass down hard. "Something wrong with her boy?"

Her boy . . . that would make Jack Sippie's brother if what she thought was true was true. And it was.

"I'm not sure, that's why I'm here." Knowing that this Jack person belonged to her as well, Sippie's sense of urgency grew.

"Well now, that's different."

"Is there some way I can get to her?"

"Well, how 'bout I go make a call, and then we can see what she says. If she says you gotta go out there to the bayou, then I'll wait for my shift to end and take you myself. How's that sound? I head out there every Monday anyway to bring the Serafinas up to date and pick up fresh produce from the gardens. They got the *special* ingredients that been makin' people come back for this same gumbo for a hundred years or so. Going a day early won't hurt. But give me a few minutes, Sippie. I can't call straight through, got to leave a message with whoever is manning the bar at the Voodoo . . . now that place. You could lose your whole life inside there."

Or find it, thought Sippie.

"And then if we can't reach her, I'll give you one of the rooms upstairs for the night, and I'll take you there myself in the morning. She won't be mad if it's about Jack. You sure he's not in real trouble? I could call—"

"All I know is it's got to be me that tells her."

I can't stay the night here. Not here. Not where Simone . . .

"All righty, then. You watch the register for me while I go try to get someone on the phone."

"Sounds like a plan, Abe. Can I have a root beer? On the house?"

"Sho' can. You want some gumbo, too? It's just finishing up its first boil. Guaranteed to make you feel lighter on the inside."

"On the house?"

"You bet."

"I'd love that."

"See those boys down at the end of the bar? You don't let them bother you. Troublemakers. Born and raised in Tivoli, people round them parts call the "The Tivoli Trash," but they ain't got nothin' inside of them. They always hanging around. . . ."

"I'll be fine . . . I can hold my own, I always have."

"You know something, Sippie? I swear, I never noticed it before, but you have a little of the shine, don't you? You a Serafina? We ain't had a new one of them here in a long while. It's good to see a young one! I'll go get your gumbo and make that call. Here's your root beer."

I got to get there quicker somehow, she thought.

As soon as Abe went into the kitchen, those troublemaking boys meandered over to Sippie.

One of them, "the handsome one," said, "You know them?" pulling the poster off the register.

"Hey!" said Sippie. "That don't belong to you. You slow or somethin'?"

"Mayyybeeee heeee isssss sloowww," responded another, even less handsome than the original. This one looked like he'd eaten the entire state of Mississippi. They reminded her of every mean kid she ever went to school with.

In ten years, you'll be nothing.

"So, do you know them or not?" the boy asked again.

Sippie decided to take a chance. She might regret it, but she needed to get to Frances, fast. Faster than that convoluted way Abe was trying. *Call here, maybe there . . . later . . .* Nope.

"You boys from Tivoli Parish ain't you? Why you so interested in these witches if you come from where they come from?" she said.

"Not all of them, Just that one there. The one who hides. She's supposed to be the real deal. Been trying to get her to tell our futures. Can't get close, though."

"Well, it just so happens that I need a ride. You think you can rip yourselves away from this"—she glanced around the empty bar—"huge party, and take me?"

"That depends. . . ." The fat one leered.

"On what?"

"If we take you there, you got to promise she'll give us what we want. "

"Sure I will, don't you know? I'm on my way to her right now. She's expecting me."

The boys huddled up, discussing. Sippie knew she was risking a lot, but she figured if they were real jerks, she'd find a way out and be halfway there. Besides, she wouldn't lead them to Frances. When they got to Tivoli Parish, she'd lose them and find her way into the bayou. Sippie was good at shaking off men with evil intentions. It was a skill she'd had to hone for years.

She wrote Abe a note. A clever one.

"Them boys left without paying their tab. I decided I had to find out once and for all what happened to Eight Track before I left. Sorry if the gumbo goes to waste. Best, Sippie."

"You ready, little lady?" asked the fat one.

"Ready as I'll ever be," she said, walking out after them and back out into the heat.

"I'm Stew," he said. "And this here's Chuck." He pointed to the almost handsome one. "And that one with the keys? He's T-Bone."

"How long does it take to get there?" she asked, climbing into the backseat of their four-door truck.

"Want a beer?" Chuck asked as they were heading out of town.

"Sure," she said. She listened to their stupid talk while she slowly drank her beer. Soon they were crossing the wide water, and she started to feel dizzy and slow. Everything blurred.

Dammit, Sippie, you know better!

"What did you do to me?" she asked, her voice sounding far away in her ears. She tried to open the car door, not caring that it was moving fast. When one of them, Stew maybe, reached over to stop her, she bit him, hard. Then he hit her right in the side of her head with a closed fist.

Well, that's one sort of answer, she thought before she passed out.

She drifted in and out of consciousness, relieved she still had clothes on. They must have continued to hit her because she felt sore on her arms and legs. One of them threw a beer can at the red-haired one—*what was his name . . . Stew, Chuck, T-Bone? They sounded like a meat lover's buffet*—who was sitting in the backseat with her, and it hit him.

"Hey! T-Bone, she's the target, not me! Watch it!" The fat one, Chuck, answered by throwing a lit cigarette back there, too. They were drunk and clearly acting more reckless than they'd planned. Sippie couldn't help laughing. *Meat heads . . . oh God, it was so funny, really. Did they even know . . .* T-Bone reached back and pulled her hair hard, slamming her head against the side window.

"We in it now boys! Didn't plan on this but can't turn back now. Just don't hit her too hard! Not the face or that witch will know. . . ."

"She gonna know already or she's no kind of witch, we just gotta change our plans. She'll read our fortunes and then we'll all take turns" Sippie passed out again.

She woke when they stopped someplace called Pete's Gas and Imports. Sippie wanted to yell for help, but she couldn't move her arms or legs. Whatever they put in her beer had made her into jelly. T-Bone went inside.

"Got it," he said, jumping back into the driver's seat with a six-pack.

As they drove, beer cans and insults flew out the windows, Chuck and Stew trying to hit passersby as they drove out of town.

I'm supposed to bring her a message and find a home. Instead I'm bringing her trouble. I'm so sorry, Frances. For the first time during the whole ordeal, Sippie felt like she might cry, and she didn't want to give those fools the satisfaction. She focused hard on trying to push the fear away. And then everything became clear inside the fog. Jack. Something was going to happen to him. Something bad. And maybe she hadn't been stupid at all, maybe she'd changed fate. Brought the bad on herself to save her brother.

The truck pulled over near a sign that read: TRINITY BRIDGE. "Get one of them boats untied, fool! We got to hustle! There's people comin'!" Chuck shouted.

They shoved her in the boat and started up the motor. As they sped away, Sippie heard people shouting.

"Damn Tivoli Trash stealin' boats now, too?" and "They headin' toward Sorrow Hall!"

"Danny and Old Jim are down in Destin, trawlin'. You gonna radio them?"

"Yeah, I'm headed to the Voodoo now. Danny's s'posed to be callin' in anyway, but they're at least a week out on the Gulf."

Please hear me, please.

Sippie hoped against hope that these Sorrow witches were all they were cracked up to be.

Hear me . . . Frances. I'm on my way, but I brought a literal boatload of trouble. I'm so sorry I didn't think this through better. I forgot to look for the exit sign.

She passed out again, waking only when she felt the boat bang against a dock. She felt the boys go stiff before she sat up slowly and looked around. Two of them were on the dock already, one was standing with one foot in and one foot out of the boat. But there, where the land rose a bit above the dock, was Frances. She looked just like she had in Sippie's dream, only better, fiercer. Because she had her finger resting on the trigger of the biggest shotgun Sippie'd ever seen.

"You want me to tell you your futures, boys?" Frances called out from behind the barrel, squinting hard so they knew she was a good shot. "Well, I don't need no magic to do that. You step one more foot on my land and you ain't got none. You hear?"

Looking up at her, Sippie felt a safety she hadn't felt before.

"Now, you lift out that beauty you been abusin' real careful like, show her the respect she deserves."

The red-haired boy lifted her out, trembling, and laid her on the docks.

"Now I'll give you what you boys came here for. I see you runnin' deep into the bayou afraid I'm gonna get the police after you, or your daddy's who I know will beat you senseless like you beat this girl. Only I'm not going to do that, see . . . what happens next is that I find you while you sleep, and none of you don't never wake up. That's what you came for and that's what you got. Now go! Git!"

Then those fools took off quick. Sippie tried to get up on her own, but her body gave out when she tried to stand up.

"Shit," said Frances, putting down the gun and rushing to Sippie's side.

"Don't you worry," she said with a warmth that finally made Sippie break down and cry. "I got you. You're safe. I got you."

She pulled Sippie up, managing to half carry her to a porch that was lit with candles, even though it was broad daylight. Frances propped her up in a comfortable wooden rocker piled up with colorful pillows. And Sippie fell back into oblivion.

She woke again only a few minutes later to the sound of a speedboat racing up to the docks. Frances came out of the little cottage, ready for a fight.

"Oh, it's you. What you doin' here, JuneBug?" Frances yelled, walking with purpose down to the dock and picking up her gun, not aiming it but making a point. "I'm busy!"

"Just thought I'd come on by, worried those boys might've done some harm, is all. Don't get yer panties in a bunch!"

"Does it look like I been harmed?"

"What about dat gal on your gallery, Frankie? They harm her?"

"She'll be fine."

"Should I call the law?"

"I got them so scared they gonna need diapers. I'll take care of the girl, and that Tivoli Trash, too."

"You takin' in strays these days? Danny won't like it."

"I could give a hot damn, Junie. When you radio him with this mess . . . Don't try to tell me you won't! You can't help yourself, and I forgive you. You just tell my *ex*-husband I'm just fine, and that *petite chère* I got visiting seems like a lost soul to me. And this place"—she gestured wildly at the ruins of the old Sorrow property—"is the perfect place for lost souls to wash up. Lost souls on lost shores. That's the way it is. The way it's always been. Leave. Us. Be."

"All right, then, I'll tell Danny you just fine," he huffed, and sped off on his boat.

Frances made a frustrated sort of groan and stomped her feet.

"I'll tell Danny you just fine," she repeated mockingly as she made her way back to Sippie. "Screw Danny! Now he'll just be over here with a mouth full of patronizing when he gets back.

"Why am I talkin' to you?" she half growled at Sippie. "You can't talk back. I been silent too long, it seems."

Sippie drifted in and out a few more times after that. Once to see Frances sitting on the wide floorboards, examining her, poking her a bit here and there.

"What you been takin', girl? Opiates? You don't seem the type. Them boys drug you up? That sounds about right. I have a cure for that. A little belladonna, a little poppy. Don't move, I'll be right back."

The sun had begun to set over the bayou in a glorious show of pinks and oranges, hypnotizing Sippie while she waited.

When Frances came back out, she put a bitter-tasting liquid into Sippie's mouth with a dropper.

"What has the world done to you, child?" she asked.

You don't want to know.

Then it was night, and the lights from the candles and the lanterns that dotted all the surfaces of the cottage glowed and shimmered. Somehow, Frances had gotten Sippie inside and was washing her up using warm, rose-scented water out of a ceramic basin. She rubbed Sippie down gently, squeezing out the water, and then doing it over again and again, before putting some kind of ointment on her cuts and bumps. Then she carefully eased a soft white cotton nightgown over Sippie's head.

Frances kept murmuring, "I mean you no harm, girl. No harm." And as Sippie's subconscious began to wake up from whatever horse tranquilizer/lighter fluid/fish shit lab-concocted drug those boys fed her, she couldn't close off her thoughts, her echoing memories. Memories of things that had been shouted at her. Words that reverberated, coming back at her in full volume. Things she hoped Frances couldn't hear.

Don't trust no one . . . come to me, honey, I got a little sumthin' for ya. You nothin'. You stupid. You wanna die, bitch?

"I can tell you are a mighty strong young woman. I know it's hard to feel weak. You just relax, I won't lord this over you. Let's get you fixed up right as rain," Frances said, placing her in a cozy bed under quilts to keep out damp air and terrible thoughts.

Sippie curled up, imagining herself a baby inside her mother's arms. It smelled of warm earth and flowers and safe things. She was wrapped up tight and held on to that feeling as hard as she could. She let herself pretend she'd always been there, because Sippie knew in the morning she'd have to be sixteen years old again.

Frances smoothed Sippie's hair back from her face as if she'd read her mind. "For tonight, you be a little girl, okay? It's always important for strong girls to have a place they can be weak. Show that soft underside. If you need that place to be here, it's here for as long as you want it."

Sippie buried her head in the softness around her, a kind of soft she'd never had, and turned her face, pretending to be asleep while she cried. She'd be brave, wild, strong-willed Sippie Wallace tomorrow. Tonight, she was a little girl who finally found her mama.

But would her mama want her? Had Frances been missing her all this time, too?

It's so unfair, she thought, *that when we finally figure out what we lost, we got to think of all the things we missed.*

8

Jack Hides with Ghosts

If Sippie had been a few hours earlier, she and those boys would have met up with Jack, and everything might have worked out differently.

But it didn't happen that way.

Their paths weren't supposed to cross, not just yet. Though each person in the world is born with a purpose, we're never given maps that take us there. And most times, it's the tragic things that lead us straight to our rightful place. Sidestepping loss is never a good idea. So, though things were about to get dark for both Jack and Sippie, it was the best sort of thing to happen. It was the only thing that could happen.

When Jack reached the bridge, he scoped out the best place to hide his bike, so it wouldn't be found too quickly but would eventually be found. He'd torn off a piece of his T-shirt and pulled out a pocketknife to make a small cut on his upper arm. It stung more than he'd thought it would, and he wished for a second that his mama were there to rub one of her salves on the wound.

But this wasn't the time to worry over things like that. He smeared the blood on the bike and on the ripped shirt. A little extra something to add flair to his plan. That part had been Millie's idea. She always did have a darker way of looking at the world.

"It's going to work," he said hesitantly. And then, "It's going to work," again, with more confidence.

Jack walked to the other side of Trinity Bridge, where he uncovered the pirogue he'd hidden there weeks before. Old Jim had given it to him for his tenth birthday, and he could maneuver that little boat anywhere.

He poled his boat down into Meager Swamp, avoiding the river, because though not a lot of people traversed Serafina's Bayou, there were always a few who ended up at the Voodoo. Meager Swamp would lead him into the denser, unexplored waters and islets of the bayou, the ones Old Jim showed him. He loved the untainted wildness of the area, with the alligators lounging in the shallow, muddy places and the strange insects fluttering about.

And so, as Frances was nursing Sippie's wounds, Jack was letting the bayou heal a little bit of his own soul. He always felt guilty for wanting more than he already had. There were plenty of people in the world that had worse things than a broken family. But there was a deeper ache inside of Jack, one he didn't really understand. He felt there was something he had to repair, that if he didn't, the ache would grow and eat him up completely. When Claudette would play those old blues albums at Sorrow Hall, every so often one would skip. That's how Jack felt, as if he were caught in some sort of skip in time. There had to be a way out, and he hoped, he believed, his "Great Idea" was the answer.

He didn't know yet that nothing is ever that easy.

As the sun began to burst into all the otherworldly colors only a bayou sky can offer, he made camp in an old shack he'd found when he was little. It was hidden in an oak grove on the west side of the Sorrow Estate. From the rickety narrow porch, he could see the entire back of the Sorrow Estate as well as the lighthouse in the middle of Sorrow Bay. He'd be able to see if anyone was coming his way—though he knew it'd be the last place they'd look. No one ever looks for anything anywhere obvious. And because Jack knew it so well, stealing off to it whenever he could, it made him feel safe as night fell over the bayou. Inside the shack there were remnants of altars and candles and spirit boards. Jack was sure it was where the infamous voodoo witch Rosella lived back when all hell broke loose in 1901. He'd gone through all of the artifacts and cataloged them in his notebook. Even brought some to Mr. Craven. Though he never said exactly where he'd found them.

When he heard the yelling from across the bay, near his mother's cottage, he crept out through the trees to see. After, he went back to his hideout, frowning the whole way.

I had to pick the most action-filled day this bayou has seen in years to hide? Idiot.

He couldn't help wondering about that girl he saw with his mama. She looked like all the prettiest girls he knew. His mama, Millie, the ghost of Mae Sorrow, and his newest find, the picture of SuzyNell from the newspaper clipping Mr. Craven had given him.

He pulled out his notebook and sat on a wooden crate he'd placed on the front porch.

WHO IS SHE?

Then he wrote:

IDEAS:

1) *Another one of the crazies who come to figure out if they have magic in them?*

Then he crossed that out, because she didn't seem crazy at all. And she was being dragged there. But also seemed to *want* to be there. Huh.

2) *Someone from the high school in Tivoli?*

No. He would have noticed her. She wasn't someone you could miss.

He was just about to write down, "3) A lost Sorrow," when he smelled the most beautiful perfume. He stood up and walked down the two steps, peeking around an oak to see if someone was coming. The lighthouse was aglow and fog swirled around the water. The moon was bright and full. The smell grew stronger, like lemons, and soap, and spices he couldn't quite name. His eyes grew wide as they fell on a woman, light hair piled high on her head, wearing a long, old-fashioned dress with a high, lace collar. She stood straight and regal, but when she turned to look at him, he felt her sadness seep straight through him.

"Helene?"

The ghost looked somewhat surprised. "I am," she said, smiling, before she turned to continue staring at the lighthouse. "It seems, however, that no one has thought to teach you any manners. You may address me as Madame Helene. And that scent that drew you out of your hiding place, that would be moonflower. Some call it devil's trumpet. It is a magnificent plant. Blooming only at night. Have you seen them?"

"The moonflowers? My mother has them in her garden."

"You mean *my* garden."

"Yes, ma'am."

"In any case, that was not what I came to inquire about. Have you seen Edmond, my husband? We are having a party, and I can't find him anywhere."

"I haven't, I'm sorry," Jack responded politely.

"I'm caught in time, boy. Reliving the pain of these years over and over again. I don't know how to leave this place."

"I've read somewhere that if you look to the light . . ."

"Don't you see? I can't leave. I'm still trying to find Belinda. I won't go without her."

Jack was just about to tell her Belinda was, impossibly, his very own Dida, but he stopped short, wondering if Dida would have to die to free all those ghosts. Jack didn't want that.

"I must go now, boy. To relive all that terror. But you must make me a promise."

Jack nodded. The scent of moonflower was fading.

"Don't believe what they say about us. There's so much that no one ever had the chance to say. It wasn't all bad. There were reasons . . . reasons."

She floated away slowly over Sorrow Bay, to the lighthouse, where she joined two other shadows in what looked like a terrible fight.

Jack was shaken. Though he'd seen Helene in the house, Edmond and Rosella, too, he'd never spoken to the grown-up ghosts the way he spoke with the Sorrow children. And he was worried about Dida. He went back to the porch, picked up his notebook, and wrote down the whole encounter. Writing things down always made Jack feel much better. Like what had just happened was the most logical thing in the world. Besides, Helene was right, there was a party, or at least the echo of one that happened long ago, going on across Sorrow Bay.

Everyone sensed that Jack had a good shot of Sorrow magic living inside of him, but no one really knew what he could do. He couldn't wait until everything was turned right again and he could share it all with his mother. He had so many questions.

He made himself comfortable, sitting on the rotting, uneven steps of the shack to watch the opulent Sorrow past play out like a movie.

The party was a glamorous affair. Multicolored paper lanterns lit up the whole of Sorrow Hall, both inside and out, hanging from porches and trees. Men in white suits held silver trays full of champagne. They moved gracefully, like dancers. Potted palms and other exotic plants were placed on all the outdoor galleries, and a brass band played the kind of jazz that beat in your blood. Jack decided he'd seen enough when the scene began to repeat itself. That's how it happened sometimes, an echo of a "bigger than life" moment that gets stuck and skips like a scratched album.

He went back inside, half dozing in his sleeping bag to visions of the beautiful Helene Sorrow, dressed in white and smiling, as the band began to play "When the Saints Go Marching In" as if it were the first time, because to them it was. Helene made such a pretty mama.

Jack's worst memory of all time was the day his mama walked away from him on the steps of the Tivoli courthouse. Jack was born with all the Sorrow "talents." At first, when he was just a baby, he thought it was fun to know things, to see things no one else could. Then, he noticed his mama could do the same kinds of "tricks," even though she tried to hide it. Only the similarities didn't make his mama happy, they made her sad. Jack was convinced it scared her so much, she decided to leave him. He knew there were other reasons. His parents fought all the time. And when they got divorced, his father wanted custody of Jack. His mama could have fought harder to keep him. But she didn't. Jack didn't like to think about that.

He was only four years old, and his father was holding him on the courthouse steps as Jack tried to wriggle out of his arms. He knew his mother was confused. She wanted to forget everything that happened and run to them, run back to the life they'd had. But she also knew the life they'd had wasn't any kind of life at all, and she couldn't figure out a way to strike a balance.

He cried out for her. "Mama!"

Her heart was beating so fast. Jack could hear it in his own heart.

As Jack reached for her, his father pushed his arms down. That's when Jack knew he'd have to use some of the magic, even if it made his mother sad.

Don't leave, he thought, looking straight at her to make sure it was working.

He could tell she heard him, but she wouldn't answer. His father saw the look pass between them and got angry.

"What do you think you're doing, Frances! Y'all see this?" Danny said angrily, looking around at the gathering of people who had come to support—some to spy on—them. Uncle Pete and his girlfriend of the moment, some old high school friends. And Millie, Millie was there with his mama. Some legal people and even a few bored souls who seemed to love other people's pain. "She's working some of that hoodoo right now!" Danny's eyes went wild.

Daddy doesn't mean what he says, Jack tried again, sending Frances an image of a picnic they'd taken out on Saint Sabine Isle the previous summer.

She still wouldn't talk to Jack. All she did was start to cry, and Jack, no more than four years old, understood what guilt was.

But as she walked away, baby Jack decided to use the secret weapon.

Why didn't you use the juju to keep me, Mama?

Jack would never forget the look in her eyes when she turned around. Something already broken broke more inside her.

I can't give you what I stole from her, she responded.

Millie put her arm around his mama and they walked away.

He'd wondered what she meant, never figuring it out and never feeling safe enough to ask.

Jack suddenly clambered back out of his sleeping bag and grabbed his notebook.

WHO IS SHE?

She's the one Mama stole from. Someone she loved first. Someone she left first. The realization sparked and exploded in his mind like a fireworks show over the bayou.

His sister.

It was as clear to Jack as if Frances were standing in front of him telling him plain.

He closed his notebook, not sure how he felt, and went back to the porch to watch the party. It was better to be with ghosts than real people sometimes.

When this is over, I'll have a whole bunch of better memories. When this is over, we'll make Sorrow Hall just like that again, he vowed. He knew change was coming, especially now, because somehow he'd already set something important in motion. Only now, what he'd started was out of his control, and all he could do was wait.

9

Daniel Amore & Old Jim Green

"Looks like heaven and hell are making love up there," said Old Jim, nodding at the sunset.

"You missed your calling, Jim, you shoulda been a philosopher or something."

"Hell no, I'm the shrimp whisperer and happy with the hard life I chose." Old Jim grinned.

They'd had a good haul in Destin—Old Jim being the shrimp god and all—and were heading back. If Danny's boat, *The Gypsy Witch,* were bigger, they probably could have stayed out longer.

Danny sighed, gazing out over the open Gulf, trying not to think about Frances, which had been his state of mind for nearly a lifetime. "If I only had a dime for every time I tried not to think about that damn woman," he said out loud to the sea.

The Gypsy Witch hadn't been that fishing boat's first name. When Danny first bought her—cheap off a Yankee who'd thought a shrimpin' life in Louisiana would be romantic and quickly realized the error of his ways—he was young and still angry about dropping out of college to marry Frances and be a father to Jack, only to get divorced four years later. The marriage had been his decision, and he loved her, but when she left him . . . none of that mattered anymore. In a fit of anger he'd called the boat *The Gypsy Whore*. But when he was trying hard to win Frances back—and she was sure as heck having none of that—he renamed her *The Gypsy Queen*. And a few years later, when Frances and Danny had settled into their peculiar and ordinary pattern of wanting each other precisely when it wasn't the right time, she got her rightful name: *The Gypsy Witch*. Danny knew the ambiguity of the last one was best. He could love her or hate her without having to rename that blasted boat again. And it all depended on his mood, his memory, or, hell, even the time of day. His feelings for her could shift with the tide, but no matter what he was feeling, *The Gypsy Witch* summed it up.

The girl Frances used to be, the one he'd admired from afar during their early days at Tivoli Elementary, was someone Danny could never hate. Back then, he'd never had the courage to tell her, because everyone made fun of the Sorrows. But her pure love of life was something he wanted to bottle up and sip from forever. Unfortunately, the woman she grew into scared the shit out of him, and the woman she became during their brief marriage was someone he could never seem to understand.

"T-Dan!" yelled Old Jim from below. "I got JuneBug on the radio. You ready?"

He switched places with Old Jim, who patted him on the shoulder as the old man came up on deck and the young man swung below.

"Hey, Junie, how's things?"

"Well now, Dan, we had quite a scare here today."

"JuneBug, don't mess with me. Is everything okay?"

"Well, see . . . I was drivin' down to Pete's around midday to get some more plywood, you know how I'm fixin' up the Voodoo. Anyway, that Tivoli trash, Chuck and his friends, were stealin' a boat off Trinity Bridge, heading for Frances. Dan, they looked meaner than any sons a bitches I ever seen. I mean, those boys got big. I swear they were just shit kids shorter than me a second ago—"

"JuneBug, I don't need you to relate an epic here, cut to the chase."

"What, Dan? What you say?"

"Just tell me!" Dan shouted.

"No need to yell, boy. Fine, fat lot o' thanks I get for goin' on over there to take care of things. They had a poor soul of a girl they were draggin' around with 'em, too. Everyone's okay, though. So I guess a 'thank you, JuneBug' is in order."

"Did you call the po-lice or . . . ?" He trailed off before adding, "Millie Bliss." Danny didn't even want to say her name. He'd only just ended what he considered a casual affair with that one. Not too many people knew about it because it would have made everyone downright livid. Danny needed less conflict, not more. Besides, Millie was crazier than a shithouse rat. He'd always thought of her as mysterious until they got close. Too close. That's why he'd broken it off right before he and Old Jim set out. Of course, with all of ten minutes of open water between the boat and the shore, he'd ended up telling Old Jim. Keeping a secret from that man was impossible.

"So let me get this straight," said Old Jim, a sparkle in those ageless blue eyes of his. "You mess around with her for over almost two years, then you wait until you're about to be gone for a good long while to end it with her. Damn, boy, every time I think you may have grown some balls . . . you run yellow, like piss in the river."

Old Jim was right, and Danny never saw the point in arguing with honesty. Unless it was coming from Frances.

"Damned right I'm a coward when it comes to them witches! You are, too. Lived a whole damn life with Dida and never married her. Why? 'Cause she don't want to get married. Shoot."

"Because that worked out so well for you, son. Thanks for the advice." Old Jim chuckled.

Danny watched Old Jim looking out over the sea and thought it wouldn't be so bad to end up just like that old man.

"You copy?" asked JuneBug, jolting Danny from his thoughts. "Police can't do nothin' now. I figure we go round 'em up when you and Jim get back."

"What you gonna do, Junie? Camp out on her porch? How you know they ain't over there right now messin' with her?"

Danny punched the console hard, creating a loud static, and closed his eyes. He was getting a headache. The Frances effect.

"Shoot, Dan. Frances met those boys with a shotgun and a smile. They're probably halfway to Mexico by now."

Dan shook his head, grinning despite himself. That woman . . . she never needed saving from anything.

"All right, then, we're heading back now anyway. Be back by Solstice Eve. But if there's any more real trouble, you go get Pete. And check in on her tomorrow, okay? Only don't let her see you, and don't tell her I asked you to. You hear?"

"Loud and clear."

"And don't tell Jack. I left him on his own for the first time. That boy knows where I keep my guns and he sure as hell knows how to use 'em. He'll run on over there with one and get himself hurt, he loves his mama so much."

"I hear ya, Danny," agreed JuneBug.

Danny went back on deck and sat next to Old Jim.

"What happened?" Old Jim asked. That man was always so calm. He'd try to stare down a nuclear bomb. Probably disarm it, too. Danny picked up part of the net, telling him what happened and how Frances had handled it in her . . . *graceful* way.

"I never learn, Jim. That woman can take care of herself. I don't know why I even try to worry," he said.

"Just because a woman says—hell, *proves* she can take on the world by herself don't mean she ain't cravin' protection. The stronger the woman, the more they need someone else to lean on. Who they gonna lay the burdens down with? Who they gonna go to when they, those that be the strongest, get scared? Right now, Frances got no one. And that's a damn shame, son."

"She made that decision."

Old Jim just looked at Danny, gave him what he liked to call "the stink eye."

"You tryin' to say she needs me, Jim?"

"Well, first off, I'm her grandpap. And I love that girl more than I should. So I hate admittin' this to you 'cause, well, you know. But second, of course she needs you. Don't act a fool. That's old news. But I think it's the other way around this time. You're startin' to realize you need her just as much as she needs you."

Old Jim sat back on his heels. "You want some coffee? I know the sun's goin' down, not comin' up, but I was thinkin' I'd put some rum in mine. Watch the sky turn into that ink-dot blue . . . make a toast to nature and all that shit."

"Do shrimp have horns?" asked Danny.

Jim went belowdecks and came back up a few minutes later, handing Danny a cup full of goodness that was more rum than coffee. Everything, especially coffee, always seemed to taste better at sea. Something about the salty air, the aroma of adventure, the taste of yet another day, where nothing, good or bad, is promised.

Danny thought that was the best kind of promise—one that can't be broken. Jim went back to his nets, and Danny went back to looking at the sky.

After Frances left him, breaking her vows and his heart, Danny's days were colorless without her. He tried to fill in the gray places but never succeeded. Jack was only four, a funny little guy who liked making his daddy smile; he'd dance around, shaking his naked butt after a bath. At first, he thought he'd really screw things up with that kid, because Jack was always so attached to Frances. But after a few weeks, he was downright proud of himself. Danny knew he was a good father, not that he had any idea what one of those looked like. His great-aunt Lavern raised him. And her son, Pete, was a sort-of-maybe-sometimes father figure. Mostly Pete was a funny, hard-ass older brother type who looked for trouble and found it more often than not.

Pete was ten years his senior, so by the time Danny was going to grammar school and beginning to watch Frances Green Sorrow with more interest than his friends might like, he was already on his way to owning Pete's Gas and Imports. (Before Pete bought it, it was Andy's, and Larry's a generation earlier, because that's Tivoli Proper for you.) On school mornings, Danny would sit in the dark little kitchen at the table, watching the chipped Formica so he wouldn't miss the gleaming sun that lit up the gloom for about five and a half minutes, between seven and five after seven A.M., because that's when Pete always left for work. That five and a half minutes was the highlight of Danny's morning, because of the scene that never failed to play out.

Aunt Lavern would sit with Danny, drinking strong Italian cof-fee, her hair in rollers that seemed permanently attached unless it was Sunday and they were going to church. She'd be smoking a cigarette while reading the obituaries and making lists of what she needed at the K&B. Then she'd lay into Pete the moment he banged into the kitchen at seven A.M., shielding his hungover eyes from the sun and rubbing his stubbly, unshaved face with pride right before doing the thing that annoyed her most—he'd pour himself a cup of coffee and leave sugar all over the counter.

"What about the sugar ants?" she'd cry out, getting up and chasing after him.

"I thought they might be hungry, Mama!" Pete would answer, looking over at Danny gleefully.

"Make something of yourself, Petey!" she'd yell, and then swat him with a folded-up newspaper. "Be like Danny. He's gonna be something! He's gonna be a lawyer someday so he can bail you out of jail. I moved you out here so you'd be away from all those crazy people in our family. And I gave you a life, a good life, and you have no ambition, none. eh, fongool. . . ."

(Lavern hated cursing but didn't consider it cursing if it was in Italian.)

Uncle Pete would leave the house, pulling on his work boots and "accidentally" slamming the door, a piece of toast hanging out of his mouth, somewhere around "I gave you a life. . . ." He'd give Danny a salute, cross his eyes, and duck out, which meant, *Have fun with her, kid.*

Pete had told him more than once that Lavern taking Danny in from her cousin Peach was the best thing that ever happened to him.

"Now you get to be the golden boy," he'd said.

At the time, they'd shared a bedroom—Jack's room now—and Danny still couldn't understand how both of them had fit into such a small room.

Pete had always talked to Danny while he got ready for a date, slicking back his thick black hair, adjusting the gold cross he wore around his neck.

"Before you came, I thought I'd grow up to be one of those sociopaths, you know, with the mama issues. Kill people and feed 'em to the alligators or somethin'. She's rough, but my mama loves hard. Now she gets to spread it around. God bless you, *son*!" he'd cheerfully yell out before wrestling Jack to the ground to give him the worst noogie ever.

But Pete was living above his gas station by the time Danny was in junior high—another moment when Danny's life had gone gray.

"I'm right here, T-Dan. Just a short bike ride away. And, do you think it's fair to be mad I get to own a gas station in the same backwater town I grew up in? Not when you have plans to fly fast and far. And I hope you do, Danny. Really, I hope that football thing works out and you get to be a lawyer. You've got a good head on your shoulders, and . . . I'm proud of you, kiddo."

Except Danny never did get very far. He tried, but then . . . *Frances.* After they were married, he worked right next to Pete at that gas station, hoping it would never become Danny's Gas and Imports. But Old Jim saved him from that. After the divorce, he took pity on Danny and helped him buy *The Gypsy Witch.* The two had been dragging together ever since. And no matter how bad things got with Frances, Old Jim never held it against him.

"You done with your evening constitutional?" asked Old Jim.

"And what is it you think you know, Jim?"

"Every night, right about now, you go off and think about all those things. Those past things. Things that you always promise you'll take care of when you get back on land. Only, when we hit land, you forget you got all contemplative out here. Seems a special kind of crazy to me. But to each their own, I guess."

"I just don't know what to do," Danny replied. He didn't much like feeling unsettled when he was on his boat. He didn't want to be worried about Frances. At least on land, Danny would feel prepared for the unease. But *The Gypsy Witch* was the only place he found peace. If someone had told him he would be thinking this way when he was twenty years old and playing football for Louisiana State, holding on to big dreams of going all-American and then becoming a lawyer, he would have knocked them out cold. When Danny was a kid, all he wanted was to escape Tivoli Parish. But here he was, the fisherman he swore he would never be. He spent years angry with Frances for the life he was stuck with, but not anymore. Now he was . . . grateful.

"Seems to me, you got a chance here, boy," said Old Jim.

"Whatchoo mean, old man?"

"You got yourself all caught up in a net made of real-life feelings and real-life mistakes. Now you got to haul it in and separate the gold from the chum."

"But I didn't leave her, Jim. She left me."

"I know. That ain't what I'm sayin'." Old Jim sipped his coffee, looking away from Danny. This was the sore spot in their relationship. Danny always admired the way the old man could look past the wreckage the divorce created. To be honest, that whole family took him back into their fold quick enough when the dust settled. Frances's family never held a grudge for too long. They just weren't that kind of people. The way those self-proclaimed "witches" organized the world and their place in it was downright odd. It hurt Danny's brain when he thought on it too much.

"Spit it out, Jim. You think takin' Jack was a mistake? Because she practically handed him over to me."

Danny could never understand that. He'd given her a hell of a time fighting over custody of Jack, but only because he thought it would make her stay. He didn't have a big family, not in Tivoli Proper, but his aunt Lavern had been raised alongside people that had nice, ordinary, middle-class lives, whereas Jim, Dida, Claudette, and Frances had magic, tradition, and history. But Danny knew Frances could have won that battle if she'd tried.

"I been feelin' guilty lately, Jim. And it ain't just because of Millie—don't start. It's other things. Things I can't put my finger on."

"Guilt's a funny thing, son." Old Jim stood up, the last colors of the sunset playing across his face.

"I feel like I should have been there for her. . . . But, hell . . . how you supposed to be a rock for someone who's all walled up inside already? It's impossible, Jim."

Danny felt a shift in Old Jim. Like the way a storm can come on quick.

"*Impossible?* Don't you think I carry a world of guilt on *my* shoulders? I was out here, on the ocean, footloose and free, when Claudette got into that lye. Danny, that child was a gift to us. We were gettin' on in years, figured we'd never have a child, so when she was born, she was our pretty little miracle. I never blamed Dida for the accident; she was alone out there, with nothin', no fancy washer or dryer. I left a happy, bouncing, beautiful . . . Goddamn, Dan, have I ever told you how pretty Claudette was when she was a baby? All she ever did was laugh. So I left this happy little girl and came back to a blind, miserable child. Then, when she finally grew some happy inside her again, I took Louis LaNuit on my trawler, and he drowned. *On my watch.* She never blamed me, but don't you think I blamed myself? Should I go on? That's why I sent for Millie, when Frances was four and getting into all kinds of trouble. I thought it would be a good thing, you know, be another set of eyes. But Millie was just a child herself. I got a letter from my people up north saying she was orphaned. And I thought . . . I know she's small, but I'll bring her to help Claudette and Dida raise that wonderful hellion while I'm away at sea. But I'll be damned if that spiteful girl didn't end up making even more of a mess of my family, driving wedges between Frankie and Claudette, you and Frankie. Oh, Danny, I got guilt. But it don't mean I leave. Can't walk around nothin', boy, you never get to the other side. Got to walk right on through."

"Jim . . . I . . ."

"You utter one word of pity and I send you to the bottom of the Gulf, you hear? It's what we lose that helps us see what we want. My ladies, they believe in their magic, and T-Dan, so do I. But what they always seem to forget is that true magic is born from sorrow. The only time we ever see clearly what we have is right before we're about to lose it *for good*."

Old Jim stared into nothing and then laughed at himself, shaking his head a bit before he slapped Danny on the back.

"You're right, Jim. But, thing is, where do I even start? Me and Frances been on this mean-ass merry-go-round for too many years now."

"Well, this Millie thing makes it different. And tryin' to weasel out of it ain't gonna help. Best own up to it, son. But you gotta remember that Frankie's been livin' inside herself for a long time, and she might not understand all the whys and the what-fors. She might act like she don't care. But that's all it is, actin'. Either way, you're fucked. Truth is, you should've never let her go in the first place. But you already know that."

"I didn't let her go. Let me say it again plain. *She* left *me*."

"Danny, haven't you ever wondered *why* she left? Dumb-ass.

Didn't I just say far too many words about guilt? That'll teach me to bare my soul to a fool. . . ."

"You're sayin' I left her first? Somehow, let her down. Left her without actually leaving. That's what you're sayin'."

"I ain't sayin' shit." But Danny knew he was right because Old Jim smiled, put his coffee cup down on the deck, stretched, and jumped over the side of *The Gypsy Witch* into the blue waters of the Gulf. Old Jim stayed under for a long time, then rose to the surface, his old shoulders, copper stained from years working in the sun, looking stronger than ever. His blue eyes got lost in the reflection of the sea, now bathed in the deep, moody shades the sun left stained on the sky. As he climbed back on deck, he pushed water back from his silver hair, his cut-off denims leaving drops of salt water in his wake as he sat on a hatch.

"Ain't you ever gonna age, old man?" asked Danny.

"I will when I decide to, and not a goddamned moment sooner. Kind of like how Claudette gave up on bein' fat. Lord, we thought she'd be fat forever. Eatin' everything she could reach after that lye accident. Seemed food was her only comfort when she couldn't see the world around her. Not that it would have been a bad thing, her stayin' fat. We never told her to be thin. But one day, she just woke up and thought, *I ain't gonna be fat no more,* and she wasn't."

Old Jim looked up at the deepening night sky with such a reverence that Danny wondered if that old coot wasn't saying some kind of silent prayer for his daughter. "Anyway, that's what'll happen to me. One day, I'll just get up and say, 'Shit, I don't wanna grace this earth no more with my beautiful face.' And that's the day I'll die."

"Shut up. You ain't never gonna die. You and Dida been old forever," Danny scoffed. Because it was true.

"Well, if I'm gonna live forever, I'm going to bed. See you on the flip side, Danny boy. We're heading' home!" he said, slapping Danny on the back as he went below to sleep.

Danny didn't want to think of losing Old Jim. He'd already lost too much.

He wished he could have acted more like Old Jim. A Yankee fisherman, originally from a colder coast, an off-season trapper with nothin' but love for Dida and the hot, humid air locking him to the Deep South. The father of a blind witch and husband to the finest healer these bayous had ever seen. He took care of his family, even when things got bad. He could have run, or ranted, but he never did.

"I'm coming back," Danny said aloud. "I'm ready now. I think."

"Good Lord, would you shut your mouth!" Old Jim shouted from belowdecks. "Romantic fool. Talk talk talk talk. You ever decide to act on those words, T-Dan, and I might just shit my pants."

10

Frances and Her Daughter

I let the girl sleep in. And I quietly made breakfast and then waited, not so patiently, on the porch. I fussed with the old wooden table, putting fruit on it, then candles and little glasses with flowers. I wanted it to be extra pretty. A part of me, that pesky instinct part I'd tried to ignore, knew from the start that this broken-up teenage girl was my daughter. My lost baby. My secret. Right age, right face, right demeanor. Besides, I'd asked for her, conjured her somehow. I'd felt more like a mother taking care of her that night than I'd ever felt when Jack was a baby. But the next morning, I couldn't for the life of me figure out how to approach it. It was so simple. But also so damned complicated. And I just felt so guilty. Facts are facts, and this girl—*my girl, oh Lord, my girl*—clearly hadn't had the life I'd wanted for her.

Messy, is what it was. I was proud, though. She seemed such a mighty little thing.

But I had to know for sure.

That morning while she slept, Millie, JuneBug, and Mr. Craven had all waved to me on their way to prepare for Solstice Eve at Sorrow Hall. So I figured I'd take her on over, walk into that house I'd spent too many years avoiding, and just tell them she was mine. They would all be there, well . . . minus the three most important people. And I'd be able to tell from her reaction whether I was right or not. I know better than to trust any daughter of mine to come right out and say something. I sure as hell never tell anyone anything.

And if she was mine, really mine, she'd appreciate the directness of my indirectness. If that makes sense.

When she finally woke and joined me on the porch, I was fidgeting nervously.

"Well, there she is, Sleeping Beauty. How do you feel today? You don't look as banged up as I thought you would."

"I'm sore, but I think I'm okay," she said.

She looked just like I used to. All pride and sadness and hope for some real magic to happen that would heal her.

"So, eat some breakfast and tell me how what I can sense is a smart girl allowed herself to get wound up with those pieces of Tivoli trash." I pulled out a cigarette, trying to hide my shaking hands, striking a match against the table. Once it was lit, I inhaled deeply as she ate some tomatoes and cream I made for her. I love tomatoes in cream with sugar, and not a whole hell of a lot of people do, but she did.

I smiled.

"I was looking for you," she said finally. "You're Frances. Crow sent me."

Crow.

"Are you talkin' about *my* Crow?" I asked.

"Crow be free. Crow don't belong to no one. He used to be caged, but never again. He's got doors in the universe that go places you and I could never go. Well, I get to go, sometimes. He's the one who showed me how to find you."

"Well then, I think it's time you tell me your name, sugar." I took an orange from the bowl, bit it, rind and all, and offered one to her.

She took the orange, drew her knees up to her chest, tucking them under the pretty white nightdress.

"My name is Sippie Wallace. And I'm here to help you find Jack."

Wouldn't Eight Track have given her his last name? Wouldn't she be Sippie St. John? For a second, I thought I was wrong and wanted to weep. *No, I told him to keep the secret, and Sippie Wallace was a blues singer, it fits.*

"You got parents?" I asked.

"Of course I do. Everyone has parents. But that's not the point. I'm here to help you find Jack."

She wasn't going to give anything up so easily. Now I was almost damned sure she was mine. But, I'd play anyway.

"But Jack's not lost," I said.

"Crow clearly said, *Find Jack.*"

"He clearly said? You talk to Crow, Miss Sippie?"

Sippie laughed, wiping orange juice from her mouth with the back of her hand.

"Yes and no. I'm not really sure. Since I was little, whenever I got to make some kind of change, he comes to me, and I fall into this sleep or somethin'. And then I'm flying with him, and when I'm with him like that, I can hear what he thinks."

"How do you know you're not dreaming?"

"I don't. But I'm here, right? I just know that more than once he's shown me things I couldn't know if I wasn't seein' them some other way."

"Well, our Crow must be getting real old, because Jack ain't lost. Come with me, let me show you something."

I walked around my cottage, through the line of oaks that made a crescent around the whole property and into the cypress grove.

"Be real quiet, Sippie, and watch your step. The ground gets soft and wet here and there," I said. Then, without getting too close, I pointed through the trees toward the back of Sorrow Hall and the bay.

"If you look close, you'll see someone moving around in that little shack back there. My Jack, he thinks he's so clever. I saw him set his whole camp up. He must be having some kind of adventure or somethin'. He's almost thirteen now, gonna spread his wings. But he sure stayed close to home. Now come on, before he sees us." I beckoned, and we crept back through the trees.

"Well, those terrible boys were on their way here with or without me. Maybe . . . maybe that's what I was supposed to do. Go with them so they wouldn't mess with him. Switch the fates up, or somethin'."

"Sounds like a good explanation to me. Crow, he always comes with change. And I've always found him to be a little . . . overprotective."

She shrugged, and we went back to our breakfast.

And then the questions started.

"So, you married?"

"Not anymore."

"Why?"

"It's complicated, Sippie."

"What's his name?"

"Danny."

"He handsome?"

"The handsomest man I've ever laid eyes on."

"You still love him?"

"I'm not talking about him anymore . . . okay?"

She stopped, pausing for a beat, then started again.

"So why don't you have Jack all the time?" she asked, taking another bite of her tomatoes and cream.

"Court said I wasn't fit."

"That the truth?"

"Almost. Maybe the whole truth is *I* didn't think I was fit. You spend any time in the bayou, Sippie?"

"No, ma'am."

"Well, I'm sure there are wild tales told all over that try to explain the convoluted nature of our bayous. Stories about alligators eating babies, hoodoo rituals, ghostly Civil War apparitions, racism, and a bunch of old folks sitting on rickety, ancient porches drinking homemade moonshine out of jelly jars while someone's great-uncle 'Beau' plays the fiddle. And it's all true. To an extent. Not that I know of any babies who got eaten, but I suppose if you're a no-account parent and leave a baby out on the banks of a shallow, swampy area, well . . . last time I checked, alligators don't discriminate when it comes to their menu. Thing is, Sippie . . . I know a lot of folks think I'm one of those no-account parents. But even I wouldn't have left my baby out for the alligators to eat. What I did was much worse. I left Jack with ordinary people trying to fill his mind with ordinary thoughts. Death by alligator, or death by ignorance. I can't figure out what's worse."

Sippie was quiet until a bunch of banging and yelling over at Sorrow Hall broke the silence.

"What's all that?" she asked.

"It's almost Solstice Eve. They always try to fix the place up this time of year. Doesn't really work. My people are all over there. I watched Millie and JuneBug paddle up this morning. Mr. Craven too . . . he runs the Tivoli Parish Historical Society and can't seem to get enough of us."

"But not Jack . . . or Danny, right?"

"I said I wasn't goin' to be talkin' about Danny."

"Fine." She sighed, disappointed.

"Old Jim isn't there either, he's your—" I caught myself. "My granddaddy. He's offshore shrimping with Danny. They'll both be back next week."

"What's this Solstice Eve you keep talking about?"

"If we go over there, I'll tell you all about it. Fascinating stuff. You want to meet my people?"

"I guess so, if you want to."

"See that dock? How it curves down to the river and up the bank like a sidewalk? Right past are the gates to the big house, Sorrow Hall. Not so far, really."

"We could go, if you want. But I figure if you don't live there, you must have a reason. So if you don't want to go, we don't have to go."

That girl was giving my plan a run for its money.

"Let's just take a walk up there, what do you say, cha?"

As we walked the docks I wanted to hold her hand, hug her tight to my chest, whisper a belated "Happy Birthday" sixteen times. But I couldn't. Not yet. When we finally reached the gates, Sippie had begun to ramble, distracting me. Almost like she knew what I was going to do.

"These oyster shells must've been hard on bare feet back in the old days," she said.

From a distance, under the stately live oak canopy that lined the path, Sorrow Hall almost looked like it once did. If you squinted really hard.

"You see them?" She pointed across the front lawns.

"Who?"

"Those girls in white dresses playing some sort of tennis. Spirits."

She really is mine.

"I used to. Jack sees 'em, though. He says he even talks to them."

"Who are they?"

"Echoes of the generation that cursed us. I mean, my family. I'm sure you'll get an earful up at the house."

The closer we got, the more apparent the damage to that once fine estate. The sagging rooftops and natural world pulling it back into a green embrace.

"I kind of like the way it looks." Sippie smiled.

"Me, too, but when you wake up to a snake in your bed, it's not quite so charming."

"But look at all the trees and flowers. It's beautiful," she said, breathing out.

"The gardens grow wild everywhere. But closer to the house, they were planted. See the fig trees? And those trumpet vines growing up so orange? I love those. But over there, by the . . . hmmm . . . I never did figure out what to call that part of the house. . . . See, Helene Dupuis Sorrow, you probably saw her back there on the lawn somewhere . . . she was a little crazy. She tore down the side of the west wing and built a chapel, and that whole side of the house was stained glass, see the bits left behind? The group of trees near there are wild oleander, don't touch any of them, or taste them . . . they're poison, and the reason we can't make our own honey here. Two things we can't do for ourselves, honey and ice. And since we can't process the wild cane, no molasses either. So sugar is out, too."

"That's three things," she murmured as we climbed the wide front steps of the lower gallery.

"You ready?" I asked.

"Yes, ma'am."

I took a big breath before opening those doors for the first time in too many years, just as swollen with damp as ever. We walked into the grand foyer. The winding staircase, like a giant's cape rising in front of us, and the gallery's windows were all open, and what little breeze there was flowed through the porticoes.

"Frances! It's the most beautiful thing I ever saw!" Sippie's eyes bloomed with delight.

"Look up. See all the birds darting around? So many of the ceilings are rotted through like the roof. 'A Swiss cheese mansion with vines and flowers and bird nests living right alongside the Witches of Sorrow Hall,' is what Craven wrote about it last year in the *Tivoli Parish News*. He did a 'spotlight' on the Sorrows. Insightful . . . ," I joked.

"I don't care about any of that," said Sippie. "This is like a dream . . . better than a dream." She was glowing as she walked up to the mural that filled the wall of the staircase.

Seeing Sorrow Hall through Sippie's eyes was like watching a film reel of my childhood.

"When I was little, I never noticed how ramshackle Sorrow Hall was either. I'd run my fingers along that same curved wall. It was damp, and the longer I left my fingers there, the colder the damp grew. Once, right before I ran off to Thirteen Bourbon, I was running my hands along it and the paint started smearing, two-hundred-year-old paint smearing as if it was new. And my hand, it sunk right into the damn wall. I pulled it out quick. I was scared, really scared. I thought I was going crazy."

"You ran away?" she asked.

"Who's there?" Claudette suddenly yelled from the back gallery.

Saved by my mama for once in my life.

"It's me, Mama!" I called, looking in on her.

"Oh, I remember you! I'll go get Dida, she'll be as surprised as me. The queen graces us with her presence, Dida!" she yelled, laughing, reaching her arm up to find a piece of rope.

"What are those for?" asked Sippie.

"So she can make her way from place to place. She's blind."

"Don't look like rope at all covered in vines like that. They're lovely," said Sippie.

"Aren't they, though?"

Claudette was making her way, too fast, across the long front parlor. Dida had emerged from the side door near the fireplace, wiping her hands on a dishrag.

"She doesn't look like you at all, your mama. With that blond thinness about her," Sippie whispered.

"I know . . . it always bothered me."

"Why?"

"A girl wants to look like her mama . . . ," I said, trailing off, and glanced at her.

Sippie opened her mouth to speak, but Dida and Claudette were already in front of us. I could tell she was nervous. Hell, I was nervous. I was about to find out, for sure, if this girl I already loved was mine.

"Frances, who dis girl?" Dida asked suspiciously.

"Be nice," I said.

"Doesn't come on this side of the property for months, only yelling across the yard for some fabric, and now comes along unexpectedly askin' us to be nice and all . . . ," mumbled Claudette.

"You're being rude, Mama. Now, call JuneBug and Millie,

and what the hell, Craven . . . I got something to say." Then I sat Sippie down on a couch inside the parlor. "Don't worry, I think it was always green, it's not moss or anything."

"What you planning on telling everyone—"

"Hush," I said.

"Junie, Craven, Millie, you are wanted in the front parlor!" Dida called out in a way that was enough to wake the dead (if they weren't already still hanging out, living life on repeat).

"That's one way to do it," I said wryly. Sippie tried not to laugh. And my mama had placed herself right smack next to me on the couch.

Millie came running down the stairs with Craven and JuneBug. She stopped short when she saw Sippie and looked at me. That's when I knew she'd been keeping secrets. Millie looked caught. But then she smiled that childlike smile of hers.

"What's all this about, well . . . lookit. Frankie! Can it really be you?" She threw herself dramatically across me, Sippie, and Mama on the couch. "You've come home! Thank you, Jaysus!" she yelled.

I turned to Sippie. "This is Millie Bliss, the closest thing a girl ever had to a sister and my dearest friend."

"Oh my," said Craven, wringing his hands. "We must finish the backdrop for the play . . . so much to do."

"Trust me, Craven, you'll love this," I said. JuneBug plopped onto the arm of the couch, placing his fingers just near enough to Mama's ear so she'd swat at the air and then pulling them away.

My heart gave a twinge. I'd missed them.

I took a deep breath.

"Okay, here goes. This is Sippie Wallace. Sippie, this is my family. Minus three. But it'll have to do. See, because . . . well, there's just no easy way . . . I have something to tell you. And if I'm wrong . . ." I turned to Sippie.

"You ain't wrong, Frances," Sippie whispered.

A door in my heart that was nailed shut shot wide open.

She's mine she's mine she's mine.

"Sippie's my daughter," I said, happy that my voice stayed strong. "Now, all of you, no dramatics. I went to Bourbon Street, and I came back all torn up, less than myself. Because I left a whole part of myself back there . . . and here she is. Which means you all got me back whole, now, too. Like it or not. Plus this little bit of sunshine."

Mama climbed over me, moving in close to Sippie. Then she cradled Sippie's face in her hands. Mama ran her fingers along Sippie's cheeks, and her whole demeanor changed. She knew it was true.

You could hear a pin drop.

I never saw my people speechless, and it was a funny thing to see. But I hoped they weren't going to get mean or bitter. I'd just decided to let them back in, after all.

"Oh my!" Craven said, flapping his hands spastically.

"Did anyone ever test you for a nervous condition, Craven?" asked Millie.

Then she turned to me. She looked so wounded. But I thought she had known. Was I destined to be wrong about everything in my life?

"It's nice to meet you, Sippie! And nice to finally know what robbed us of Frankie all those years ago—Wait, I didn't mean it like that! It's the shock, is all." Millie quickly added, "Junie, Craven, let's get back to work and let these Sorrow ladies get acquainted. Frankie? You, me, the Voodoo, later, okay?" I nodded, but we both knew I wasn't going to be there.

Mama was all over Sippie's face again.

"You really are blind, Miss Claudette," said Sippie. "Like, really blind."

Damn girl. Just like her mama. Can't hold her tongue to save her life.

"What other kind of blind is there?" Claudette frowned, her fingers dropping.

"Well, it could mean, like . . . not being able to see emotions or somethin'," Sippie responded.

"She's blind that way, too," I said.

"She's got to learn some manners, if we're gonna keep her," said Claudette.

"She's not a puppy, Mama."

Dida walked forward and took Sippie's hands, pulling her up into a tight hug. Then she held her back by the shoulders so she could get a good look.

"Well, ain't you beautiful. I love you already. Come on, child, help me in the kitchen so you can catch me up on . . . what? Sixteen years? That's right, ain't it, Little Bit? All those lost years makes sense now, everything always makes sense if you give it enough time."

"You gonna be okay, Sippie?" I asked.

"I am."

"You go on home, Frances," said Dida. "Let us have some time with dis here girl of ours."

"Well, actually, I'd like to help with the celebration this year, so there are some things I could be doing in the garden."

Mama and Dida were both silent, but I could tell they were pleased.

"You'll find your way back later, Sippie?"

"I know how to get there, the walk ain't too far."

"That's right, Sippie. You tell her. She's been putting a million miles between us for years. Would have put up a damn wall if she could. Put all those wisteria trees in so they'd block out any view of this house. She's spiteful," said Claudette. Then she turned to me and added, "And I'm *still* too young to be a grandma."

Sippie piped up suddenly, "Ms. Claudette? Did you know that they got surgery now that might be able to fix those eyes of yours? They advertise it on TV. You should look into it. I mean, check it out! Sorry . . ."

I was laughing on the inside so hard, I might burst. Sassy Sippie Sorrow would be her new name.

"She really is yours, it seems," said Claudette.

"Ours." Dida smiled, moving Sippie toward the kitchen, talking her ear off the whole way. "Old Jim, he gonna be so excited to have another child around . . . you want to be all grown? Or do you want to be little, it's your choice, we ain't got no rules like that here. . . ."

I made my way to the hall. I felt so full and alive and . . . tired.

Millie caught me before I left; she was twirling around on the first landing.

"What a bat-shit crazy turn of events," she said.

"Millie, stop acting like you didn't know. I'm not mad. I know you were helping me keep my secret. And I get it, when Simone died, you would have wanted to protect me then, too. I love you for it. Try to get to know her, Millie. She's like us. Like both of us."

"You gonna take over the role of Serafina in the play again?" she asked, ignoring my speech.

"I'm not taking over anything, I'm helping. You been asking me to help for years."

"Help is one thing, eclipsing everybody else is another. A secret child is so . . . *ordinary*. Taking the lead role in this pageant is another thing entirely," Millie replied, an edge to her voice.

"I don't care, you decide . . . ," I said.

Something wasn't right with Millie. And I was scared it had more to do with me than her. I'd missed her. I'd let her in during those years, but it hadn't been the same. Because I wasn't the same.

Guilt, another gift that keeps on giving.

11

Sippie at Sorrow Hall

"You ever had a crawfish boil, Sippie?"

"In town I have."

"Those places never do it right. You gotta have it out here on the bayou. The *right* way. With plenty of beer and old bay. We gonna have one come Solstice Eve. Just you wait. Today, though, we're all gonna have some bread puddin'. Millie brought all this honey. Just look at it. Ain't it fine?"

Sippie followed Dida into a huge kitchen—at least it looked like what a kitchen might have back before the wheel was invented. Part of the roof was missing, so that it was as if they were outside with walls around them.

"What do you do when it rains?" asked Sippie.

"Well now, Old Jim, he's handy. He got these tarps rolled up like sideways sails, and all we got to do is untie 'em. Got hooks to hitch 'em up on all over this fine hall. Why you ask, Cha? You think a roof would be better?"

"No. Not at all. It's like a secret garden, with jars," Sippie whispered, looking at all the ledges and sills and bits of wood and stone that were lined with jars full of honey and jams and pickles and some things that weren't meant to be eaten at all. Dark things.

Dida went to a large, open fireplace and pulled a pan of steaming bread pudding out with a long wooden paddle. It smelled like every good thing should smell.

"It might seem peculiar, us living this way, but it's clean. It's a good clean life. Simple and true. Which is the best kind of magic. We wash the floors and the windows with vinegar, and keep out the rot where we can. Let's let this cool, and I'll take you to meet the others."

"The others?" asked Sippie.

"The dead ones . . ."

"I think I already met some of them, out on the front lawn."

"You saw them? Well now, then you really do belong here, cha! So, now let's go meet them proper like."

Dida took her out the side door of the kitchen, and Sippie noticed that Helene's chapel glass hadn't gone to waste. A dozen or so wind chimes and suncatchers had been fashioned from the shards. They clinked and glowed bright in the sun. Sippie heard whispers of them everywhere she turned.

She followed Dida through the gardens toward the family plot, noticing that other bits of the colored glass made up strange mosaics on the broken saints in the cemetery. Lopsided, grouted crowns, dripping edges of robes, and St. Therese's roses, the petals glued together with red glass.

There was a black iron gate enclosing a series of marble tombs overgrown with wildflowers. Dida lovingly placed her hands across each one as she walked by.

"Here they all are," she said. "Helene, Edmond, all my sisters, and my baby brother, Egg. *Cher bébé Egg.*"

"Dida, you that old?"

"I am. It's why the magic is so strong in our bloodline. And it's why your very own mama was born to save the family, only . . . she refused. Denied her own self."

"Why?"

"It seems she lost her faith. But maybe she just got it back, what do you think, cha?"

Sippie didn't know what to think. A lot had happened . . . fast, and it was hard work to catch up to this new family of hers.

Dida turned to leave, lingering over one grave she hadn't spoken of.

Elsie Mae Sorrow

"Who's that?"

"I'm not sure, I've always wondered," Dida said softly, leading the way back. "I feel close to her, *ça va*? Dis the only grave makes me cry, sometimes. Think maybe I just feel bad no one knows who she is."

"You ever ask Mr. Craven?"

"Dat fool? He thinks he knows things he simply do not know, child. I don't trust one thing he says, but he sure does entertain us. I know this place seems like a wonderland, but it can get hollow feelin', too. Craven thickens us up like a dark roux"

"Do you miss your family all the time? You can see them, right? I think that would hurt too much, to see the ones we love, and not be able to touch them, feel them . . . to say things."

"I think you might be talking about yourself, Sippie. But in case you're talking about me, a fever came and cleared everyone out and cleared my memory, too. So, it don't hurt, the missing. I feel them all around me. And when it's my turn for my soul to leave my body, I'll be with them again. And my memories, too."

"Ain't you afraid to die?" Sippie asked.

"Nah, I look forward to it, *ça va*? It's part of the cycle. Think of the life span of a flower. Shorter than ours . . . but no less beautiful. *Mais non*. These gardens are as much about life and death as that cemetery."

"The gardens are like a fairy tale," said Sippie.

"That is a true thing, Sippie. A real true thing. You'll love it in the fall when the spider lilies bloom. Such perfume and beauty. Those lilies wait underwater to bloom, then, as soon as the sun hits them and the waters are low, all you want to do is run into those boggy fields and throw yourself right on top of them, except that's when the snakes and gators are at their most ornery . . . meaning' you got to watch them, smell them, and love them from far away, so you won't get bit. Reminds me of all of us."

"What do you mean? Beauty with a bite or being underwater till you bloom?" asked Sippie.

"Clever girl. You belong right here where you washed. With us." Dida squeezed her hand as they walked back into the kitchen.

"No, no, no! That's not it at all! Not at all, JuneBug!" yelled a voice from the east side of the house.

"What's all that about, Dida?"

"That's Craven. He's helping JuneBug get the set ready for the pageant. Each year on summer solstice, we reenact the trials and tribulations of Serafina Sorrow, our original matriarch."

Craven huffed into the kitchen, hands aflutter, smoothing down his black hair and mustache. "That man is an imbecile. Oh my. Yes, he is," he said, pumping water out into a large bucket and soaking a cloth. "He's gotten the blue paints mixed up! Put the water where the sky should be. Come with me, won't you, Sippie? I may need your help to fix this. And you can watch a rehearsal of the show." He walked out.

"It's in the ballroom, cha," Dida said, giving her a nudge toward the door. "You'll love it. It has a complete roof, so we hang all the herbs in there to dry. Nice and earthy. Enjoy, *ma chère*! Learn a bit a your history."

"You see, Sippie," Craven said, walking upstairs to the east side of the house, "though there is much about this family that I believe is conjured out of thin air, I do suspect there are places on the earth that are ripe with unexplainable forces. And this is one of them. You see, *time* moves differently here. Or, at least, it has the possibilities of that type of shift. Some say older generations of Sorrows, even Serafina herself, moved through time. And that's why I think"—he lowered his voice reverently—"that Serafina was a *real* witch. What a wonder that would be! To explore the world sideways like that."

"Or . . . ," said Millie, flinging open two enormous doors to the largest room Sippie had ever seen, "people could just stay home and see the wonders they got right in front of them. Wouldn't that be magical? To see the magic in ordinary things . . . like love and sky and friendship?"

Sippie followed Millie into the room that was even bigger once she was inside.

Rows of mismatched chairs were lined up in front of a strange, colorful stage. Ancient sets leaned against the walls. Large, wooden waves of blue and white paint splashes; orange and red swirls as the fires that burned down much of Bourbon Street in 1788; and in the distance, a flat board ship could be seen resting behind deep red velvet curtains.

"Let's start! Places! Places, everyone!" cried Craven. "Take a seat up front, Sippie."

The waves began to move, a cityscape behind the stage rising to reveal a vast ocean expanse. Millie stood at the center of the waves as they shifted back and forth. She wore a handkerchief around her head.

"*When Serafina came across the sea, a casket girl of only ten and three* . . . Ah, screw this, Frances is going to do it this year anyhow," Millie grumbled.

"She didn't say that," said Craven. "And this is by far our most important segment! At least stand there so we can get the ship positioned right."

So she stood there and decided to put on a little show of her own.

"Sippie, you want to know what you just fell into? Here you go: When people from these parts mention 'curse' and 'Sorrow' in the same sentence, everyone thinks of the curse that began with that crazy killer nun taking down a whole generation of Sorrows.

"But I'm going to tell you about a different curse—the lesser-known Frances Green Sorrow curse. The one she brought on herself.

"Each summer solstice, we Sorrows dress in our traditional Serafina clothes and make our way with lanterns lit, around the Sorrow property, throughout the hall, then sail from the front docks to the back bayou, ending at the lighthouse. And this, *this* is the most important right of being a Serafina, because we believed one day, when the time was right, Serafina herself would speak to the 'chosen witch' and reveal a spell that would restore the Sorrows to their former glory. Imagine! Only she never did speak to Frances. Special, *chosen* Frances, did she, Dida?"

Dida suddenly appeared by Sippie's side. "Pay no mind to her, Sippie," she said, moving them both toward the door. "She's just a little . . . high-strung. She loves your mother so much, she don't know where to put it all, *ça va*? Either way you and me should exit Toute de suite, I can feel a Nasty Millie Moment comin' on."

"Simone had a voice like silk, didn't she, Sippie?" Millie yelled after them. "Maybe you should take over the lead?"

"Hush your damn mouth Millie," said Dida who ushered Sippie back to the safety of the hallway.

Sippie felt as if she'd been slapped. She turned around and narrowed her eyes at this "friend" of her mother's, as a tide of curses came too close to bursting off her tongue.

"Leave it be, child." said Dida as she closed the ballroom doors.

"Why is she so unhappy?"

"That, Sippie, is because she wasn't born a Sorrow. If she'd been born a Sorrow, nothing would have been able to hurt her because we're already born into pools of it. Now, let's go fix you up with some new clothes, what you say, cha?"

"Got anything with leopard print?" asked Sippie.

"Lordy, we got some work to do, don't we," said Dida.

12

Sippie and Frances

Cast a Spell

Frances

I went to weed my garden. With my hands in the earth, everything began to sink down straight into my soul. I felt the pain coming, like a wave, and I wanted to fight it, shut down, sleep, be angry. But after all these years, I knew it was time to sift through all that pain. So I just let it come. In *The Book of Sorrows* there is a passage that states: "There are many ways to die, and many parts of us, dead already that need to be severed or we risk gangrene of the soul."

It's the most terrifying thing, removing all the dead time and loss and anger. I knew it myself, the weakness of weeping. It might wash away the dead parts. So I cried.

"I want to go back—" My voice broke, my mouth full of regret. "I want to choose differently! There's this young girl inside of me sitting on a beach with this crazy fool of a boy, and it was the first and last time I was completely myself. No contrition, no past, no worries. And I walked away! Oh God, I walked away. I was never brave at all; I just walked away from everything."

I walked away. Me. Not Danny. Danny never walked away. Not even that first time. It was always me doing the running.

My cries filled me until there were no more wails to be found and all that was left was my ragged breath breaking the silence.

Sometimes you make a mistake so large, but so quiet, hidden inside a second, you forget to remember why you walk around with that terrible ache. The idea that everything happens for a reason is swell, until you realize you're using that to hide behind your fuckup.

Danny was my first mistake.

All I had to do was wait; Exercise a little patience and see if he'd come back to me from that fancy college. Instead I created my own personal hell with my fear.

The truth is complicated.

I sat up, wiping the dirt from my hands. Exhausted, but full of lightness, I went back to my porch to wait for Sippie, remembering the time before the hope inside me died. Clearing away some of those dead parts set the best parts free.

I always loved the way the sunshine poured in through the old lace curtains in the kitchen. They always smelled fresh and new, and Dida made them frame the lopsided windows so that they almost looked straight.

Dida would put together the most beautiful outdoor dining rooms, entertaining on old china while shooing cats off the garden tables. Then, later, when I didn't know I still cared, I'd watch Old Jim play with Jack in the gardens. Danny, too. The unbridled joy they all seemed to have with one another. A joy that wasn't stolen from me—I'd given it away.

When Sippie finally came back, she was flushed and wearing an old dress that Dida must have fixed up to fit her. I didn't realize until I saw her that I'd been afraid she wouldn't come back at all.

"You're a vision in that Sorrow lace, Sippie!" I smiled up at her.

"Thank you," she said, sitting across from me on the porch.

"So, Miss Teenage Daughter, tell me, do you want to talk or to let things work themselves out? You're a Sorrow. And for better or worse, we do a lot of letting things just work themselves out. I've been sitting here, thinking and thinking, and I'm out of ideas on how we should . . . proceed."

"You said you had to work in the garden, you all done?"

"You like to garden, Sippie?"

"I do! I used to help Simone garden in the backyard of our old house, then after . . . well, Eight Track wasn't much good at that kind of stuff."

"Then we have a plan," I said.

I showed Sippie my saint garden, how I fill up Helene's broken statues with flowers and greenery. A wisteria plant growing up from inside St. Michael, camellias around the hands of Jesus. It was Sippie's idea to plant wild roses inside the Virgin Mary in such a way that the blossoms filled out her eyes.

"I'm sure that during Helene's time, this was a beautiful garden," I said. "And I'm sure she'd call me a heathen if she saw what I've done to it. But I think it's far more beautiful now than it ever was. I think the statues like it better this way, too."

"I do, too," said Sippie, digging in the earth. "Can I ask you a question?"

"Of course, my dear."

"Why'd you get married?"

"When I found out I was pregnant with Jack, Danny insisted. We don't usually marry in this family, just partner for life, like wolves."

"Well, technically they don't. They just have one mate at a time. But you could use sandhill cranes there. That would work. So, why'd you get divorced?"

"We didn't like each other much."

"I don't believe you." Sippie eyed me wisely.

"Fine, we liked each other too much."

"Better. Who's my grandfather?"

"My father was a fisherman, or rather boy, that fell in love with poor, blind Claudette, which surprised the whole bayou. But before I was born, he drowned. Drowning is what terrifies Claudette most. His name was Louis. But I always had Old Jim, and growing up, Eight Track was like an older brother."

"He's a good man," said Sippie, who had gone quiet at his name.

"You miss him . . . well then, tell me about him!"

We spent the rest of that night like that, with Sippie telling stories of growing up and the things her Eight Track taught her.

"He always reminded me of Old Jim. All that wisdom. I suppose Crow gave you a taste of him, too?"

"Yeah, but Old Jim too white to be like Eight Track."

"There is no white or black or purple or orange or anything here in Serafina's Bayou. You got to try not to think like that anymore."

"I think I lived too long in a world where it's all anyone looks for, so long that I started to look for it inside myself. I think I'll stop looking for it now. The more I look for it in myself, the more invisible I become. You know?"

I nodded.

Sippie hesitated. "So . . . who is my father?"

"Maybe we should start with how I feel about fathers."

"There was this high school counselor; he was a strange little man. I saw him at a strip club just last month and he put ten dollars—"

"Stop there." I grabbed her hands; I wasn't ready to hear about the terrible way I'd left her.

"Well, anyway, he used to say I had 'daddy issues.'"

"Honey, we all have those. It's like . . . an American crisis or something."

"You aren't answering me."

"I don't have an answer."

"You don't know?! You're worse than me! How old were you again? Fifteen?"

"Don't be a sass mouth. And you already been with someone? Tell me, I need to know. And don't say something like 'You been my mama for a day and you want me to tell you everything?' Just tell me that one thing."

"I been wanting you for too long already, so the more mothering you have for me, the more I'll take. And no . . . I've never . . . I mean, almost. But never because I wanted to."

"Those boys rape you, Sippie? Those meat boys?! I'll kill them!" I started to get up.

"Wait! They didn't, they didn't touch me in that way. But they weren't the first to beat me either. Foster care is another great American crisis, I guess. It's why I always look for the exit signs. Eight Track always said . . ."

I smiled, joining her.

"Be kind, be clever, be safe, know your magic, and always look for the exit signs."

"You loved him, too," she said.

"Daddy issues . . . ," I said, laughing.

"You still ain't answer my question."

"You still *didn't* answer my question."

"You talk just like me, why you tryin' to correct me all the time?"

"Honey, Sorrow women know how to speak. We got our 'home' speak, where we be all relaxed and inside and out like that watahhhh, movin' all slow like, and even a bit a Cajun French now and again, *ça va*? But then, we got proper English for when we are out in the real world and must speak in a way that gives us power. How we use words carries powerful magic, Sippie."

"And what makes you think I don't already have the ability to use my words that way? I have a stunning vocabulary and can hold my own with the classiest of classies. It's something I pride myself on . . . *de bon coeur*."

With her whole heart. That girl, my girl. Getting to know her was like opening a never-ending Christmas present. Each layer of bright paper bringing a new, shiny thing to enjoy.

"But, you still ain't answerin' my question."

"Beast. You are a beast of a child. And I get it, you know how to speak . . . fine. But let's have that conversation over dinner. I need to get my strength up."

"I ain't a child."

"You are *my* child," I said. And with that declaration planting us firmly together on this Sorrow soil, for the first time in forever I felt whole.

That night we feasted on red beans and rice, tomato salad, and bread pudding Dida sent over for dessert. We sat on the front porch as the candles burned low and the tree frogs chirped right alongside her many questions. I couldn't stop looking at her, examining every feature.

Her head, so like mine, resting on her hands. Her thin, elegant wrist turned upward, tilting her exotic face toward the warm light of the candles.

The world amuses her. But it also hurts her, confounds her. She's been an observer so long, she hasn't had to feel. Only now the feelings are leaking inside.

We were almost through with dinner when I saw her begin to search my face the way I searched hers, ready to strike or laugh.

A smile teased the corner of her mouth. Always chattering, she was, a loud kind of quiet that hung over her. She was loud so that she could keep her hurting soul quiet. God, I wanted to kill the world for her, to steal back anything that was stolen from her, including me. I'd give myself over to her. I would take care of this girl.

"Now that we're just sitting here," she said pointedly.

"Ah yes, the father question," I said. "I hope this doesn't disappoint you, Sippie, but for all my . . . whatever it is people say about me, I've only ever been with two men. And they were both . . . well, timing is everything. So, you are either the child of the most unruly union there ever was, me and Danny, or, you are the child of Eddie the Jazz Man. And I don't know his last name so don't bother askin'."

"Was Eddie black?" she asked.

"What? Why do you care?"

"'Cause my skin . . ."

"Is like *mine*. A little tanner, but like mine," I said.

"Still . . ."

"Girl, Eddie was Cuban and Haitian and Portuguese, with the most beautiful green eyes. He was all mixed up. And Danny is Italian, not dark skinned, but his hair . . . Lord. And then there's my own poor, drowned lost soul of a father, Louis LaNuit, who was a Creole, and so there's no rhyme or reason to how we look. And if you ask me, Sippie Wallace, that's the way this whole damn country should see things, the more mixed up we get ourselves, the less we got to argue about, *ça va?*"

Sippie looked confused and relieved at the same time.

"Well, fine," she said. "I don't reckon I have to know everything with a certainty, as long as I got you."

I forced back the tears. I couldn't cry anymore. "What else happened over there?"

"Dida told me a whole bunch of things. Millie, too."

"Like what?"

"Well, lemme get this straight. You were supposed to save this whole family? You were the most powerful of all of them. That's what they said."

"Exactly, that's what they *say*. But I still believe that's just a story. I could do *things*. It used to be on and off, even then. Magic is temperamental. It demands payment if you ask for something big. So I gave up on all of it." I saw Sippie start to smile, then we were both laughing. Then? It was that kind of laughter that is something else entirely . . . one you can't stop. And I was trying to breathe through the tears and said . . . "But now, it's coming back. I think you brought it back. You brought *magic* back into my life!" Which pushed us both into new waves of laughter.

When the last bits of it ebbed away, we were lying on the ground, looking up at the stars.

"I know how to do that, too, you know . . . get all funny when something hurts to talk about," said Sippie. "So tell me . . . come on. No foolin'."

She had me there. We sat back at the table, and I tried.

"It's not that easy to explain, Sippie. Magic, and I don't even like that term, it's a hard art to master. And for a long time I just turned it all off because I couldn't figure out what was real and what was an act."

"Tell me something small you used to do."

"Well, I could light candles and put them out again. Without any matches."

"Do it now! At least try!"

I put out the candle with my fingers.

"No fair!" Sippie glared at me.

"Shhh . . ." I looked at the candle hard. Nothing. It didn't work.

"Guess I don't have it anymore," I said quietly.

"How'd you do it before?"

"I'd think about something that made me angry."

"Here, hold my hand." She reached out over the table, taking my hand. "Now, think about those boys, the no-good ones who brought me here, the ones who left me bruised."

The candle wick sputtered to life, a strong, deep flame.

"You did it!" she said.

"It could have been you, honey."

"Then we did it. Teach me? Teach me more."

"We'll teach each other. And Jack, too, when he comes home. He'll be over the moon. He's spent his whole life trying to get me to teach him things."

"I love him already, out there on his own. He's so brave."

"Blood does that, girl. Now, enough of this talking . . . I got an idea," I said. I felt reborn, filling up like the moon.

"What?"

"Well, we're gonna try something from *The Book of Sorrows,* you and me, together."

"What?"

"It's a surprise."

It was the perfect night for it. The moon was on its way to waxing, change of heart and all that.

I had her make a circle out of salt in the middle of the saint garden. Then we placed all the elements in the corners. A bowl of water, a candle, a pile of dirt, a jar we both blew into, capturing our breath, and *The Book of Sorrows* in the middle. We sat as I flipped through the pages.

"As soon as Old Jim, your great-granddaddy, came back, I was gonna have him hunt down those boys and make them into alligator food. But maybe . . . Here it is. Turning evil into good . . . let's try this."

"What's it supposed to do?"

"Well, those boys? It should make them kind. As kind as they are dark. Which means they might all grow into good men with good hearts who do good things. They'll be good."

Sippie thought for a minute. "That's worse, isn't it, than killing them. It's like . . . the best kind of spite."

"I met this woman once," I said. "Vivian Pratt, a tourist from up north. She came to see me a month or so before you were born. She said she was looking for her sister. And when I pulled the cards . . . I swear, I told her I saw her sister losing someone she loved, that she was full of hurt and pain. I thought it would make her sad. Only it didn't. Vivian paid me more than she should have, and walked out of the parlor at Thirteen Bourbon laughing. 'Oh, Frances, thank you,' she said. 'For what?' 'For the proof.' Oh, Karma, she is a cruel bitch."

Sippie started laughing.

"Now, our Eight Track, he'd been teaching me a little philosophy from the time I was a bit of a thing. About Karma, you know . . . and I think maybe that's the best idea."

"He taught me that, too. So, yeah . . . Frances, let's do it. This is exactly what they deserve," said Sippie.

"Well," I said, examining the book in the lantern light, "unfortunately, this will have to wait until tomorrow. I'm missing something. These witches, I swear, I take a fifteen-year break, and they let the devil's bit die out. I bet there'll be some at the farmer's market in Tivoli. An old Cajun lady always used to have what we needed, when we needed it. We can check the garden at the Voodoo first, but they mostly got vegetables now. Millie never did have a knack for herbs or root work."

"You know something, Frances?" she said as we made our way back, "I remember her."

"From where, honey?"

"From a long time ago, from when my mother, I mean, Simone . . . the night she died. Millie was there. At least, I think it was her."

So that's it. Oh, Millie.

"Look, I'm going to tell you something right now, and I want you to hear it as the truth," I said. "I gave you to Simone and Eight Track for a lot of reasons. Because her voice always made me think of what love should feel like. Because Eight Track always kept me safe. And now, here you are, and I know you might've walked a thousand miles of grief to get here, but you *are* here. And we're gonna walk through whatever comes our way together from now on."

We walked up the porch stairs, hand in hand.

"You think mistakes are lessons or just mistakes, Frances?" she asked.

"I think it depends."

"Why?"

"Because a lesson stays a mistake unless you learn something from it."

"So, we're learning now, right? You and me together?" she asked.

"Yes. We are. But let's go to bed now because I could listen to you talk forever, and Lord knows we could both use some rest."

13

Day by Day

Frances

The Voodoo garden had nothing useful, as I suspected. Millie stood over me, yammering nonsense. I'd sent Sippie in to get JuneBug so he could take us into town.

"I know it's hard to keep up, needing dry soil and all, but devil's bit is one of the more important ones, Millie. Hoodoo aside, it's something that we use when people come to us for pregnancy . . . helps stop miscarriages, you know that."

"Frances, when was the last time anyone came to Sorrow Hall, or Bourbon Street, for that matter, for anything other than a fortune?"

I sat back on my heels. She was right. I hadn't seen many people coming to Dida for herbal remedies of late. But I thought she still did her root work when they were at 13 Bourbon. "What types of things does that store sell now? None of Dida's cures?"

"Hell, woman, that all ended years ago. Now it's all that stuff tourists eat up. Crap from China."

I rolled my eyes.

"You got no right judging us, Frances. One could say it's your own damn fault, you know."

"You're right, Millie."

"Anyway, it's been ages since we used that root. It's good you're 'back' and all, Frankie, but what about baby steps? You diving in so fast, girl."

"Well, I've never been real good at doing things halfway, have I?"

"Guess you have a point. But you got a lifetime to reclaim what's lost. Take it slow."

"I don't want to wait. I want it all back now. I should have had it back ten years ago." I stared at her, hard.

I hadn't intended on letting Millie know I knew she'd kept the truth from me. I thought that after Sippie was settled and Danny was home I'd sit her down and ask what happened the night Simone died. I was sure there was some sort of reasonable explanation, and my anger took me by surprise. Millie looked up at the sky, then back at me, like she wanted to say something, but instead she shook her head and walked away. Maybe I should have followed her. But I was downright vexed at that moment, and me and Millie were as famous for our fights as we were our follies.

Sippie and JuneBug passed Millie as they walked out of the bar. JuneBug tried to say something to her, but she looked away from them as well. She was isolating herself and knowing she felt cornered made my anger melt back into love.

Breathe. Millie will be fine. All this change is hard on everyone. After the solstice we'll have a night, just the two of us, where we confess all our sins and dance under the stars like when we were kids so she knows I'm still here for her.

"We goin' to town or not, Frankie?" shouted JuneBug banging the hood of his truck.

"We sure as hell are." I said.

"You okay, Frankie?" asked JuneBug as we drove off toward Tivoli Bridge.

"I'm fine," I said.

Sippie looked confused.

"I haven't been over this bridge in nine years."

"'Bout time, then," she said.

The drive into Tivoli Proper was easier than I thought. Right up until we crossed the bridge, I worried that the memories of my time living there with Jack and Danny would drown me in guilt. Once we crossed it, I was filled with lightness instead.

I feel like I could fly . . . I thought.

JuneBug dropped us off at Pete's, who gave me a big hug. I wanted to ask him if he knew Jack was off on his own, but I didn't want to ruin Jack's adventure.

"Grabbin' a beer," said JuneBug, disappearing into the market.

"It's good to see you on this side of the world, Frankie! You gonna stop by and see Jack?" he asked.

"No, not now . . . he'll be coming to Sorrow Hall soon enough. But Pete, here's the thing. We're gonna have a really big Solstice Eve celebration this year. Spread the word, okay . . . I got something to announce." I winked at Sippie.

"You messing with all that hoodoo again, Frankie?" Pete was never comfortable with things he didn't understand.

"So what if I am?" I said, but I smiled and he warmed up again.

"Who's this pretty gal you got with you?" he asked.

"Part of my solstice surprise."

"When you get what you need, I'll be right here with Pete," said JuneBug walking back out into the sunshine with a six-pack.

"Where else?" I asked.

Sippie and I headed off down Main Street to the sound of Pete saying, "What's gotten into her? She sure seems happy. . . ."

The farmer's market was held daily from early spring through midsummer. And as we walked toward the white tents, we passed the Tivoli Parish Historical Society. A small, dinky storefront with an elaborately ornate sign. The juxtaposition always made me laugh.

We'd just walked past when Craven came running outside.

"Oh, Miss Frances, look at you, here in town! And it's a lucky day for me, I guess because I have something to tell you, well, ask you. And tell you . . . I was just going to make a trip into the bayou, and now I don't! It's fascinating, really . . . you see—" He broke off suddenly, noticing Sippie. "Well, hello again, Miss . . . Wallace. How are you getting on?" He turned his attention back to me, not waiting for an answer. "Anyway, I found an old newspaper article from a French paper called *Le Matin,* and the society pages! They state that SuzyNell Sorrow was returning to America to claim Sorrow Hall. This explains so many things, Miss Frances. I gave a copy of it to Jack, and I wanted to show it to you, only I can't seem to find him (or the original for that matter). And I must either find HIM or IT as this stellar find gives me actual *proof* that . . . well, suffice it to say, I think there has been a terrible misunderstanding. . . ."

"Oh, Craven. You fixin' on spoiling every single mystery?" I asked, wanting to be on our way to get the devil's bit. "What are we without the shadow of the unknown? Now, why don't you go add Sippie to that crazy family tree you keep up for all of us?"

It was like hanging something shiny in front of a bird. "Yes! Oh my, *yes*. Oh! But could you just tell me where to find Jack—"

"No, sir, got to get to the market before it closes, but you know you are always welcome at Sorrow Hall. And by the way, better start boarding up your things, we're expecting a big storm."

"How big?"

"Big enough, Craven."

"Oh my, I should pack all this up, then, and bring it to Thirteen Bourbon. Will there be a room for me? Should I go now?"

Sippie and I smiled at each other. He's easy to fluster, and I could tell we were both holding back needling him more than he deserved.

"I'd wait, I mean, until after the solstice, because we need you there," said Sippie.

"But our, I mean, *your* history is so much more important. Maybe I'll skip this year's. Oh, my . . . yes. Yes, I'll start packing right now."

Sippie tried not to laugh.

Mr. Craven hurried back inside, muttering packing plans to himself.

Alva Vidal saw me before I saw her.

"Frances, *ma cha,* you come to me again aftah all dees yeahs? And dis time, look, you be wit dat young one you lost. You've grown up into a beauty, Sippie Wallace. I figure you bot be finding yo' own selves now dat you found each other, no?"

"She's the real thing, ain't she?" whispered Sippie.

"Used to scare me to death when I was little, though I wouldn't admit it. Let's not stay too long. I always swear she can look right inside the soul, maybe even steal it."

"For someone who decided not to believe in magic, you sure believe in magic."

"Oh, Sippie, I decided not to believe in my family and their magic. I never said anything about other things in this crazy world." Then I turned to Alva, who stood watch over a foul-smelling table of roots.

"Alva, it's been too long. And I'd love to stay and catch up on everything, but I need something."

"Here you go, cha, devil's bit. All wrapped up for you. And some bulbs, too, so you can plant dem in your own garden once again . . . now dat you back."

"*Merci,*" I whispered.

"A storm be comin', cha, take care of your babies. Don't make no deals wit no devils, you can't afford to pay dat fine, girl. You hear? Now go, tings about to get all kinds of messy. Just when you ready to give up, you remember dis, the tantrum, it set you free. The mad inside, you let it go, you find your way. Tell her, Sippie Wallace. *Tell her.*"

Sippie had my hand and was dragging me away. We started to run, fast and free. JuneBug let us ride in the flatbed on the way back. We were wind tossed and wild, laughing the whole way home at the strange world.

When we finally got home, we did a discreet check in on Jack. "I can't wait to meet him tomorrow. You think he'll be okay with all this?" asked Sippie.

"I'm sure he will . . . but even if he isn't, he'll learn."

As we cast our spell in the night garden, the one to make those Tivoli trash boys good, I could feel us growing together, curling . . . unfurling and interlacing like the vines growing wild all around. It was beautiful. We had missed so much time because of some stupid, stubborn girl.

Me.

"You sure are somethin', Sippie," I said when we were done. "Let's turn in."

I'd rigged a feather bed on a platform on the floor close to me, so we could talk. I fell asleep listening to her voice, it was such a delicious thing. I wanted to talk to her forever. I wanted to know what her first words were, when she learned to walk . . . but couldn't ask. Those questions were too full of sad.

"What did it feel like, when you gave me to Eight Track?"

"Well, at first, I wasn't going to give you up at all. I'd wake up crying. I'd never cried like that before. When I finally saw you, my first thought was, *I'm not giving this baby up.* I couldn't give you up; you were the most beautiful baby, *my* baby. I fell in love with you, and that was the problem. It happened too fast. I had no time to think clearly."

"What do you mean?"

"We had it all worked out, and Eight Track, he tried to make me keep you. He did. But I was stubborn and felt like everything had to happen immediately. So, he took you out of the building, and I ran to the window and yelled, 'I'm not ready, wait, come back.' But he couldn't hear me, Sippie. Everything had already been set in motion. And by the time I woke up the next day, the missing you was another layer of hate I laid across the world."

"So, you put your magic away. Because of me?"

"Of course not. You were just a baby. I put it away because I couldn't understand why it didn't help me figure out what to do. I was so young," I said.

And then, in perfect Sorrow fashion, she turned the conversation around.

"You ever get mad at how people make witches out to be ugly? Like in the movies and books and stuff. Or even if there's one that's pretty, she's all old inside or ugly when she looks in a mirror."

"I don't pay much attention to those things, Sippie. And there's not a lot of TV or movie watching in these parts."

"That suits me fine. And just because you sell yourself to the devil don't mean you have to be ugly, right?"

My stomach hurt so hard from laughing at that one. Sippie Wallace was waking things up inside me that I thought were dead and buried. She was bringing me back to life. Hell, she was even digging up new parts of me I never knew existed.

As I fell asleep, I was eager for the next day. The solstice celebration, seeing Jack. But I had no idea what that next day, our sacred day, would hold. And if I did, I swear to God, I might have thrown it all away and slept forever.

The Full Moon on the

Eve of the Summer Solstice

If the moon be full, the magic be full.

It is time for us to rid ourselves of unwanted things.
Work your protection Magic.
Let go of habits that hold you back from the truth.
Direct the moon's light inward for revelation.
Revealing yourself to yourself.
Only then are you never complicit in harm.
The lies we tell to ourselves make us weak.
Always stand tall inside of your truth.

—Serafina's Book of Sorrows

14

"I Should Have Stayed Fishing"

Danny

On the morning of Solstice Eve, Danny and Old Jim could see the faint outline of Saint Sabine Isle. They were heading for the mouth of Tivoli River, when a dense fog (that hadn't been in the maritime forecast) rolled in and forced them to drop anchor before they could get to Lafourch's seafood to off-load. Danny was anxious. The water did not feel friendly or peaceful. He wanted to see Jack. He wanted to tell Frances how much he needed her. How much he wanted to try again. Maybe get it right this time. But that fog had them stuck with nothing but time and worry.

Old Jim and Danny, one man old with a young heart, the other young with an old heart, stood silently, watching as the unexpected squall skimmed off to the east.

"That there fog ain't right. It's that damn solstice tradition of theirs. Those people, I swear," Danny grumbled.

"Those people are my people, boy. And those people have been good to you. Don't you dare forget it." Old Jim didn't usually snap at Danny. His tone unnerved Danny even further. The radio kicked on below, and Old Jim went to get it. Danny breathed a sigh of relief. He hated stepping on Jim's toes.

"Dan! JuneBug's on this here radio for you, again. Next time we stay out this long, I'm shootin' this thing. Point is to get away from everything as far as I'm concerned. Not to be bothered with all them hens back home."

Danny smiled slyly. "What happens if we get stranded? Besides, you love them hens."

"Just go see what new fool thing that boy wants from you."

Turns out it wasn't a fool thing at all; it's what his old coach back at Louisiana State would have called "a game changer."

"Yeah, Junie, I'm here."

"You fellas close to home?"

"We here already, damn fog rolled in. When it clears, we'll be at Lafourch's. You all ready for a haul the size of kingdom come? We got shrimp comin' out our ears over here."

"That's fine! Fine, but, ah, well, I got something I think you should know. Now, it ain't fact, and no one told me not to tell you, but I got a feelin' maybe they don't want me to tell you and—"

"JuneBug Lafourch, if you don't speak your mind I might shoot up this damn radio."

Old Jim let out a snort from up on deck.

"Turns out that girl them boys brought to Frankie's? Well, turns out, she's Frankie's daughter, Dan. Got a funny name, too (not that I'm one to talk). They call her Sippie."

Danny dropped the radio receiver.

"You there? T-Dan . . . you there?"

"I'm here, I'm here," Danny sputtered.

"Well, anyway, she had her over there on Bourbon Street

way back when she was still, well, you know, as sane as them women ever get. And—"

Danny interrupted, "Okay, uh, thanks for the info, Junebug, we'll . . . we'll be in soon."

"Will do, Danny."

Dan waited a few minutes to go up on deck. His heart was beating so fast, he thought he might have a heart attack. He was still trying to catch his breath when he rejoined Old Jim.

"What's he fussin' over?"

Danny didn't answer. He just looked out over the water again. The fog had begun to shift, and he could see more of Saint Sabine Isle.

That damn fog.

"That's where it all started, Jim. And here we are stuck looking at it."

"What started?"

"Me and Frankie."

"When?"

"Well, you were gone that summer. Out on a big rig, remember? And I was gonna go off to college in the fall. And Frankie was walking down that beach, playing in the ruins of that fancy resort."

"I remember, she sure loved going there. But, you gonna get around to tellin' me what Junie said?" Old Jim wasn't easily distracted.

"In a minute. Anyway, I was there, too, by accident. But you all know I'd loved her for ages. I just never told her."

"You never had the courage to go against all them people in Tivoli Proper who made fun of her. Sons a bitches."

"Jim, she came to school barefoot, dirty clothes, no manners, no lunch. How were they supposed to act?"

Old Jim sighed. "You right, boy. You right. Can't tell that girl nothing, never could. So we didn't argue. And, when your mama is blind, you don't always have the best outfits."

They both chuckled, the way they always did whenever things got too serious.

"So I was walking one way up the beach, and she was walking the other. And damn, Jim . . . she was only fifteen, but her hair, blowing in that wind. Her confidence, her body—"

"Enough of that, boy," scolded Old Jim.

"We spent the summer there. Didn't tell anyone. I gave her a strange little key I found on the shore, and she strung it up on a piece of ribbon."

"I know. She never takes it off. To this very day," said Old Jim.

Danny knew, too, and it made him happy. Though when they were fighting, he wanted to rip it off her neck.

"Jim, that summer was the beginning and end of everything. She wanted me to stay, but I needed to go. I knew I'd miss her, but I didn't know how much. So on my way to college, I stopped at Thirteen Bourbon and went walkin' in like I owned her or somethin'. And that's when I saw her with that Jazz Man. I almost lost my damn mind."

Danny roughly pushed his hands through his hair and sighed.

"You gonna keep strollin' me down memory lane or tell me what this is about? This about somethin' JuneBug said?"

"I don't know if I'm the right person to tell you this mess of news, Jim. Because in the end, it's gonna be about you, not me."

"Boy, you actin' like a woman. Just tell me."

Danny recounted the radio call with JuneBug. "Her name is Sippie. Wallace" he finished.

"So, I got me a grown great-grandbaby I never knew. Hell, it feels like Christmas! Sippie, Wallace huh? Like that blues singer.

Frankie musta' given that baby to one of them musicians to raise. What a turn of events . . . a granddaughter. Tie me up happy and shoot me to the moon."

After taking a flask from his back pocket, Old Jim took a swig. "Want one?"

"Nah," said Danny.

Old Jim got too quiet too fast as knowledge swept across his face. "All that you've been tellin' me about Saint Sabine Isle . . . that's when all the love happened, right? Dammit, Danny, you got no sense. She was too young! And then you kept her a secret. And thought she'd trust you again? No wonder she ran off to Bourbon Street and lost her mind. You're the reason I didn't get to bounce that Sippie girl on my knee. You better walk to the other side of this boat, boy. I feel an anger comin' on me quick."

"But Jim," began Danny, just as Saint Sabine Isle started to come into view through the lifting fog, "I can't wrap my mind around it. Why didn't she ever tell me?"

"You really askin' me why Frances kept some sort of secret from you? Something that hurt her or broke her up so bad she came back from that time in her life all beaten down and bitter? You more of a fool than I usually give you credit for, son."

Danny sat back against a pile of nets on deck. "So that could be why she was so messed up when Jack was born. Dammit, Jim! It answers so many questions. If she'd just told me, we coulda worked it out."

"You don't seem to recall those fights you had. How you didn't listen to a word that woman said? How you blamed her for wreckin' your life? Tell me, Dan, give me one time during your whole godforsaken marriage that she could have trusted you enough with something she didn't trust her own grandpap with. Stop bein' an ass."

"You're right. And I know it."

"Good. Now, the fog's liftin'. We best get to work fast so we can get on over to Sorrow Hall and meet that girl of hers." Old Jim angled the boat toward the docks.

"You know what, Jim? I'm gonna look at it like you. I'm gonna look at it like a gift. I'm not gonna be mad about it."

"It's good to hear you're gonna stop bein' an ass, boy. But you might want to tell me a little bit more about you and our Frankie. It ain't that I want to know the whats and the wheres or none of that shit. But I think you ain't considering one important fact here, boy."

"What's that?"

"Timing."

"Timing?"

"When did you say you went up to Thirteen Bourbon?"

"End of August, right when I was going to school."

"And did the two of you . . . shit, boy, put two and two together afore I lose my mind and beat you senseless."

"We did. But she was already with that Jazz Man."

"Don't you know anything about the birds and the bees, son?"

Danny felt the world crash and break over him, like he was drowning with only a speck of sun to swim toward.

"That girl could be mine," Danny whispered. And he knew that he'd known it to be true the second Junie mentioned it. It was taking a journey from his head to his heart.

"We got to figure out how we gonna string those Tivoli trash boys up by their balls. Mess with one of my own and there aint no savin' you. Skin 'em, I say. I never been more unhappy about being on the water, I tell you what," Old Jim muttered. But Danny wasn't really listening,

"Jesus, Jim. She's mine. I know she is. I just know it. Let's swim to shore."

"I enjoy your enthusiasm, boy, but I think we better dock first."

"Then hurry up, old man."

Danny's land legs were wobbly as he drove out from the island onto the mainland. He thought about stopping at the Voodoo for a drink but didn't want to be a coward. Or run into Millie, which also made him a coward. The Voodoo always seemed to complicate things for him.

Frances and Danny had many "dances" in their lives. The Christmas pageant when they were thirteen. The summer on Saint Sabine Isle two years later and that crazy night at 13 Bourbon Street (that may have resulted in a daughter he didn't know he had). But the night at the Voodoo, that night would lead to their longest, meanest run of passion.

They'd repeated the whole dance again. Between his junior and senior years, he came back to Tivoli Parish with those fool boys who wanted to drink at the Voodoo. Get in some bayou culture . . . slum it. And there she was, sitting at the bar looking like a movie star and drinking like a lush. It felt like they were back on that beach before the big bad world made them grow up too quick. They spent that whole summer and fall together (Danny making frequent trips back home to see her), free and in love, trying to re-create the past. Neither of them suspecting that within a few months, Danny would be out of school, and they'd be married with a baby on the way. Looking back, Danny knew that the Frances he swept up at the Voodoo, the Frances he married, and the Frances who left him . . . all those versions were never the same as the girl he'd first loved when they were both kids. He kept waiting for her to come back, got mad at her for changing. But now . . .

"I'm such an asshole," he said, parking his truck next to Trinity Bridge and heading to the boat he kept docked there to go out to the Sorrow Estate. Then he saw Pete's truck speeding from Tivoli.

Pete fairly skidded to a stop and jumped out.

"Dammit, Danny. What took you so long?! Jack's gone. Been gone for almost a week already, but I only found out today. Millie come by the gas station askin' if we seen him. And I said no, because, Dan, I'm so sorry. He said he'd stay close to home and I didn't think to question it because he's such a smart kid. I'm so sorry, Dan. We been lookin' for hours now. Got some boys from Tivoli Proper in trucks. But we ain't checked over here, 'cause Millie said she'd take care of it. And no one wants to tell Frances."

"Wait, slow down, Pete. Frances doesn't know?"

"Not that I heard."

"Well, that don't make sense. She always knows when something's going on with Jack. Those witchy ways of hers. She has to know!"

Pete shrugged. "Maybe she's got him with her, like, hidin' him or somethin'."

"That's crazy talk, Pete."

"Maybe so, but I think it's time we call the police. Don't forget, those Tivoli trash boys were in rare form last week, too. Could be a whole host of trouble."

"Now I *know* you lost your mind. You know a full-out search of this bayou will bring a lotta things out in the light that people don't want found out. We do things different. You ready to bring all that down on this place?"

"Look, Dan, I don't care who's poaching or who's growing or who's trafficking. All I want is to find Jack. You left me responsible, and I failed you. And I failed that boy. So let me do it now."

Danny tried to talk him out of it, but he knew as soon as Pete was out of sight he was just going to go back to Tivoli and get the police. Pete slammed the door to his truck, tires squealing as he pulled away. And then Danny hopped in his little boat so fast, it almost capsized. Soon enough he was on his way to Frances, watching the Sorrow Estate come into view. He watched and waited. He was scared, and he didn't know why. Danny pulled his boat over to the side. He wasn't worried about Jack, not yet. He was sure the boy was pulling some kind of stunt. He was worried about whether or not he'd ever be able to make things right. Millie, arriving late, saw him and waved her arms like, *Don't come.* Don't come? Screw that. Like Old Jim had said, it was time he grew a pair. And with one defiant step after another, Danny made his way toward his ex-wife, his ex-lover, and a young girl he was convinced was his daughter.

15

Clever Jack Gets Out-Clevered

Jack

While his father was facing that thick fog, Jack woke up and had to face the facts. His week outsmarting his family with that Great Idea of his hadn't worked out so good. No one seemed the least bit worried. He was hungry. And though he'd never admit it, he was tired of being quiet. It's hard to hide when you're a boy. He'd read *The Legend of the Sorrow Women* cover to cover, twice. Learned a few racy details about Serafina and her years running 13 Bourbon as a brothel. But not racy enough . . . seems she used a whole bunch of herbs in her bar, and those men didn't ever touch a lady at all, just thought they did! It was sure as heck funny, but not sexy. He also saw a few more of the Sorrow ghosts, but none of them spoke to him the way Helene had. He was glad it was finally solstice. He could make his big reveal, even if no one made a big deal out of it.

He snooped around after his mama and his new sister. Sippie was her name. His mama and Dida were yelling it so loudly, it was as if they needed to hear it echo off the universe to make it real or something. He'd thought it over and decided he was downright giddy about having a sister. If he hadn't inherited a double dose of stubborn from both his parents, he'd have forgotten the whole plan and run over there to spend time with her. But he convinced himself that the Important Work he was doing to Save His Family would benefit her as well.

"It's my first act of brotherly love, is what it is," he told himself. "Don't need both of us dealin' with all that crazy."

Then he changed his mind again and decided to just head on down to Sorrow Hall to help everyone get ready for the solstice.

That's when Millie Bliss knocked on the door and walked in with a bottle of root beer and a plate full of bread and molasses.

"Hey, sugar, how you doin'? I missed you."

"I did okay, but I don't think it worked."

"Of course not, your mama saw you, you know. That first day. She's just been waiting for you to come out."

"So she wasn't even worried?"

"Nope. She's been too busy with that Sippie of hers. I suppose you've been watching."

"Yeah, it's a fine mess. Maybe I should just throw in the towel, Millie."

"No, sir, you just need a little more time. And you got something working in your favor."

"What's that?"

"A storm is coming, Jack. A big one. And they'd be worried sick if you were lost in something like that."

"But where would I go?"

"I have an idea," she said, taking a little bottle out of her pocket.

"What'll it do?"

"Put you to sleep. Like Dida."

"But Dida didn't wake up for one hundred years!"

"That's because no one knew where she was. I'll take you somewhere safe, and you'll emerge triumphant and safe after the storm. Think about it, Jack . . . everyone will be all cooped up at Thirteen Bourbon riding this thing out, with no escape route. This storm is a happy accident."

"Then why can't I just wait it out awake?"

"These herbs have special ancient properties so you won't need food and water. Like, slow-release nutrients. That's how Dida stayed alive. I don't want you to be runnin' around in a hurricane tryin' to find a cheeseburger and a Coke. Do you?"

"I don't think I want to, Millie. I think I just want to go back. And ride out the storm with everyone else. Maybe the change wasn't this at all. Maybe it was Sippie. I've been spying on Mama. She looks happy."

Millie sat back and looked thoughtful.

"I guess you're right, Jack. And she is. She's mighty happy. How about we have a root beer, and then I'll take you back home?"

That root beer was dripping with cold. He took it gladly.

"Thank you, Millie. Really. I'm sorry I was so mean about you and my daddy," he said.

"It'll all be okay, Jack. I promise you. Just go on to sleep now. You ain't got a choice in it."

"What?" he asked, looking at Millie. There were two of her, then three. Bright, white fear washed over him as he reached for his conjure bag, but no amount of salt or hope or silver dimes could help. Then, the blackness came.

Jack wakes up inside a dream. Only Jack knows the language of dreams, and this is different.

He's in a place he's never been. Tucked in an unfamiliar bed. He tries to move, but his body won't listen to his mind. Mama called that "body rooting." He'd watched a TV show with Uncle Pete where they called it "sleep paralysis," and the people on TV said sometimes you could die like that. Jack said it was a load a shit, and Pete made him put that nasty bar of soap from the gas station bathroom in his mouth. And when he had come back spitting out soap bubbles and reaching for a root beer in the cooler, Pete had laughed and said, "I didn't really mean it, boi! You ain't got enough a your mama's ways to read my mind?"

Jack knew better than to tell Pete that reading minds wasn't like pumpin' gas. You had to concentrate, and it took a lot outta you, so it had to be important. Besides, Jack wasn't so sure he wanted to go into Pete's mind. Nothing but beef jerky, boobs, and booze in there.

Jack lies still in his rooted place and thinks he may have been too hard on Uncle Pete. He doesn't want to admit it, but he's scared. He closes his mind again, trying to reach out for his mama.

"Mama?"

Jack opens his eyes. He's in trouble.

His mother always told him that dreams are mysterious things. She didn't teach him much about anything else, but she always answered his questions about dreams.

"No dreamin' is ordinary," she'd say. "Most people have dreams that tell them some kind of truth about somethin' they worry over. Only most people don't know the language of dreams, so they push them aside like food they don't like. The best kind of dreams are the ones you can reach right into. Be careful with those, Jack. Listen, look, and feel all around inside those reaching dreams. They can take you places you can't get out of, so you watch your step, boy."

"Close your eyes, Jack . . . see me."

"Mama?"

"No, boy. It's Serafina."

"Everything is dark."

"Try to look deeper."

Greens and blues and all sorts of colors burst behind Jack's eyes. He's in a perfect painting of the bayou, and Serafina is there, leaning against a tree, looking too much like his mama.

"I'm not here, right? Millie gave me something and I'm not even really here?"

"Maybe yes, maybe no. But aren't you the least little bit curious about why you may or may not be here and who the hell you think I am, little one?"

"You're Serafina, I'd know you anywhere. And I'm here because I want to make my family worry. Wait, it doesn't sound good when I say it like that."

"I think I like you."

"You don't even know me," he says.

"Why do you say that?"

"I . . . I think I made a mistake. And if I'm here with you, maybe I'm dead. Mama said Millie don't know shit about root work. Damn, I'm not ready to be dead yet," Jack says, fear filling his voice.

"Oh, cha, you ain't dead. You are on the grandest adventure of your whole life. And you got a job to do for me. That's why I snuck into Millie's little spell."

"Her spell?" asks Jack.

"Aye, her spell. She's fixin' on taking you for herself. Gonna pretend you died in the storm and scoop you up and away."

"She can't do that! I won't let her," Jack says angrily.

"You are in way too deep here, boi. You let your mama and daddy and your new sister, Sippie, take care of the living side of things. I just figured, while you're here, you could help me with something."

"What do you want me to do?"

"You'll figure it out. Just remember, there's a purpose to you wandering around inside this chasm."

"Don't you have any real answers? You're just like one of those magic eight ball. But bigger. And prettier."

She laughs wildly, with her head thrown back, before morphing into trees and the sky and the aerial map of the bayou, and suddenly Jack is flying, listening.

You're strong, like your mama, your sister, and me. You gonna need it. Trust.

Then the world is dark again.

Nothing's there, not even the light that plays behind your eyes when you close them.

"Dark ain't never really dark, Jack," Dida'd told him when he was little and afraid. "There's light everywhere. You just got to look. But if you ever get to a place where there really ain't no light at all, open your eyes fast, Jack. Open 'em fast."

Stay calm, he thinks, looking around. There are windows nailed shut from the inside, with a bit of light filtering through. *Dark ain't never really dark.* He breathes out, relieved. He knows the room is comfortable and old-fashioned with high ceilings. Nothing dark, dank, or dangerous looking. He hears all the women in his life talking to him in a loud whisper. Dida, Mama, Claudie . . .

"Think about something safe. Something that makes you feel like you float. Think about it real hard and then don't try to move your whole self, just one tiny part, like a pinky or a baby toe. It's like quicksand, that kind of dream, the harder you fight, the longer you stay stuck."

Jack thinks about water. Of floating down the bayou in a pirogue with his mama in the summer, leaning back against her, feeling the safest he ever feels, the silence between them full of love and light, the only sound the soft ripple of the water as they glide through the shallows. Jack tries to wiggle his little finger.

It still feels heavy and stuck, but part of it has grown weightless.

Keep trying.

Pinky to hand, hand to arm, arm to neck, neck to head, shoulder, arm, hand, fingers.

Jack sits up. But when he looks down, he's still there, sleeping. Only part of him—the soul part—is moving. But it doesn't matter to Jack, because something is always better than nothing. And he doesn't feel like a shadow. He looks at his hands; they still look like his hands.

"Well, if that's the way this works, what the hell," he says, standing up to look around, pulling his legs free. He knows it should be scary, seeing himself lying there, unmoving. But it's not.

"You're not dead, Jack," comes a voice from a corner under an eave.

"I didn't think so," Jack responds with a start. "And it's rude to talk to someone you don't know. Come here where I can see you."

A girl a little younger than Jack walks out into the middle of the room. She's wearing an old-fashioned white dress, and her hair looks as if it might have been neat once upon a time, but now it has a red bow falling down the side. She tries to push it in place but it slips back down.

"Here, let me fix that. You don't have to be afraid. I'm Jack."

"I'm not scared, and I don't need your help. I'm Belinda B'Lovely Sorrow. And I've been here longer than you. Besides, I'm more like a boy than a girl anyway."

Jack almost runs to squeeze her, while yelling, "Dida!" But he stops himself. Maybe she doesn't know she's lost. Or grown into an old lady. He doesn't want a weepin' little girl on his hands. It seems strange that Dida could be two places at once, but here he is, about to straighten a bow in her little-girl hair, while his body is still on the bed behind him.

"Just come here and let me fix it. I like messy things, but that looks a half-cocked kinda crazy."

"I've tried, but when we're like this, we can't see our reflections."

"Maybe we're vampires."

"I don't think so."

She walks to him and he reaches out, half expecting his hand to go right through her, but it doesn't. He unties the bow from its tiny knots and smooths down her hair gently.

"There, now, where do you want it? I'll put it back."

"Here," she says, pointing to the side. She pulls some of her black hair across and shows him where to tie it so it stays out of her face. After, she pats it. "You did a fine job . . . for a *boy*! *Merci!*"

"Are you stuck here, Di . . . I mean Belinda?"

"I guess."

"Forever?"

"That's the part I don't know."

"You get lonely?"

Belinda is quiet. "What's your full name, boy?"

"I'm a Sorrow, too. Jack Amore Sorrow."

"Well, that's a relief. I don't know you, though. And you're dressed funny. I've been away a long time, haven't I?"

"My mama says you can't measure time. Says time is all around us, and we just aren't evolved enough yet to move between."

"Evolved. That's funny. My daddy has this big old book, *The Book of Sorrows*. And it says you shouldn't try to move through time 'cause you could go crazy."

"I've read that book, too."

"So if you have my name and you've read our book, then you know things I don't, things that happened already, right?"

Jack pauses, not knowing what to say.

"Never mind, Jack . . . Time travel, or whatever this is, is complicated. Anyway, I have an idea." says Belinda.

"Oh yeah?"

"Want to leave here?"

"You know how to get back? Why didn't you just—"

"No. At least I don't think so. But I've been by myself for so long, and maybe if I show you what I've learned here, you and I can put two and two together."

"Well, I don't feel like sittin' here watching myself sleep. How do we get out of here? Wherever here is."

"You got to think of where you want to go is all." She holds out her hand. As soon as he takes it, they are outside, on Trinity Bridge, and everything is quiet and still. Not a person in sight. The water doesn't move under them, the clouds don't move over them. The sky is a perfect shade of blue.

"Everything's stuck." He looks around in awe.

"Most things. But some things still move. Come on."

"Where we going, Belinda?"

"Call me Bee."

"Fine. Where we goin', Bee?"

"First we got to figure out where we are in time. See, I notice that time jumps all around like leapfrog here, only I don't ever know where I'm going next. There's one place, though . . . it's not always so nice there," she adds quietly, before continuing, "That helps me get to other places. It's like the X on a treasure map or something. Sometimes I hear people calling me when I'm there. Maybe someone is calling you, too, Jack."

Jack clasps her hand once again, hoping she's right, and together they smudge the blue sky.

16

A Not-So-Festive Solstice

Frances

I should have known the minute I decided to participate in the solstice that it would spell disaster. The storm had fallen from the realm of instinct straight into the reality of the national news and was now looming, dark and angry, off our shores.

Mama and Dida had come down to my house that day, making their way slow up the twisting docks, holding lanterns and dressed up for the play, looking like crazy pirate explorers. Their long hair whipped in the wind behind them; their skirts were half-damp with the water splashing up through the planks. They were a colorful mess of fabrics, bangles, canes, hats, and bags. Mama had her hand on Dida's shoulder, tentatively following behind her.

I'm gonna ask Old Jim to put back those ropes connecting us.

"How's my new great-grandbaby doin'?" Dida asked as we met them on the grass in front of my porch.

"She's just fine," I said.

"Can't the girl speak for herself?" asked Claudette.

Maybe those ropes could stay cut a little while longer.

"Don't start, you two," said Dida. "Anyone seen Millie? Craven and JuneBug are up at the hall putting the last few touches on the set. Craven keeps on yellin' about people bein' on their way. How many people came last year, Claudette, two? And with this storm, we'll be lucky if anyone comes at all. Just in case, though, I got some girls in from Tivoli Proper gettin' the food ready. Now, Frances, I just want you to know, it's been real nice having you back with us. Just like the old days. Really, though, where is that Millie Bliss?"

And as if Dida'd conjured her up, Millie came from around the back of my shack, swatting at the gnats that were growing thicker as dusk fell.

"I feel as if someone is calling my name," she said spookily, like a witch called from the grave in one of those old movies we used to sneak into town to see.

"Girl, where you been?! There's still a lot of work to do. And people . . . well, if they come, they'll start rowing up to our dock in less than an hour!" said Claudette.

Millie walked up my porch steps and threw herself down on a chair, laughing. "One, ain't no one comin'. Two, you don't need me. Frances the Great has come back from her exile to take over her rightful place in the Sorrow world. Now, let's see . . . she made all the tinctures and teas, prepared all the herbs and flowers, and she got the lead role in our play. So, what is it you needed? Did you need me to babysit this new kid? Because, I thought for sure I was done babysitting."

I wasn't sure if Millie was drunk, tired, or just plain mad. And, we Sorrows—and I always considered her one of us—really do love our sarcasm. But this was over-the-top, even for Millie.

"Now, you just wait a minute—" I started.

Sippie tucked her hand quickly inside of mine. "It's okay, Frances. Everyone's just all worked up."

"You know what, Sippie?" Millie said, standing up. "You right. The whole world is humming. You feel it?"

"Sure is. Especially you. You in rare form, Miss Millie," said Dida.

"I hear a boat," said Claudette. "Come on, ladies, let's head back and get ourselves all ready. It's time."

"Oh look, it's Danny," said Millie, who sat on the bottom step of my porch, lit a cigarette, and looked like a cobra, those green eyes shining like slits.

I looked up the bayou to Danny and back at Millie. "What is the matter with you?" I asked. "You look about ready to kill someone."

"Oh, Frankie. Hush. Just go on, run to your man," she said, suddenly very sad and waving me away in a plume of cigarette smoke.

"That's him?" asked Sippie.

"Yep."

"This gonna be weird?"

"Yep."

She gave my hand a squeeze and then let go.

Danny was tying off his boat. I waited for him to start walking up the dock and then couldn't help running to him with my heart beating wildly in my chest. He picked me up in his strong arms like I was nothing but half a feather. Wrapping my legs around him, I buried my head in his neck. He smelled of salt and sweat, hard work and fish, but I didn't care. He smelled like home. Before I knew it, our faces were pressed against each other, and out of some kind of sheer, hot will, we were kissing, his full lips finding mine over and over again. I didn't ever want to stop, each kiss seemed to take an edge off all the old pain. It was better than a sedative, better than a stimulant. It was Danny.

It was always Danny.

"Danny, I got so much to tell you, I've been listening to everything you said to me over the years, and it's like I can finally hear you, you know? And look, just look at me, I'm gonna help these hens out with our solstice, and then, well, I got somethin' to tell you. And it's, well, it's a big sort of thing."

I felt like I was a rambling twelve year old.

And Danny, who usually liked it when I went all childish and excited—*"You're so pretty when you smile, Gypsy," he'd say*—he was just standing there, dead quiet.

"Has everyone lost their minds?" I asked.

"Frances?" Sippie called from my porch. Millie, Dida, and Claudette were just standing there, the moon rising behind them, watching us. "You okay?"

"I'm fine," I said.

Danny was just staring at her.

"You got something wrong with you?" I asked.

Danny pulled me into another, tighter hug.

"I already know about Sippie. JuneBug radioed. And there's so much in my heart and on my mind. So many questions. But I have to tell you something. And you aren't going to like it. So when I say it, you can't think I'm not interested or don't care about that beauty waiting for us up there," he said, nodding his head toward Sippie.

I reached up and touched Danny's face. He had the start of a beard from his time on the boat. "You can tell me anything, Danny. I won't hold anything against you. I'm done with that."

He took in a deep breath. "It's Jack. He's been gone all week. Pete says he's missing. And even though I think he's nuts for doing it, he's called the police. Probably gonna mess up your whole night, but Frankie, have you seen him?"

That's when I laughed. I'll never forget that, how I laughed. It shames me to think on it.

"Oh, Dan. Always worried," Millie spoke up from behind me.

I jumped. "You can be like a cat when you wanna be, Millie," I said. Her tone, too quiet and loud at the same time, was nerve-racking.

"He's safe," I told Danny, but I was looking at Millie. Giving her our secret little eye thing we do when we want the other one to shut up. "He's over at the juju cabin thinkin' we don't know he's there. I been secretly checking on him every day."

"*Every* day?" asked Millie.

That made me right mad. Millie was playing me, and I didn't know why. She's my safe person. My friend. So I didn't understand this dance she was doing.

"Not today, not yet," I said.

"Why do you think he ran off?" asked Danny, who was visibly relieved but also seemed to be giving Millie that same overly familiar *Shut up* look. I frowned.

"I got a feeling he wants to make us worry. He's mad about somethin'," I said, a knowledge blooming inside me that I really didn't want to know.

"Everyone okay down there?" asked Dida.

"We good, Dida," Danny yelled.

"My Jim comin?"

"Sho' is. I rushed off and left him to off-load. He'll be by soon."

"We gonna go up to the house, Frankie. You come on up when you done with whatever you doin'. Millie, why not leave those two alone. A lot has happened this past week," said Dida.

"Hush your goddamned face, woman!" Millie yelled . . .

loud. Too loud. "Christ, these witches." She leaned on a piling and lit another cigarette.

Claudette and Dida started walking the docks toward the house with Sippie between them. She looked back at me. I nodded for her to go.

"Look, you two," said Millie. "Jack told me he'd be coming back tonight, make his big entrance right in the middle of our play. Like Huck Finn or Tom Sawyer or somethin' like that. Whichever one walked in on his own funeral."

"How did you know that?" I asked.

"How do you think? *He told me.* Seems like you're turning into that kind of mama you never wanted to be, all cold and closed up."

Danny cleared his throat. "Thanks, Millie, I think we both feel a lot better now. I'll just go on back to the Voodoo right quick and try to cut off those police before they cross Trinity Bridge. Then I'll come back here, and Frances"—he turned to me—"I love you, honey, and can't wait for you to catch me up on everything and meet that girl of ours . . . properly."

"Isn't this just adorable," Millie said, voice like too-sweet frosting. "And really, I can't wait for that family reunion, but there's . . . One. Small. Problem."

"Which is?" I asked.

"Jack's not there. I just went to check on him since his mama forgot today. And he's not there."

"You sure?" asked Danny.

"Yep, all his stuff is gone, too. Everything except his scrapbook." She reached into her big velvet bag and pulled out Jack's prized possession.

"But the storm, it's coming. Maybe he went back to Tivoli?" I asked.

"Pete would have known that," said Danny. "When did you see him last, Frances?"

"Yesterday. I left him some oranges. He looked like he was gettin' scurvy," I said. "He left his scrapbook?" My mind raced. "Danny, he wouldn't have left that. Now . . . now I'm worried."

"Let's go double-check," said Danny.

We searched the cypress grove, checking the lean-to again and again. Blue lights flickered everywhere as night fell around us. *Feux follets.* The souls of the lost.

"I can't do this. Danny, I can't find one child and lose another—" My voice broke. We were back at the dock, getting ready to take Danny's boat up and down the river and into Meager Swamp.

Millie started to laugh. This time it was a mean sort of cackle.

"Shut up, Millie, I swear to God," Danny said harshly.

"What is going on?" I asked, arms crossed. "Is there something I'm missing here? Other than my son?"

Danny hung his head.

"I was just thinking about why that boy ran away to begin with. I was trying to save *you* a little guilt, Frankie. Because it ain't your fault he's gone. It's Danny's."

"You best tell me right now what the hell you're on about, Millie."

Millie and Danny looked at each other, and that thing I didn't want to know, I suddenly knew in my bones.

"The two of you? Really? Will wonders never cease? Millie, hand me one of them cigarettes." I lit one and inhaled. The night was coming on full. Old Jim skimmed by in his boat, waving at us, heading straight for the docks at Sorrow Hall for his lady. We all waved like nothin' was goin' on. "How long?" I asked edgily.

"Two years, give or take," said Millie.

Two years.

"Well, I mean, Danny has to have some sort of life. And why not choose to be with someone who looks like me?" I added harshly.

"Wait, you're mad at me? What about him?" asked Millie.

A fierce kind of mean boiled up from deep inside me just then.

"Danny and I have a love *you* will never understand, Millie. And it belongs to *us*. Hell, we don't even understand it. But you? You come over here and you lie to me. You know where Jack is, you know why he left. So I'm thinkin' maybe I should be angry with you. Real angry. Because you know how much I ache for Danny. How many times I cried to you about it. Then you gonna lay that body of yours down on his? What the hell kinda friendship is that?" I said, steel in my voice as my eyes went dull and quiet. "And you knew about Sippie, too. For all those years *you knew*. She remembers you, you know, from that night when Simone died. I've been trying to convince myself that you were protecting me, but now I'm thinkin' you just wanted to let her suffer."

I didn't really think the stuff about Sippie was true, but I couldn't help saying it anyway. And then I saw her eyes grow wide with surprise, and I knew all the worst things I could conjure about her right then and there just might be true.

"Say that's not true, Millie," said Danny.

"You two don't deserve any of what you got," she said. "You got one boy who's so mad at you both that he runs off into a storm. And you got a little lost girl that you gave away who washes up on your dock. That's what you do, isn't it, Frances. You just give everything away. And what do I get? Nothing. I came here, lived with you, was as close as a sister to you. And you run off because of this ass"—she gave Danny a little shove with her hand—"and then next thing I know, I'm asked to go and run the Voodoo. And then, when you get back, I got to take on everything you discarded with none of the love attached. You ever think of that, you selfish witch?" Millie's eyes took on a glint. "And you know what? You're right, I did know about that damp little girl. All dirty and raised up by those lowborn people you Sorrows love to pal around with. And I wasn't gonna bring her back here and give myself one more child to raise. I'm done raising your children with nothing in return. It's *my* turn now."

A fire rose up inside me so fast, I was on her before she could even finish, slapping, punching, kicking, until we fell right off the dock into the water. I tried to drown her. I really did. Danny jumped in, pulling us apart and helping us back out of the water. Millie just stood there dripping, coughing, and bleeding while eyeing me. The sight of her knocked some sense back into me.

"Oh, my God, Millie! I'm so sorry! You okay? I don't even know where that came from! I just want to understand why," I pleaded.

She glared at me, wiping some blood from the corner of her mouth. Then, with a sly half grin, she mouthed, "Thank you."

I'd never been so confused.

"Frankie, you're okay; she's okay. It's all gonna be okay," said Danny.

"But I love her. I need to know," I said.

"When we love, we get hurt. Your people taught me that," said Millie.

"I don't even have time right now to argue about how ass backwards that is," I said.

Police sirens suddenly rang out in the distance.

"Thank God!" Millie practically swooned. "The cavalry!"

Her predilection for fake dramatics made me wish I *had* drowned her.

"Did you find him?" Danny asked as the police boat slammed into the deck. But he didn't get an answer.

"Did you find our boy?" I asked in case they hadn't heard Danny.

"Frances Green Sorrow?" asked a police officer.

"Yes?"

"You are under arrest and charged with possible kidnapping and let's add what looks like assault. You pressing charges, Millie?"

"You bet I am," she said. And I thought Danny would hit her next.

"What the hell is goin' on over here?" yelled Old Jim, who had run down from Sorrow Hall with Sippie. The police were putting cuffs on me, and Millie was just standing there, smiling.

"Get her outta here, Jim!" yelled Danny, walking up the dock.

"What did you do, Danny? Did you call the police on her? You fuckin' creep!" Sippie screamed. She had lost control, and I saw, for the first time, the pain she'd lived through. "This is who you married, Frances? This coward? He ain't brave or strong or mighty. That handsome face you got sure do hide all that nasty underneath, don't it, fool?"

She was about to gouge out his eyes when Danny grabbed her, wrapping his arms around her tight. "Shhh, Sippie, it's gonna be okay. It wasn't me, I swear it, but I'm gonna fix it. Don't you worry."

"You got your daughter under control, sir? Or do we have to drag her in as well?"

"I got her," said Danny. "It's been a long day."

"Find our boy, Danny," I said as they put me into the boat. And then we were gone, away from Sorrow Hall, away from everything. And with the sirens off, that little police boat was almost peaceful.

The water glowed under the waxing moon. I stared out over it, numb and half-crazy, like I was on some kind of drug.

"You know what?" I said to the younger of the officers. "The whole bayou reminds me of a woman, her head thrown back in laughter. That dark water snakes against the land in uneven, almost surreal ways. Kinda like the people of the bayou. No distinguishable boundaries, uniform flood paths or predictable tides. It just slinks itself forward and back, depending on the day or mood. You ever notice?"

"You right, Nick, this one is crazy."

I didn't care, I just kept on talking. "I always loved the subtle ease of stubborn, languid waters. Until tonight when I wanted to set it all on fire."

"That kind of talk ain't gonna help you none, ma'am."

"Or maybe it's more like Medusa," I mumbled, closing my eyes so I could see Serafina, the first witch. She was everywhere, like a map of the bayou. Her long curly hair was drawn with the bayou waters, tendrils curling around in spirals, leading to smaller wisps of streams and broad, thick, swampy pools. Her face reflected in Saint Sabine Isle. The sand, toasted golden by the sun, was open, ready for the adventures lurking out in the Gulf. Jade stones for her eyes and the teahouse a glowing refuge for her thoughts and dreams. And then it hit me. *She has him.* Millie took my boy.

"Give him back to me, you good for nothing half-assed witch," I yelled.

"That'll be enough of that, Ms. Sorrow," said one of the officers. I made a mental note to find out who he was so I could make sure his first child was born with six fingers.

17

Shall We Gather
at the Voodoo

Sippie

While police searched the bayou, further spreading the news that
Frances was in jail, everyone gathered at the Voodoo. Sippie
couldn't believe the joint could hold all the people pouring in.
Friends and family and strangers, too. Pete was helping Junie in
the kitchen, food was coming out on big trays. It was like a party,
only it wasn't a party at all.

"This ain't quite the soiree we would have planned for you, Sippie girl," said Old Jim, "but at least you get the chance to witness
that it don't matter how bad a thing gets here in the bayou, we
always find the love."

"And the liquor," Millie said on her way to the second-floor
porch.

"Shut your damn face," yelled Claudette. Sippie thought she
might be starting to like that blond wisp of a grandma.

The sound of Danny yelling at some police officers outside

carried right on through the windows, conveniently open so everyone inside could hear to the best of their ability.

"Boys, you got to let Frances go. I'll get Millie to drop those charges, you know I will. And Jack, well, Millie said he ran away. Ain't nobody done any wrong here. Please let her go."

"Too late, Danny. We found his bike thrown into the woods by Trinity Bridge. And blood, too, on a ripped T-shirt Pete identified as Jack's. Now, it don't take much to put two and two together."

"What about them Tivoli trash boys? You think of them? God. This goes from bad to worse."

"Look, Danny . . . Someone took him. We're sure of it. Don't you worry. We'll find him." They threw the police cruiser into drive and headed off.

"I'm tellin' you she didn't do nothin'!" he yelled, running after the car as though he could catch it, change fate, turn back time. And then he stood there sadly, in the middle of that dirt road, in the dark.

"Come with me, Sippie." Old Jim tried pulling her away from the window. "Let me comfort you some. I've missed that kind of thing. You afraid of thunder?"

But Sippie just watched until Danny came back inside. Then she watched as he sat at a table, alone, his head in his hands. Finally, Sippie went to him, Old Jim following. And she sat there between the two of them, the image of those police officers putting handcuffs on Frances on loop in her head. It was too much for her. She started to cry, leaning into Danny's arms. "It's all my fault, it's all my fault," she whispered over and over.

"No, honey, it's mine," said Danny.

"I'm sorry I tried to hurt you," she said.

"You don't have to be. I'm proud of you."

"How come?"

"You were protecting your mama. And I've been piss-poor at that. Sippie, talk to me some."

"Look here," said Old Jim. "I'm gonna go check on Dida over there, and then I'm comin' right back. I can't wait to get to know you, Sippie, after this mess is cleared up. But what I seen? Well, even if I didn't know you were my blood, I'd sit here wishin' you were." He kissed her head and walked off toward Dida, who was sitting at the bar, holding Claudette in her arms.

Sippie couldn't understand how fast she was taking to everyone. It was like she'd known them forever. Blood ties, Sorrow Soil. No matter. She'd found home and somehow ripped it apart. She sat there willing everything to go back the way it was, even if it meant she wasn't a part of it.

"That man, he's got more class than anyone I ever met. I wish I could be that graceful." Danny turned back to her. "So, here we are, Sippie. You and me. And I'm just gonna talk and hope some sense comes out of me."

Sippie thought that was a fine idea.

"You know something, Sippie? At some point a man wakes up and suddenly his youth is gone. People is always going on about women and how they age: the unfairness of men getting distinguished and women getting ugly, blah blah blah. But no one talks about the terror a man faces when his eyes dull and his body won't cooperate. I know I'm only thirty-five, but Sippie, I can feel the grassy smell of my youth fading and my memories playin' tricks. Sad, scary, *lonesome,* is what it is.

"And so much of what happened with Millie came from that fear. Frances didn't seem to want me. And I don't blame her. We kept making the same mistakes over and over. But now, look at this mess."

Sippie rested her head on his shoulder, not knowing what to say.

"See, the second JuneBug told me about you this morning, everything I ever thought I knew about Frances just . . . changed. Because knowing about you makes everything else make sense. Which means I'm the worst husband there ever was."

"How do you mean, Danny?"

"Okay, this one night, right before she left us for good, Jack screamed all the way through. But we didn't even know because his bedroom door was closed and locked from the outside. Frances was so torn up, she threw up all day. She kept saying she didn't deserve him. She was filled with grief. She said, 'I left him. Alone. He must have been so scared.' But it wasn't her, Sippie. It was *me*. I closed the door. Locked it, too, because I wanted some privacy with her and he was always climbing in our bed. I forgot we couldn't hear him with the door closed. But she blamed herself, and she left. I thought she was being weak. But she was facing her biggest fear with no support at all. So, see how that changes things?"

"It doesn't change anything," said Millie, who came in from the back and was drying her hair with a towel behind the bar. Danny stood up quick. "Don't get any ideas, I'll throw your sorry ass in jail, too," she said, smirking.

"You still here? Thought the devil might have ate you up whole, Millie," said Dida. The whole room went quiet.

"What do you mean, Dida? I live here. I run this place. And the devil don't eat his own." She pretended to bite at Dida and laughed. She stopped laughing when Dida stood up and banged her beer against the bar, getting everyone quiet.

"Listen here, all you wandering fools. Millie don't run this place no more." Then she turned to Millie. "You are no longer a member of this family. I don't know what you did, or how you did it, but I know this whole thing, even Jack, is all about you."

"Did you take him?" asked Danny.

"You can't be serious!" Millie scoffed.

"Dead serious," he growled.

"Would you step outside with me for a moment, Dan?" she asked coyly, a fake smile plastered on her face. Sippie knew Danny didn't want to go, but he did anyway.

"I tell you this is just like what happened to me. A hurricane, a missing child. So, if I'm fine," said Dida, "then Jack will be fine."

Sippie listened to the voices around her, to the TV flicker in and out with news about the devastating storm pressing down on them. But what she heard above it all was something Simone had said years ago. *If you don't never love, Sippie, you don't never cry.*

She felt a hand on her back. Claudette.

"I know what you be thinkin', Sippie. But you can't listen to that voice in your head. Trust me, I know. It's true, if we don't love, we don't cry. But the trouble is, we can't seem to avoid love, and if we hide it away, make it a secret, all we do is cry harder. And without any of the joy. I know Frances thinks I'm a terrible mother. Truth is, I am. But we had laughter. And she'll remember that. Maybe you'll help her. Now, come on and give your Claudie a hug. I can be a mean bitch, but that runs in the family."

Sippie broke into a smile, hugging her grandmother tightly as Millie's arm gestures grew more animated through the window.

"Excuse me for a moment, Claudie," she said, and headed out onto the back porch of the Voodoo.

"But don't you see? I lost both of you! You took that girl and made a mess of her," Millie was yelling. "But that look, the one you give her . . . *I* want that look. I want that feeling, too. Why can't I be that for you? Danny, we could be good together."

"Millie, I'm gonna ask you one more time. Did you take Jack?"

"Danny, please . . ." Millie was trying to hold on to him, but he grabbed her wrists. Sippie knew he was on the verge of something everyone would regret.

"Danny?" she interrupted hesitantly.

He dropped Millie's arms instantly.

"You okay, Sip?"

"Could you come inside?"

"You bet, baby. I'm done out here. Done. And you're gonna drop those charges, Millie Bliss. Right now. Get on that crappy phone and call them police right now."

Millie pulled at Sippie roughly.

"She took everything from him, just like she took everything from you, her own daughter . . . it seems to be the only way she knows how to love. It's the only way any of us Sorrows know how to love. You ready for that?" Then she let go of Sippie and slammed back inside.

"Thank you," he said, leading her back inside.

Millie was on the phone, and Sippie saw a big old scrapbook on the bar.

"What's this?" she asked Danny.

"This is Jack's, your brother's, scrapbook of all things Sorrow."

"Can I look at it?"

"Of course, sugar. Let's look at it together."

The two of them paged through the book, Sippie marveling at the detailed notes and neat tape lines. There was so much information, so many interesting facts.

"Danny, look at this," she said, pointing to the newspaper clipping about SuzyNell returning to Serafina's Bayou in 1910. It was a picture of her whole family, with names.

"What am I looking for, honey?"

"There!" She pointed at the little girl seated on SuzyNell's lap. Her daughter, Elsie Mae. "When I was in the family cemetery with Dida, she got all kinds of quiet and said she wasn't sure who Elsie Mae was. And just when you were outside, Dida was telling us Jack would be safe because she went missing during a hurricane and she was safe. Only she didn't, did she?"

"No, baby. We all like to believe the fairy tale of it, but always knew somethin' wasn't quite right. But none of us ever really put it all together before. You are some kind of wonderful, Sippie. . . .

"Dida?" he asked, loud enough to quiet everyone down. Then, tentatively: "You said that this was just like what happened back when you were put to sleep, right? The hurricane . . . 1901?"

"That's right. It's like a mirror image, Danny boy," said Dida.

"Well, then, why wouldn't it be that someone might think they could put a sleeping spell on another Sorrow child in a similar situation?"

"That is my point, cha. I'm telling you, Miss Millie over here is playin' us all for fools. She knows where our boy is at. She put the same spell on him," said Dida.

"Well, that would just be stupid," Danny said. "And Millie's a lot of things, but you're not stupid, are you, Millie?"

"Why would it be stupid?" Millie frowned.

"Because Dida's not really Belinda Sorrow. We all just like to play that she is. Gives us hope in the miracle of things. Everyone needs something to hold on to."

Sippie just stared at him, shaking her head. Men never did know when to take the soft approach.

"Dida?" asked Sippie.

"Yes, cha?"

"Because of the sleep, you would have still been a little girl when you came back to Sorrow Hall. Who raised you?"

Sippie spoke low and calm. Everyone had to lean in close to hear.

Dida sighed, a dazed smile spreading across her face.

"Well, my mother, she was a wonderful woman with rich, deep black hair. I mean blond. Yes, blond. I wore this red bow, and she didn't like it. My mother . . . died young. But I remember her love. My father, he remarried, but then he died, too. He was a king, I think. And my stepmother raised me. Her name was . . . her name . . . Jim? Where's Jim. I need my Jim."

"I'm right here, sweet lady."

"Dida, you know you ain't Belinda Sorrow," said Danny.

Dida let out a low moan and her eyes went in back of her head. Old Jim glared at him.

"What? She's a Sorrow, just not Belinda Sorrow."

"How do you know, Dan? I mean, we always wondered, but we didn't know for sure," said Old Jim.

"We got it right here," said Danny, holding up the newspaper clipping. "She's SuzyNell's granddaughter."

That's when Dida started rambling. "I remember planting things and washing windows with vinegar. I remember being hungry at first, then cold . . . the damp, you know. But I found linens in the Sorrow Hall closets and washed them up in the creek and hung them to dry. It was quiet, back then. My name is Belinda B'lovely Sorrow. I had a family. A family who loved me. And I had a little brother who I worried over, and a mother who I could look at for hours. And my father. Oh, he was the finest-looking man I'd ever seen." Her eyes glazed over in some kind of delirium.

"So what really happened?" asked Pete.

"There wasn't a sleeping spell?" asked Millie too tentatively above the growing mumuring in the bar.

"No, you stupid witch. That's what I'm trying to tell you," said Danny. "Jim, you want to take Dida outside?"

"Yes, son, I think that's best."

When Old Jim had Dida out on the porch, Danny continued.

"Frances and I used to talk about this a lot, only we never had real proof and no real reason to upset Dida. We always thought it had something to do with that fever that hit fifty years ago, wiping out a lot of our families down here. But we didn't know that Dida's mother was Elsie Mae."

"So, Dida didn't die, she just got all jumbled up with fever?" asked Pete.

"Oh God!" said Claudette. "Now it makes sense. She must have been all alone out there at the house. Wandering and waiting . . . with just those Sorrow ghosts for company."

"So how come no one said anything?" JuneBug asked.

"She probably needed to believe it. It helped her," said Sippie. "It meant she was the one that got lost, the one everyone was looking for, instead of the other way around. No one wants to know there's not a soul in the world to love them."

The room got quiet and Danny just put his arms around her and kissed her head.

"You know something? Lies are so powerful," said Claudette. "I never actually thought she was Belinda B'lovely. Because it was too fantastic, you know? But you live with something like that for so long, you come to believe it. No matter how unexplainable. Poor Mama. No wonder she's always so listless near Elsie Mae's grave."

"Anyone see Millie?" JuneBug asked suddenly, looking out the window.

"No, why?"

"Because she ain't here, and my truck is missin'."

Danny about had a tantrum. "That damn woman. I got to go after her. She took my son!!"

"But why would she do that? Steal Jack?" asked JuneBug.

"Millie loves and hates Frances. Wants what she can't have. Wants what Frances threw away," said Danny. "Practically screamed it at her down on those docks."

Claudette sighed sadly.

"You okay, Claudette?" asked Sippie.

"She was alone. Mama was alone," Claudette whispered.

Everyone grew quiet, but they knew it was true. Dida made up a fairy tale about her life. A lie to tell herself when she was lonesome and frightened. And she told it so many times that it became her hiding place.

"And Millie, she *believed* that story. It was her favorite one," said Claudette. "No one ever thought to tell her we didn't know if it was true. It's our fault. All of us. We are all to blame."

"We'll find him," Danny said. "She wouldn't hurt him, she couldn't."

"We might have a problem," said Claudette.

"Which is?"

"I know that girl too well. If she ran off while we were talking about Dida, it only makes sense that she tried a sleeping spell. Which means she's hidden him somewhere, thinking he could be safe for a hundred years. It's why she disappeared when she found out; she's trying to cover her tracks. I swear, for people who can all see, you're completely blind."

"She's right," said Sippie.

"I know," said Danny.

Everything felt surreal after that. Dida was reassured that she was, in fact, Belinda Sorrow because she just didn't need to believe anything different. The police from Tivoli had given way to the police from New Orleans, and as no one could tell for sure where Jack had been for a day or so, the feds got called in, too. The night bayou was lit up like a fluorescent nightmare. Everyone was looking for Jack. Probably the whole goddamned country.

Sippie watched Danny get restless. Then he stood up and made for the door.

"Where you goin', boy?" asked Old Jim.

"To get my girl."

"'Bout damn time." Old Jim nodded.

18

Betrayed by Bliss

Frances

I sat in that cold police station waiting for those fools to figure out what to do with me. Half of them were scared to look at me, the other half wanted to burn me at the stake, colonial style. Hate mixed with fear and scented with ignorance is a potion for disaster. So I just sat there, thinking on how I came to be where I was sitting.

I'd tried to be a good wife. But I'd also tried to be someone I wasn't, and when you do that, every little thing explodes. Before things got really bad between us, I'd wake up in our sweet yet suffocating bedroom, with my skin aching. It felt bruised from the inside out. . . .

Everything wild inside me was yearning to break free of the tame confines I'd agreed to in order to keep Danny's love and raise Jack the way everyone felt he ought to be raised.

By the time Danny and I had our second go-around, I had almost awakened again. The summer he came back too handsome for words, I was nineteen and living a life of nothing but freedom at the Voodoo. And when he walked into that bar and our eyes met, it was all over. For both of us. From May until August we ran the beaches again. Rode through all of southern Louisiana, got to know each other. More than once I tried to tell him about that baby. But I didn't know how. Hell, I didn't even know if it was his.

When he left to go back to his senior year, I was fine. I felt like we'd stay together. And I cherished his letters, running to the mail boat all lighthearted. I'd almost decided to tell him about the baby I'd given away and daydreamed about me and Danny scooping her up and bringing her home together.

But then I found out I was pregnant. Again. And all that fear came rising up inside. Old Jim convinced me to go on over to the Voodoo and call him at school. And it was killing me, because I was the only one who knew that this wasn't my first time. One mistake, it's a lesson. Two mistakes, and you got no one to blame but yourself.

"I don't want him to know, Jim. He's got that nice football thing goin' on and he wants to be a lawyer! This'll ruin him!"

"What's done is done, Little Bit. This baby changes everything. If Danny chooses to make it a wall in his life, that's on him. Not you. Either way, you got to let him know. I know Millie always says an honest person knows when to tell a lie, but honey, trust this old pirate grampa of yours: A liar lies when he's too scared to tell the truth. Now, you really believe with all your heart it's best not to tell him, then by all means, don't call. But if you ain't callin' him 'cause you be afraid to call him? Well now, that there's a liar's lie."

I have to give Old Jim credit, because when I made that call, Danny came running. He dropped out of school and asked me to marry him. He got down on one knee right there on the second-floor porch of the Voodoo. I remember thinking, *It's a good thing me and Millie washed this floor down with vinegar this morning, because it wouldn't be right to start off a new life on a dirty note.* As it turned out, we didn't need to worry much about that. Things got messy all on their own.

"I don't know, Danny. I was thinkin' you could go back to school and then we could try raising him together when you graduate. Take things from there, you know? It's probably best to just live together or something. Later, I mean. When you get your life just like you want it. And besides, we don't really get married in this family. You know that."

"It's a boy?" I could practically see the visions of playing catch filling his head.

"Yes. Sorry if you didn't want to know."

I'd had to know. I'd made Dida do all her root work to find out, because if it was a girl, I was putting rocks in my pockets and walking into the sea.

"It's a boy! You hear that, Old Jim? I know you're all in there listening. Hot damn! It's a boy. How did you find out? Oh, right!" He had winked then, happy about my magic for once.

That's how I knew he wasn't going to listen to reason. Sometimes the present can color the future way too bright.

"Don't you see?" he'd said, trying to convince me. "This is what you've wanted your whole life. You get to be *normal*. All those nights we spent last summer at the cottage over at the Sorrow Estate, you did nothing but complain. About being alone, about having to live the way you did, about not having a phone or TV. You even complained about the magic. Now you can start over, Frankie!"

I'd stared at him with wide eyes. Gave him a look, *They are listening.* He'd just shrugged.

"I never complained about phones or TV, Danny."

"See? We're so in love I can't even tell where you leave off and I begin. Let's do this thing, honey. Let's have this baby and grab this life. Come build a home with me."

I'm not sure his logic made sense, but it was sure as hell romantic. And I'd already taken a glance at my future. Bartender at the Voodoo. Hermit. Maybe alligator hunter. I hadn't made up my mind. The idea of a lifetime of nights next to Danny and a bathtub that ran hot water, now *that* was appealing. And I thought it would give me some kind of second chance, I really did. That one baby would somehow substitute for the other.

So I did it. I got married. We went to a justice of the peace in Tivoli. Dida, Millie, and Claudette all wore black and stood in the back, weeping.

"It goes against everything we stand for! Marrying, giving yourself over to a man. What would Serafina say?" Dida cried.

The whole thing was clinical and cold. Pete came, with his girl of the moment. They stood up for us. She popped gum the whole time. Old Jim was out trawling.

Pete was going to let us live in the trailer out behind his gas station and let Danny work there until we got on our feet. Danny didn't want me going into New Orleans while I was pregnant, and he didn't like the idea of me telling fortunes or using any type of magic while Jack grew inside me. I thought he was ashamed, and that feeling grew into quiet resentment. But it did it slowly. *So* slowly. Like most things, it just festered until it exploded into a world of bad news. So when we left the courthouse and drove right past Pete's, I was confused.

"What's goin' on, Danny? We got us a honeymoon you didn't tell me about?"

"Nope, not quite yet, though Pete's givin' me a nice wage as we're family and all. So if we save up I can take you somewhere real exotic in a few years. No, it's not a honeymoon, Gypsy. But it *is* a surprise."

We turned off of Main Street and ended up in the neighborhood where he grew up. One of those ticky-tacky places with a crooked basketball hoop in front of a two-car garage that some half-assed do-it-yourself husband put on what probably started out as a nice house somewhere along the line.

He pointed out things he'd already pointed out a thousand times before on those endless drives we took the previous summer. When you're young and you got a car and just enough money for gas and a six-pack, you drive around a lot. I'd oohed and ahhed back then, because I was falling back in love with the football star. And he was in love with me. But that day, with a silver band on my finger and a baby growing inside me, all I was was carsick.

"You okay, honey? I bet you're tired. Let's get you home."

"Thank you, Danny. I hope I didn't ruin the surprise. Maybe we can come back tomorrow and you can show me where our boy will play Little League." He smiled at that. Just like I knew he would. I could give a shit about Little League.

"Well, that's just it, Gypsy. Here we are. Home *is* the surprise!"

He pulled into the driveway of his aunt Lavern's house. The house Danny grew up in. I knew it well enough to know it wasn't one of those "bigger on the inside" homes. It was what it was. All my words stuck in my throat just then. Making myself look and sound happy about his surprise should have won me an Academy Award.

We moved into his aunt Lavern's house the next day. And I'd put on shoes. It was a fine mess.

When she'd died a few months earlier, Danny had been pretty broken up. But Aunt Lavern had left the house to Danny, and the estate was settled the very day we got hitched. So he felt it was serendipity, while I felt, *knew*, it was bad luck. But I tried to convince myself he was right. That this kind of place *was* better for raising up a child. It had wall-to-wall carpet and plastic-covered furniture. I spent a full month spiffing it up. Ripping things out and adding a little bit of comfort and greenery wherever I could.

"We ain't in the bayou, Frankie," Danny would say.

"Hell, your aunt likes it. Says she never really wanted to keep her things all covered up like that."

"You see her. She's here?"

While I was trying out my normal life, I had let a little of the magic back in. Because it annoyed Danny—which was always fun for me—and because I was homesick. Kind of like falling off the wagon when you hit a whole bunch of stress.

"Of course I see her. She can't cross over. I'm trying to figure out why. She's as stubborn as always. Still has curlers in her hair. Says she won't meet Jesus until it's set."

"She watch us in the bedroom?"

"Not that I know of."

"I sure as hell hope not."

We started to argue right after Jack was born. About everything. And I started to wonder what the hell I was doing.

"What do you want from me?" I'd whisper at first. And then shout. And then, in the end, scream. *"What do you want from me?!"*

"I don't want you to forget to go to the stupid store," he said harshly. "I want you to cook a decent meal once in a while. I want you to stop reading those damn hoodoo cards and pay attention to your son. And while you're at it, I think everyone would appreciate it if you brushed your damn hair."

It doesn't really matter if you know that a person speaking in anger doesn't mean the hurtful things he says. It stings just as bad. I'd counseled enough of those love-lost ladies who came to me complaining about "her man" this and "her man" that to know "his mouth is acting the fool" and "can't leave a man because his stupid lips don't know better."

Only this wasn't happening to any of them hens. It was happening to me.

I was so hurt by those things he said that I knew for sure if I said, *"Go to hell!"* a crack might spring up right between us in that cheap linoleum floor and he'd get sucked under that prissy, ordinary house. And once the earth had filled up his sorry lungs, he'd be forced to spend a good amount of his eternity making amends to me. It was one of the few times during my "I am not a witch" life that I wanted all that power back.

But at the end of all the roads in my life, there was Danny. Danny, whom I loved even if he didn't love me. Danny, Jack's father. And because of that, I figured that he didn't need to go to hell after all.

At least yet.

So instead, I got real quiet and asked, "How is it you call yourself a man, Danny?" And I meant it. I thought men were supposed to love, adore, protect. Listen, partner, admit to their failings. I'd watched Old Jim and Dida. I'd heard the stories of Serafina and her two lovers. I'd read *The Book of Sorrows*. And Danny wasn't acting like any man I ever saw. He was acting like a spoiled child.

"Oh, good. You gonna take away that, too? Strip me of the one thing I got left? That's low, Frances," he said, glowering at me.

Honesty can hurt more than a hundred lashes.

"Not as low as I could have got, and you know it. You think it's manly to bully me? You know I can't fight back. You hurt me, you make me angry, and I have to worry I might do something to you that neither of us intended."

"Speak for yourself, Frances. Speak for your goddamn self. I'm sick of worrying that one day I'll do or say the wrong thing and you'll work those evil ways on me. I see you fight it. I saw you fight it a second ago. How do you think that feels?"

For one single, solitary moment I thought we'd be okay. Because he'd told me a deep truth, one I understood. So I knelt by him and put my head on his lap, the denim of his jeans rough on my face.

"Is that what this is all about, Danny? Why didn't you just tell me that you were scared? I can handle—"

Suddenly he flew into an even bigger rage, throwing me off of him. I slid across the floor. The man was about to have an honest-to-God tantrum right in front of me, in his aunt Lavern's house of all places.

"You've ruined my life, Frances Green *Sorrow,* so I don't really care what you do. Do your worst. I ain't got nothin' to lose! *You already took everything.*"

All I could think about was that I couldn't remember the last time I wore socks. It's funny the things the brain will do to protect the heart.

That tantrum he had is one I played over in my mind for years. Every word he said cutting me deeper and deeper. Being a Sorrow, I knew a thing or two about love. I knew how much it hurt people and how much damage it could do. Love is a dark thing.

"I can't turn you into anything. You know that. That's magic from a storybook. But I can sure as hell make you disappear."

"Trust me," he said, "if I could be anyplace else, I would be. I got an idea, why don't you zap me right out onto my boat. Put a fishing pole in one hand and a beer in the other. Come on, do it," he said sarcastically, closing his eyes and puffing out his chest.

How did we get this way?

"I can't do that either, Danny. My plan was to remove you from my line of sight by leaving you. This time for real. No bluffing. I'm sorry, I tried," I said sadly. And I walked out of that kitchen to the bedroom and started throwing my clothes into a bag. Then I got my crying toddler, gave him to Danny, and walked out of that ticky-tacky house.

"Where are you going?" he yelled.

"Oh, look! Poof! I made you disappear," I said with a flourish of my fingers.

What he didn't know, what I never told him, was that I couldn't stay because the ache for my lost baby was too much for me to bear.

We punished each other for dreams deferred. Both knowing, deep in our hearts, that the dream was what we could have had together if we just learned how to get over ourselves. Been more patient, given ourselves more time. Isn't that always the truth? I laughed a little, sitting there in that gray room thinking that all I had right then and there was time.

That's when I heard things in my own head clear for the first time. Right there in that police station. And I was still trying to escape just by being there because I couldn't think about how Jack was missing and how I couldn't seem to find him. How I'd been a terrible mother.

Too much honesty was making my face hurt.

The door to the little gray room opened up and a young, baby-faced officer walked in.

"I need to get out of here. Can one of you fine men in blue call my ex-husband, Danny? I need to talk to him."

"Ain't got to make no phone call, Ms. Frances. He's been here the whole time, waiting on you. We got no charges anyway. Millie never come in to fill out the papers. So we got a lot of nothin' holding you. Come with me, I'll take you to him."

I saw Danny through the glass, waiting on a long wooden bench. He was ripping off pieces of a Styrofoam coffee cup bit by bit, balling them up, and putting them in the cup. He always picked at things when he was nervous. His shoulders were tense with worry, and when he looked up as I came through the doors, his eyes were all bloodshot.

19

Finding the Bones

Danny

"Why are you here and not out there lookin' for our boy!" Frances yelled irately. The five people in the small precinct turned to stare, but Danny just fell more in love.

"Mind your own damn business, fools," he said to the officers and then turned to Frances. "I told them to go find her."

"Her?"

"Millie. She took him, and she's hiding him. I know, I know. But listen, Frances, we . . . I . . . look . . . the whole goddamn world is looking for them."

"I knew it," she said incredulously as they walked out into the humid night.

"Danny?" she said, stopping him before they got to his truck, parked haphazardly on the curb.

"What is it, Gypsy?"

"Once, when I was pregnant with Jack, I was in the grocery

store, with its canned music and fluorescent lighting. I was already uncomfortable. And I saw this lady holding her daughter's hand. She would have been about Sippie's age, and I just . . . I left. And you thought I forgot to go to the store."

"Gypsy," he said softly.

"No, wait. Every time I looked at Jack, I saw her. Each time he did something new, I cried. I thought the aching would go away. That he'd replace her. How could I think like that?"

"You got to stop, Frances. Come with me."

"Wait!" she cried out. "Back there, when I yelled at you? I didn't mean it. What I wanted to say was, 'Dan! I was just tellin' these fools I wanted to call you and there you were, right when I needed you.' Only that's not what came out of my mouth."

"You remember back when we were first starting to fight and Pete suggested we see some kind of crazy doctor, and you said we didn't need anyone messing with our minds? You said we needed a translator. You remember?" asked Danny.

"Of course I do."

"Well, you were right. Our whole problem has always been a lack of translation." He opened the passenger side of the truck, helping her in.

"You think he's okay, Danny?" Frances asked quietly. "Do you think she hates me enough to hurt him?"

"I think he's fine. He's a strong boy. He's *our* boy. We'll find him, Frances. I promise."

"I can't feel him, Dan. I can't feel him when I close my eyes. But I don't see him on the dead side either. And I don't know what it means. It's like, he's not dead, but he's not alive. I can't figure it out." She was crying, but they weren't the angry tears Danny was used to. It was a steady stream of remorse.

"You aren't alone, Frances. I said we'd find him and we will. *We*. Now, come on over here and let me put my arm around you while I drive you home."

She slunk over close to him, tucking herself in nice and tight.

"I'm sorry about Millie. It's all my fault, you know," he spoke up again once they were on the road.

"And I'm sorry about Sippie. I'm sorry I . . . there's too many sorrys, Danny."

"I know," he said.

"Danny, pull over."

They'd just passed Pete's and the lights of Tivoli Proper were fading in the rearview mirror.

"You gonna be sick?" he asked, pulling the truck to the side of the road.

"No. Come here, look at me." Frances pulled him in close. "Translate this," she said, and kissed him.

That's when the police cars started flying by them, all headed out of Tivoli, which was never the case. Bayou people had bayou justice and took care of their own.

And just as quick as she'd kissed him, Frances smacked Danny. "Whatcha waitin' for?! *Go!*"

Haste and speed and fear-laced panic brought them to Tivoli Bridge, where Danny slammed to a stop and JuneBug was already waiting with his boat to follow the police boats back to the Sorrow Estate. The entire back of Sorrow Bay was lit up. The glow from what seemed like hundreds of boat lights and lanterns illuminating the night bayou was as disturbing as it was beautiful. A helicopter hummed with a loud buzz above as divers gave a thumbs-up sign just before a stretcher twirled up into the sky.

"Is that a body? Danny, oh God, Dan. Is that a body?" Once docked, they pushed through people—where did they even come from?—to get closer to the shore. Sippie saw them and ran down the back steps of Sorrow Hall toward them. Frances turned, opening her arms. Danny watched the two of them fall into each other and felt weak for a moment, as though he might crack open.

The officer in charge brought them inside Sorrow Hall. Lanterns and candles lit the front parlor where Danny sat, arms around Frances and Sippie. He'd been talking on and on about policy and procedure. Danny knew it was the most action the sergeant had seen in a while, but as much as he wanted everyone to keep searching for Jack, he also wanted the damn officers to leave them in peace.

"So, to finish up the briefing, the bones do not in fact belong to Jack, or anyone who has died recently. I'm no expert, but I'd say they must be over a hundred years old." He went to switch on a lamp and noticed it had a wick, not a plug. Danny lit it for him.

"Did you lose power, or do you live like this?" asked the officer.

"Ain't you never heard of livin' off the grid?" Old Jim asked grumpily.

"Just tell us what we need to do, Officer," said Claudette.

"Nothing. Not a damn thing. See, that hurricane you all predicted? It's moving faster than anyone thought. Landfall. We got one day. Come on, folks, you know the drill. Evacuation time."

"I ain't goin' nowhere," said Frances.

"You don't have to, baby," said Danny.

"Sippie, if you want to go, I won't be mad at all. In fact, it might set me at ease. I can't have you both missing. Not now," said Frances.

"I'd like to stay with you," she said softly.

"We'll keep her safe, honey," said Old Jim.

"Mama?" asked Frances.

"Um-hmmm."

"Can I stay here? Can I come home? I want to be home with all of you. Me and Sippie. And Danny."

"Sugar, I been waiting for you to come home since the day you left."

"I take it you aren't going to heed my mandatory evacuation warning," said the officer.

The whole Sorrow clan just stared at him.

"Well then, I'll be on my way, but I want you all to know that none of my men are leaving Tivoli Parish until we've turned it upside down for Jack."

"Yes, sir, thank you," said Dida, showing him to the door. "Now, Frances, why don't you go on up to bed? I always keep your bed made just in case. I'll take care of Sippie. Give her a nice room and warm up some water for a bath. That sound good?"

"You okay with that, Sippie?" asked Danny.

"I'm fine, Danny. You gonna take care of her?"

Frances was already fast asleep against the arm of the couch. Danny lifted her in his arms.

"Forever."

20

A Sorrow Solstice

Sippie

Sippie sat on the docks, watching the exodus of people from the bayou. For a place that seemed deserted most days, there sure were a lot of people hiding out, living their lives deep in that wild country.

She didn't come here to be the same as the rest of them, sitting around, waiting for something to happen. She was different, raised different, and maybe there was a reason for that. Crow brought her here on the wings of a dream. And if she could fly again, even on her own, maybe she could find Jack.

She went back to Frances's cottage, laying herself back down in the cocoon of blankets Frances had made her that first night. Closing her eyes, she thought about being safely nestled inside her mother's womb, one that Jack grew in three years later. They had to be tied; there had to be a cord. She fell asleep knowing how peaceful it would be when they were all together, finally.

Memories floated in and out and away, liquid and undefined.

Where she was at, the past and present were one. It scared her. It was as if all the walls in the universe had come down and she were swaying in between. There was blackness all around.

"Jack? You there, Jack? I can't stay . . . I'm trying to fly on my own. Talk to me if you can."

"Sippie?"

They sat on the floor, hands together, in that little closed-up room. Familiar sounds surrounded them.

"You okay? Everyone's so worried," she said. "I'm your sister, Sippie Wallace."

"I know. I think I'm okay. But I can't wake up."

"Do you know where you are?"

"No. I've never been here. And it's so lonesome."

Sippie hooked her pinky in his. "I'm making you a promise, Jack. I swear they will find you. I swear it. And if for some reason they can't, I'll come back here. And I'll stay. I won't leave you alone. Ever."

He hugged her tightly right before she began to fade.

"I'm waking up, Jack. But I'll be back. You're not alone. Sippie's here!"

As her eyes fluttered open, she remembered tapping, silver shoes, brass bands, horns, music. He was somewhere close to Bourbon Street. She knew it. She jolted up, bumping her head on a low shelf that crashed down, leaving a pile of half-broken glass jars, feathers, and old letters scattered everywhere.

"Great. Just great."

One letter, older than the rest and encased entirely in wax, caught her eye. She picked it up curiously, gently attempting to free the paper from the sticky coating, only to rip the letter when she tried to pull out the paper inside too quickly.

"Dammit . . ." She sighed and unfolded the letter.

It was written by the nun everyone thought killed the Sorrows. Only it seemed the truth everyone had come to believe wasn't the truth at all. The tear she'd made in the letter went directly through the address on the top: 13 Bourbon Street. Signs, omens, ghosts, magic. In the end, it all came down to instinct. Jack was definitely in New Orleans.

Sippie walked purposefully back to Sorrow Hall, straight inside and up the stairs. The house seemed to somehow be more alive, rotting floorboards repairing themselves, damp spots slinking away, as the people inside were breaking over Jack and Millie. She opened the doors to Frances's room. It looked like something out of an old plantation museum, only it had bits of the outdoors sneaking in through cracks in windows and walls.

"Sippie," said Frances, "do you need anything?"

"Yes. You. It's time to get out of bed, Frances."

"When you gonna start calling me Mama?"

"It's been what, a little over a week? Give the girl some space," Danny said, pulling on some boots.

"Are you really asking *me* to give someone space? All I've done for too many years is give everyone space!"

"You two just can't quit, can you? Look, Danny, can I talk to Frances alone?"

"Be my guest, Miss Sippie. I got to go get some more plywood."

"Don't mind him," said Frances. "He gets quiet and mean when he's not in control. Look, honey, I know it's been hard on you, coming here, then all this . . . I'm trying to figure out what exactly I did in this sorry life that makes every single good thing that happens to me get followed up by a bad thing."

"Goodness! Stop with all the apologizing and rationalizing! I need to tell you somethin'!"

"Sippie, love, come here."

Crying, Sippie rushed to her and fell into her arms.

"What's all this?" asked Frances, smoothing back her hair.

"I saw Jack. I went to sleep and found him. I think he's safe, but he's scared, Frances. And we got to find him. Soon. I can feel it."

"Where, Sippie? Where do you think he is?" Frances's eyes stared at her with the kind of trust Sippie couldn't believe she'd already gained.

"I don't know exactly, but it's on Bourbon Street. I heard it. Or at least somewhere in the Quarter. And look—" Sippie held out the letter. "Look where the rip is. Everything happens for a reason, right?"

"I lost you there. You lost Simone there. Jack has to be there." Frances smiled and hurried to dress. "You amazing girl. Come on, quick! Let's go."

Frances and Sippie ran out of the room together, skipped over rotten stairs, and rushed out the front door, heading to the docks as though they'd been shot out of a cannon made of pure joy.

"How we gonna get there? Everyone's runnin', evacuating or fillin' up their trucks with sand and plywood." Sippie followed, gasping for breath.

"Just come on," Frances called back to her.

They took Frances's boat to Trinity Bridge, and then the woman Sippie couldn't seem to keep up with just stopped. She leaned against the railing of the bridge, unmoving.

"It's sort of lucky that not many people live here anymore, and those who do won't leave, because this road would be all jammed up already," Frances said. "Still, we better hurry up or else we'll get caught in the traffic north of here."

"What are you talking about?"

"Come on, help me." Off to the Tivoli side of the bridge, hidden back in the trees, was a truck. Covered in tarps and cared for.

"Whose is it?" asked Sippie.

"It's mine. I know something about exits, too, you know."

Maybe it was the confines of the truck, or the freedom of driving, or the long lines where Sippie and Frances had fun making up stories for everyone in all the different cars. Or maybe it was because they were beginning to trust each other. Whatever it was, the drive was magic, and the two began to speak (without words) the way Old Jim liked to do. Under and over the radio stations and songs that they'd sing. Screaming their heads off to "Baby, I Love You" and "I'll Be There," Sippie knew, her whole body humming with peace, that once they found Jack, nothing would be able to tear any of them apart again.

About a mile outside of New Orleans, Sippie suddenly grabbed Frances's arm. "Oh, my God, look!"

And there they were, those meat boys, *helping*. They were out there directing traffic for all those families who'd gotten their cars tangled up in the traffic while getting out of Dodge.

"They're smiling, but you can tell they sure as hell aren't happy about it!" said Sippie.

"We did it!" said Frances. "And Sippie girl, we're gonna find Jack, too."

When they pulled up to 13 Bourbon, Abe was bringing in some coolers to keep the produce in when the power went out.

"Well, look who's here! I think this building missed you, Frankie! And look, I got the last bunch of coolers at the store.

Hope we have enough. You ladies gonna find your way inside all right? I'm battening down the hatches, if dat's all right wit you, Frances."

"Of course. Thank you, Abe."

He paused and looked at her again carefully. "You sure you okay?"

"I'm sure."

"What's that about?" asked Sippie.

"I haven't been here for a long time."

"Since when?"

"Since . . ." Frances cleared her throat. "Since the morning after I gave you to Eight Track. I ran to the bayou and never came back."

"Here," said Sippie, taking her hand tightly. "You face your demons, and I'll face mine."

They walked slowly into the deserted building, hand in hand. "No one's here. I thought you said people come here to ride out the storm?"

"Not yet. First, the overly cautious leave. Then the suddenly terrified. *Then* the damn crazy ones wait till the last possible second to come get drunk. Now, let's climb these stairs and get to searchin'. Right?"

"Right."

Frances opened the door to the third floor into a large, sunny living room filled with antiques, richly textured carpets, and plants. Next to a tiny kitchenette off to the side was a hallway that led to three closed doors at the back.

"What do those lead to?"

"Bedrooms. That one was mine. That's where you were born, Sippie. Millie shares that one with Claudette, and Dida has her own." Frances kicked off her shoes with disgust and fell onto the couch. It was old and narrow, but plush like a big, blue velvet pillow. Frances seemed stuck. Fidgety.

"It must be hard, being back here . . . with me," Sippie whispered.

Frances rushed back to the present and went to Sippie. "No, love. It's just the opposite. It's like a gift I don't feel I deserve. If Jack was here . . . well, see . . . this is so close to the life I thought I'd ruined. I feel like I've been given a second chance, only . . . Jack."

A loud-pitched noise suddenly rang through the room, causing them both to jump.

"What is that?" asked Sippie.

"An intercom, I plumb forgot about it. Eight Track put it in years ago, scared I'd get into trouble up here when I was reading fortunes. I bet it's Abe. Hold on."

Frances pushed the button. "What's goin' on, Abe? You need me?"

"No, Miss Frances. I got Danny on the line down here. You want me to send the call up there, or take care of it on this end?"

"I'll take it. I don't want to, but I will."

The black, heavy phone on the side table near the atrium rang.

"He gonna be mad?" asked Sippie.

"I'm not sure. If you'd asked me last week, well . . . hell, last week I wouldn't have answered it." Frances picked up the phone. And urged Sippie over so that they were both listening in on the receiver.

"Hello?"

"Well, listen to you on the phone," he said. "So, how about you tell me why you are *there* and I am *here*? You got something you got to tell me, Gypsy?!" Sippie started to move away, but Frances pulled her back. Her eyes said, *You're not leaving me on this phone alone!*

"I'm sorry, Danny. See, Sippie had this dream, and then I had this tantrum, and then we found . . . anyway, the important thing is . . ." Frances looked at Sippie and smiled. "We believe Jack's here, in New Orleans. And you have to trust me on that. And I thought I'd come here and find him, you know, because, he's here. And Sippie's here . . . on the line with me."

"Sippie! You okay, honey?"

"Yessir."

"Look, if you two think he's there, he is. Do what you need to do, Frances. And Sippie, you listen to your mother. Now, if you'll excuse me, I got a blind woman, a deluded matriarch, an angry, displaced Yankee fisherman, a drunk, and a womanizer to deal with. No one is leaving, they're staying put. We've been boarding up what we can. But I'm coming to you as soon as I get these fools situated. Should be fun," he grunted.

"Millie didn't come back?" asked Frances, moving away so Sippie couldn't hear anymore. She paused, and Danny must have asked about Sippie because Frances said, "She's good. Better than good. Thank you, Danny. Drive safe, hear?"

She hung up the phone. She pushed back her hair, smiled, and then got all teary-eyed. "How come beautiful things hurt so much, Sippie? Got any idea?"

"My mama . . . I mean, Simone—"

Frances interrupted her. "Sugar, I may be your mama, but so was Simone. She took good care of you until she couldn't no more. And I'm nothin' but grateful for it."

Sippie smiled. "Okay, then, my *other* mama, she sang this song . . ." Sippie began to sing in a low, bluesy tone, gazing off in the distance. "'Being happy is beautiful, beautiful, so beautiful, being happy is beautiful until you realize what you had.'" Her eyes rested on Frances again. "I always thought it meant that when we're too mad and too scared, it's easy to be blind to just about everything. And when we feel light, when we can see beauty again, we got to remember all the sad that comes with it. All the things that get left behind in this leave-behind world."

"Well, if that ain't one of the truest things I ever heard, Sippie." Frances squeezed her hand. "Now, let's get to work."

"Where do we even start?" asked Sippie.

"We search every nook and cranny of this building."

They walked back out into the odd little third-floor hallway and Sippie stopped, placing her hands against a smaller door in the corner.

"What's in here?"

"It's a small room we use mostly for storage. But from time to time, when all the other rooms were full, or someone who couldn't pay needed a room, that's where we'd put them."

"I been here."

"In that room?"

Sippie gulped. "This is where she died, Frances."

"How about I look there, and you take the first floor. Then we'll meet on the second, okay?"

"Thank you," said Sippie.

Half an hour later on the second floor, they found each other.

"Anything?" asked Frances.

"No . . . but he doesn't have to be here, right? He could be somewhere else nearby."

"I suppose I'm just getting tired. Sippie, what if we never find him? Millie, she's smart. I don't think she'd hurt him, but I do think she'd take him. Far away."

"We *will* find him," Sippie said. "I made him a promise."

"Then I believe you," said Frances, forcing a smile. "You know, that room on the third floor, it's all boxes now. No ghosts at all, if you want to take a look."

"I don't think so," said Sippie.

"Sweet girl, sometimes we got to lean inside of something in order to let go. I just learned that, this very week. You taught me that. Made it easy for me because you didn't give me a choice. But see, you got a choice. And it's harder that way, to choose that walk back in time."

"I know," she said.

"Miss Frances! Miss Sippie! Oh my, yes. Just the ladies I need to see. Come!" Craven cried out joyfully as he emerged from the first room in the hallway.

"Mr. Craven! You scared me half to death! I forgot you were here," said Frances.

"We haven't found Jack, Mr. Craven. Can we talk about some long-lost history later?"

"Miss Sippie, Miss Frances, I *insist*. You need to hear me out. Come see what I've found. I believe it might help us find Jack. You see," he said, shuffling through boxes, "this place used to be the office of A. A. Monroe. Yes, right here!"

Frances and Sippie looked at each other. The tear in the sister-nurse's letter was directly across that very name.

"This desk, you see, it has a secret panel in the back of the drawer, isn't that fascinating!" He flapped his hands excitedly.

"Oh, my goodness, what did you find, Craven?" Frances asked impatiently. "Some secret, hidden journal or something? Just tell us!"

"Well, yes, actually. But not in the hiding spot. I found mouse poop there. But right there in the drawer itself, I found this. " 'The Journals of Albert Monroe.' He was the—"

"We know!" Sippie and Frances grabbed the musty pages and ran back to the apartment upstairs. "Promise we'll bring 'em back!"

And so, as the humid day filtered a lie of sunshine through the windows and the sounds of people boarding up their windows and heading out of town grew muted, Frances Green Sorrow sat curled up with her daughter. They shut out the world, taking turns to read to each other. And though Sippie knew Frances couldn't put the thought of Jack, out there somewhere, out of her mind, she was as present with Sippie as if there weren't a thing wrong. Which made Sippie feel more loved than any type of wordy declaration.

The reunited pair were once again finding a balance of dark and light. But at least they were together doing it.

They read fast and frantic. The answer was there.

It had to be.

The Sorrow Papers

21

Reflections and Revelations

Albert Monroe

June 22, 1902

As the caretaker for the Sorrow Estate, I, Albert Monroe, compile this document full of thoughts, revelations, and notes I took during the questioning of Sister Vesta Grace concerning her alleged involvement in the demise of the Sorrow family. My purpose is simple: When another Sorrow finally steps forward to claim what is rightfully theirs, they will have an accurate account of what transpired during the darkest hour of their history. I have written letters to all members of the family that reside scattered across Europe, and though not many have written back—indeed many of my letters have been returned unopened owing to faulty address information—the few that have responded sent their regrets. They are fearful of the perceived curse, and though they are full of kind words, they do not wish to return.

SuzyNell has set up a small stipend for the upkeep of the estate

and granted me guardianship over the business at 13 Bourbon
Street. I must admit, reading her letter filled me with despair. I
hope she may find the way back to her bayou someday.

But I cannot begin this accounting with the end of the story. I
must begin where it started, which is, oddly enough, at the end of
an era. This document begins with a transcription of the questioning over a period of days during the weeks following Helene
Sorrow's death. And it ends with a full recounting of the events
that followed the hurricane of August 14, 1901, that caused so
much devastation. The events herein still shock me to my very core
and call into question what is truly right and wrong. The world
is, it seems, full of shadowy areas that only the bravest of us can
learn to accept. I am not one of those brave souls. But I believe
Sr. Vesta was.

It was June 1, 1901, two years to the day of her arrival. The District Attorney of Tivoli Parish sent me a note stating that its citi-
zens were convinced she had bewitched the Sorrows and were
demanding an inquiry.

*Mr. Monroe, as you can imagine, this situation is much too big for
our small justice system. I plan on inviting the New Orleans District Attorney to take over the case as the family has stakes in both
Tivoli and Orleans Parish. But out of deference to the bond you
secured with Edmond, and assuming you will take Sr. Vesta's case
were it to come to that, I am offering you the opportunity to come
question her yourself. Once you feel you have built a good defense,
we can quiet the growing rage of this community. And if we fail, then
you will at least have the opportunity to construct a solid case on her
behalf.*

I have instructed Vesta to remain on the Sorrow Estate and have

placed an officer at the dock for her protection. I suggest you make
arrangements for immediate arrival.

Regards,
Clifford Levoy

I cleared my schedule, packed my valise, and left within the hour.

Until my trips to the Sorrow Estate became those of mourning, I always looked forward to meeting with Edmond in his bayou paradise. We would walk through the citrus groves and he'd tell me of his many troubles—most revolving around women or money. Edmond was always terrible at managing his finances.

"You must employ an accountant, or at least a bookkeeper, Edmond. I'm your lawyer, not your financial adviser. I'm quite ignorant when it comes to money matters," I would tell him repeatedly.

"Ah, but you cut a fine figure in front of the jury."

"Thankfully, your malingering hasn't ended you up there yet, old boy."

"Not yet," he'd say with that gleam in his eye. As a man that shared his taste for women, whiskey, and gambling—the reason why I was in his employ—I am man enough to admit that Edmond Sorrow could charm the devil.

As the driver brought me in from New Orleans, I let my mind reminisce over our walks through those lush estate grounds and our boat trips through the wild, forgotten areas of Serafina's Bayou. But as we crossed into Tivoli Parish, I began to prepare for what would be the first of my sessions with Sister Vesta Grace. I myself was overcome with the loss of that fine, eccentric family. But the pain and anger etched across the faces of the people in Tivoli Proper and ingrained even deeper on the faces of those in the bayou chilled me. Rosella, Edmond's childhood friend, was kind enough to meet me at Trinity Bridge.

"Good to see you, Albert."

She was always an alarming beauty. Dark hair and dark eyes, but a mystery about her that seemed at once free and in need of capture. She was a woman you looked at and wanted to possess, knowing full well you never quite could.

"And you, Rosella. Though I wish I could say we'd been estranged for longer. Helene is only a week in the ground, God rest her."

"You are here to question our captive nun? She has been graced with such a fine, gilded prison, don't you think?"

"You believe she did this? I'm surprised."

"I don't believe it. I know it, Albert. Everyone thinks I'm the witch, my mother, too. All because we hold tight to the old traditions and do terrible, monstrous things like heal people. God forbid you try and help someone these days. But that woman is guilty as sin. And trust me, she knows sin better than anyone. Don't let her beguile you. She'll try."

We were silent as Rosella deftly moved the pirogue through the low-lying swampy areas. I began to question my decision to wear a suit. The air was as humid and damp as ever, but it held something else, something even more oppressive. It held hate.

When we reached the long dock that wound up to the white, shell-covered road leading to the Sorrow Estate, Rosella pulled in close but did not tie off the boat.

"Don't look so alarmed, Albert. The officer will signal me when you're ready to come back. I have not set foot on that property since we buried Helene. And I don't intend to ever set foot on it again."

"*Merci,*" I said.

"*Ça va,*" she said, pushing off easily from the dock. Even the ripples in the water seemed to mock me.

I walked up the path, fanning myself with my hat. Sister Vesta must have seen me coming because she was running down to the gate. I'd always found her pretty. Edmond, when he wrote to me of her arrival, had likened her to Jane Eyre. And I quite agreed. Plain at first and then simply magnificent. There was an officer at the gate, as promised.

"How do you do, sir?" I asked.

He nodded at me, more perfunctory than personable, and turned to unlock the chains that held the iron gates together. I remembered when Edmond had them commissioned, not long after he brought Helene home as a new bride. They were made by a local artisan and had crescent moons and stars decorating each ironwork arch. Helene had become hysterical, yelling that she had to endure heathen culture even when she asked for something practical, like a gate. Edmond and I had laughed over that. And it was, of course, his intention to annoy her. He'd wanted to keep the estate open, as it had been since it was built. But Helene was different, an outsider from Royal Street. She didn't understand the freedom that came with living in seclusion.

Sister Vesta looked at me through the bars, waiting for the officer to fumble the lock open. It was more like visiting a client in Angola than I realized. And in that moment, I was scared for her.

We walked up to the house together, past her whitewashed cottage. She'd lived there the first year of her employ, but as she grew closer to the family, Helene gave her a set of rooms right next to her own.

"Do you miss it, living there?" I asked as we passed it.

"Yes. Especially now. It's terrifying to be up here all alone. But somehow I feel closer to all of them when I'm there. So I spend my days taking care of their things, and I come here to sleep. It's not a bad arrangement."

As we stepped onto the lower gallery of the house, I looked out over Helene's saint garden to the family plot. Eight raised stones shone in the sun. The marble, still so new, shocking next to the weathered graves of Sorrow ancestors that died appropriately.

"Too many, too soon. It's haunting, is it not?" said Sister Vesta.

"Indeed."

"I won't speak of it, you know. And I know that's why you've come. It seems you may have wasted a trip," she said as we entered the large front parlor. She had all the windows on both sides open so that the breeze from the front and back galleries made the interior of the home comfortably cool.

"Won't speak of what?" I asked.

"How they died."

"Sister Vesta," I said, placing my valise on the ground and laying my hat down on top of it, "I am not here to accuse you. I am here to help you."

"Mr. Monroe, would you care for a drink? I've learned to make a wonderful julep."

"I would like that very much." I smiled.

"Good. Meet me on the back gallery. Oh, and Mr. Monroe?"

"Yes?"

"Please call me Vesta. And I'll call you Albert. I seem to lose a vow each day."

What an odd creature, I thought as she went off to fix our drinks.

When she returned with two drinks in hand, I was already settled on a wicker couch facing the teahouse, right in the center of the larger mouth of the bayou in the back of the house. The arching oaks and magnolias framed the setting sun perfectly.

"Here you are." She handed me a glass and then turned, leaning against the baluster to face me. She took a sip of her drink and winced. "I'm still getting used to spirits," she said. "Both alcoholic and otherwise."

"I have to admit, Sister . . . I mean, Vesta, I'm at a loss. I assure you that the district attorney is not overreacting. If you do not want to talk to me about your opinions and ideas of what may or may not have transpired here, you must at least tell me what you plan to do."

"To do?"

"For example, do you plan on returning to Baltimore?"

That's when she laughed. And I tell you her whole face lit up with that laugh.

"I don't think they want me, Albert."

"So I ask again, with no disrespect, what is it you plan to do?"

"Die here," she said. And there wasn't an ounce of falseness to her declaration.

"You mustn't!" I said.

"Calm down, Albert. There is nothing left for me. I do not take the accusations lightly. I've seen what can happen to people when this parish has decided to take the law into their own hands. And I know that is exactly what has happened. So, I'll stay here for as long as I can, search for Belinda, and when the mob comes for me, they can have me."

"This is insanity, Vesta. You did nothing!"

"How did they die, then?"

"That is what I'm here to ask *you*." I almost ended the statement with "darling" and was reminded of Rosella and her comment about beguiling.

"Well, if you are here to gather proof of my innocence, then you must have an idea of what actually happened."

"It was a bizarre set of accidents! That's all. A horrifying case of coincidence. But these are people who believe curses, and the fact that the fatalities began right after your arrival two years ago is all the proof they need. What I need from you are facts that can outweigh the fiction they are creating."

She turned away from me then and looked out over the sunset that had now turned the entire vista into a vibrant painting of pinks, oranges, and violet.

"It is Eden here," she said.

"It is."

"Or perhaps hell. At least, that's what Helene always thought."

"Ah, Helene. She always seemed to be, how shall I put this, tormented."

"Oh, she was," said Vesta with a certainty that made me curious.

"I must tell you, Vesta, I have toyed with the notion that she may have been the one who was the catalyst for much of what happened. If there is any grain of truth to that idea, tell me what you know and I can clear up this whole mess. You can come back and I will let you have a room at Thirteen Bourbon. You can start life anew."

"It was most definitely not Helene," was her simple, solid answer.

"How can you be so sure? She wasn't in her right mind for years. Everyone knew it. It's part of why you were employed here."

"I am sure, Albert, because there isn't much I don't know about her. About who she was before she came here, about whom she turned into and why. I was honored to have her so quickly consider me a friend and confidante. Helene was full of longing and loss, but she was not a murderess. And no mother ever loved her children the way Helene loved hers."

"Well, if you won't help me figure out a logical explanation to feed to the hungry masses, why not tell me about Helene? I was always closer to Edmond. Tell me what you know."

"Are you planning on staying here for a while, Albert?"

"I came with my valise, did I not? I intend on staying in Tivoli Parish until I can clear your name."

"That won't happen. But I am glad you planned an extended visit. We will talk about Helene by and by. It will feel good, like she's with us somehow. And I know she'd want me to tell her story. Sometimes I think learning their stories is the whole reason I came here. As if the future knew the past and needed a translator of sorts. Is that very odd?"

"Not odd at all."

Vesta took a seat next to me, and as she began to speak of Helene, she grew more at ease. The cool evening set in around us as she spoke.

"Well, let's begin with the day I arrived and we can skip around a bit."

"Yes, that sounds like a good way to proceed."

"On the day I arrived, June 1, 1899, Helene was standing in her bedroom window . . ."

22

Heathens and Hoodoo

Helene Dupuis Sorrow

Helene watched the children from her window high above the front lawn, saying her rosary. The beads, handcrafted from precious metals, had been handed down through Edmond's family. He'd given her a set before they were married, and now, all of her daughters had sets as well. Each was different, some with leaf motifs etched onto the beads, some with florals. Helene's was the largest, the most ornate. And the chain was wrought in the form of vines. She cherished those beads and was never seen without them wrapped around her hand or pinned to the waist of her dress. They helped her remember that the Sorrows, for all their heathen ways, had once been holy.

Always a devout Catholic, Helene had fallen deeper and deeper into a zealous practice of the faith as she grew more disillusioned with her life as a Sorrow. Her growing fanaticism irritated Edmond. She'd even had a chapel built by knocking down the walls of the staff quarters, which meant that those who worked and lived on the estate before her arrival were forced to move. For Helene, it was a double blessing. First, she would no longer be required to leave the estate to attend mass, which meant she no longer had to take one of those awful little boats through the swamps, then wade through the muck of Sweet Meadow, with its foul, fishy smells, or see the Cajun trappers hanging creatures by their feet in the market square. It all soured her stomach so. She'd begged to travel into Tivoli Proper, where the church was grander and reminded her, if only a little, of home. But when Edmond finally gave in, Helene discovered that the journey was an all-day event and that the children fussed too much. Nothing ever turned out the way Helene thought it would. Second, with everyone but her own children and Edmond gone, she no longer had to suffer through those mixed-race lowborns and their sidelong glances. She no longer had to listen to their unhushed whispers about the way she mothered her children, or her fancy ways, or what a terrible choice Edmond had made when he married her. *A terrible choice?* she'd think. *I'm a Dupuis, from New Orleans. Finally one of these Sorrows has gotten it right, not wrong.* But it didn't matter what they thought of her anymore, because *ces abrutis,* as she called them, would now come and go during the day only, and Helene would not have to worry about their ridiculous judgments or influence over her children.

Though she never liked to admit it, she'd wanted to marry Edmond from the second she'd seen him. She'd had her doubts before her father introduced them. More than once during her marriage, she'd asked herself why she hadn't listened to her instincts instead of her heart all those years ago.

"Papa," she'd said when she was still a young, vibrant girl growing up in the Quarter. She was confident and spoiled back then, with thick blond hair and a list of suitors a mile long. "Why should I consider this proposal? Alexander Dumond will ask you for my hand any day now. He's handsome and a good Catholic . . . and just think! I won't even have to change the monograms on my linens."

They'd been sitting in the garden room of the grand house she'd grown up in on Royal Street. Her father had prepared a fête so that Edmond Sorrow could come and court her properly. He poured a drink for himself and gave her a small glass of cordial, then sat with her under the potted palms.

"*Ma belle chérie,* you don't understand the history. It's an *honor* to be invited into the Sorrow family. Tivoli Parish will be all yours. The bayou, the quaint town of Sweet Meadow, the cane fields, and that wonderful building on Thirteen Bourbon. It's a prized piece of property, you know. Not to mention, you'll summer on Saint Sabine Isle, the finest and most *haut monde* retreat on the Gulf. Who could want more?"

"Papa, I don't know a soul there, and I don't see myself on some pirogue casting nets, either. *Mon Dieu,* it's as if you want to feed me to the alligators! And I'm not completely unaware of that place or those people. That . . . *lifestyle.* How am I supposed to live like that?"

"*Mais non, chérie.* Let me explain. Tivoli Parish is a magical place. Don't laugh at me, it's true. You are my only child, your dear mother has gone to God, and I want the best for you. I want you to be safe, because I can't live forever. Though our country has begun to make strides towards women's rights, I fear for your independence once you are no longer my sole responsibility. Whoever you marry will be, in effect, your owner. It is but one of the terrible truths of our times. Now, the women of Tivoli Parish . . . Oh, how can I explain this to you, darling? It's a different kind of life for them. You'll have your rights, your children will have more power."

He halted for a moment when he saw Helene's expression. "Young girls care nothing about their rights until they've been undone. So, *c'est la vie* . . . do as you will. Of course, in the end, the choice will be yours. See if Edmond pleases you. If he doesn't? Marry Dumond. *Voilà*."

In the end, the entire conversation was for naught, because as soon as Edmond entered her home the next evening for the party, Helene fell madly in love.

"They all have it, those Sorrows," said her father. "I knew a Sorrow woman once. . . ." He trailed off. But he didn't have to finish. The dreams she saw there in his eyes told the entire story.

That night, Helene and Edmond danced in wide circles on the ballroom floor. Helene watched how everyone watched them. They were luminous and irresistible together. And when his hand touched her back, a million butterflies took flight inside her heart.

Edmond and Helene spent their honeymoon on a riverboat that took them up the Mississippi. It was so grand, that ship. Helene even forgave Edmond for gambling, because, oh, how they danced! They danced throughout the ballrooms and across the endless decks. Helene would never forget those twirling, decadent weeks where she drowned in love. She conceived SuzyNell on that boat. Their lovemaking was so inspired that her back felt permanently arched with pleasure. Edmond's natural fire lit up a hidden sensuality in Helene. "Don't stop, Edmond . . . I never want you to stop touching me," she'd said.

But all honeymoons, however lovely, must come to an end, and too soon Edmond and Helene were traveling southward to Tivoli Parish.

"Allez vite! Allez vite!" the coachman called out, urging his horses forward while shaking their reins.

"Must he make them go so fast, Edmond?"

"Leon is excited to bring us back home, *chérie.* And in these parts, we like doing things fast so the air moves around us, *c'est bon?"*

Helene sat back, not wanting to admit she was scared. Things had been so sublimely wonderful that the sinking feeling growing inside her as the land separated into a damp, watery mosaic was sadder than any other sort of disappointment.

"If you don't stop pouting, Nell, I'll ride up on top with Leon and you'll have to see the sights for yourself," Edmond joked as they crossed the isthmus connecting Tivoli Parish to southern Louisiana.

Helene hated that nickname he'd given her. Nell. It was the name of a servant. Or a horse. But she smiled and pretended, because that was what she'd learned marriage was all about. It never occurred to her to speak her mind. Instead, she let the unease grow slowly inside her like a disease.

"There's so much water, Edmond. What do you do when it floods?"

"Well, *chérie,* we climb high up into the trees, that's what we do," said Edmond, and he laughed.

The sensible roads had ended, and the pitted dirt roads ahead forced Leon to drive the coach slower. Helene looked out the window once again.

"We're ridin' into Tivoli now," Edmond said. "It's not much. But bigger than Saint Sabine Isle. We think of it more like a boundary than a city. Other people, though, from the *ville,* they come on down to Tivoli Parish and spend time right here. And those that summer on Saint Sabine Isle, this is where they go to get their necessities. The fishermen, too. I suppose it's a right useful little town."

Helene thought it quaint, with its wooden cottages and tall trees, the branches spreading out in the back like great quilts.

There were a few shops she thought she'd like to visit, and just when she was going to tell Edmond how *relieved* she was, she realized the main road had ended, and there were no other houses in sight.

"Where did the town go, Edmond?"

"It goes wide, east to west. But this south road is all you have in or out of Tivoli Proper. Now, look close, because here's where the magic starts. . . ."

Helene looked close. All she noticed was the trees getting thicker, the smell of must growing stronger, and the road getting thinner. Water practically dripped from everything around her.

"Where are we now?" she asked.

"We are on the edge of Serafina's Bayou. The most beautiful bayou in all of Louisiana. As a matter of fact, we're 'bout to drive right over Trinity Bridge, the center of the whole parish. When I was but a small boy, I'd listen for the ti-gallop of the hooves against the wood of this bridge. That's how I knew I was almost home. Once over the bridge there's a three-way fork in the road. If we drive straight, we cross another bridge onto Saint Sabine Isle. The cane fields are down the west road, and our home, Sorrow Hall, is down the waterway east. There's no choice but to take a boat there. Either from here or from the inlet of the bayou behind Sweet Meadow. See the boat there?"

Helene leaned over Edmond to look out his side of the carriage.

"*Mais non,* Edmond. I can't see anything but mud."

"It's right there—" He pointed to a small boat that looked more like a raft than any sort of vessel one would expect to carry one to a grand house. She sank back in the velvet seat of the coach.

"Are you unwell, *chérie*? It really is silly to go all the way to Saint Sabine Isle. Leon can tie the horses off here, and then take us to the house. Are you sure you want to see the resort first?"

Helene was very sure. She wanted to put as much time between herself and her new bayou life as possible.

Edmond put his arm around her. "I know this is difficult, Nell. But you'll have to look harder. The people who live in this community are our dearest companions. Tivoli Proper, Serafina's Bayou, and Saint Sabine Isle: We are a trinity, like this bridge. The sooner you learn that, the sooner you'll feel better."

"I feel just fine," she lied.

When they crossed onto Saint Sabine Isle, she once again felt the same hopefulness she had in Tivoli Proper. The resort was absolutely lovely. Rows of idyllic cottages set amid gardens and the sandy beaches of the Gulf. She could clearly see herself spending time there. But then they were back on the other side of Trinity Bridge, and Leon was lifting her out of the carriage and placing her in the small boat, and she felt nothing but an ever growing sense of despair.

"Leon, will you bring the trunks across later?" asked Edmond. "I'm afraid, with all the things my Helene has brought with her, she'd sink us quick."

"May I at least bring Goldie?" she asked. Goldie was Helene's yellow canary. But as his elaborate cage was large and heavy, the two men said no and laughed.

Edmond climbed into the boat beside her, and they wound their way through the dark waters. Every so often, a low-lying branch would touch Helene, and she would be forced to stifle her fear. She knew Edmond wanted her to be brave.

As they came to a bend in the bayou, Leon turned the boat, and Helene saw the gardens leading up to Sorrow Hall and then the grand, wide docks. There were several small cottages filled with people clustered around one area. "We will stop here first, and then it is just a short ride up to the main docks."

When they were safely on solid ground, the people gathered around them, welcoming them, warm for a strange, mixed-up lot.

"Who's who?" she asked softly as Edmond made his way through the crowd, smiling and shaking hands.

"What do you mean?" he asked through his smile.

"Who are the wealthy and who are the poor? I can't seem to discern the society from the rabble. And where are they from? This is our home, is it not?"

Edmond turned to look at her, annoyed.

"*Ma chérie,* there is no such division here," he explained. "The only thing that divides us is the water and land between our homes, and until recently, Sorrow Hall was a gathering place for any who needed shelter. The founder of this parish was very clear on how she wanted things done. So that's how *things are done*."

It was the first time he'd been harsh with her, and her eyes welled with tears.

"No, my sweet. Don't cry. You're just tired. Let's get back in the boat and take you home, *ça va*?"

Helene nodded.

"I'll take it from here, Leon. *Merci beaucoup* for your kindness. When you come back with the trunks, you'll have dinner with us, no?"

"Of course, Edmond."

Dinner. With the coachman. The Negro coachman. Helene felt faint.

Edmond rowed the boat easily, and soon every bit of civilization was obscured by the canopy of trees and the bits of pink-and-gold sky peeking out between rounded spaces in the Spanish moss. Bits of leaves and moss fell onto her, and she'd jump from time to time, making Edmond admonish her, "You'll tip us, Nell! Sit still. You are in Nature's castle now. Nothing here will hurt you."

"What about them?" she asked, pointing at a pair of lazy alligators sunning themselves on a bit of dark sand.

"*Voilà, oui,* you are right. If you were to bother them, they would bother you. The secret is to find the stillness inside of yourself, then the things you fear will still themselves as well."

"Why, Edmond! That sounds like poetry. Do you write?"

"No, no, cha. That is a quote from *The Book of Sorrows.*"

"What is that book? I have not read it. And I have read all the books there are to read in Papa's library."

"There is so much for you to learn. You know, of course, the story of Serafina Sorrow?"

"Of course. She must have been very powerful to have been allowed so much control over the governance and the business of this parish," said Helene.

Edmond stopped rowing and let the boat glide softly on the water.

"Did I say something wrong?" she asked.

"You are going to have to change the way you think, Nell. Serafina wasn't 'allowed' anything. She was the creator. Her book, *The Book of Sorrows,* is . . . how shall I say this . . . our Bible."

Helene smiled, silent.

Finally, Edmond turned the boat down a smaller tributary, and the sky, all purples and greens, golds and pinks, opened up before her. The trees arched up and around, creating a magnificent frame. It was so beautiful that Helene almost began to understand why the house was set so far out.

Edmond rowed up to the dock and helped her out of the boat.

"Will there be people greeting us here, as well?" she asked.

"No, I gave them the day off. All but Rosella, a dear friend and wonderful cook. But she's busy preparing our dinner. I wanted to show you this myself."

The dock was long, and the path up to the house was lined with live oaks and bursting with bushes and flowers of every color imaginable. Then, as they rounded a small bend, there it was, the Sorrow Estate house, standing tall and magnificent against the kaleidoscope sky. Edmond reached out for her with tangible excitement.

As they walked closer to the house, Helene took in the entire vista. Majestic and beautiful. Hope entered her heart yet again.

With its sprawling porches, columns, and welcoming staircases stretching up what seemed like forever, the house dominated everything. It appeared to glow with a light blue reflection thanks to the painted undersides of the porch roofs. And there were endless windows, pocket ones, that ran the length of the rooms they opened up to, and small round ones with arched stained glass. It was a messy sort of architecture, but Helene saw it the way most did on first glance—as mesmerizing. And it quieted her anxiety.

"It's beautiful," she breathed out. Edmond picked her up and swung her around, laughing boyishly. Helene laughed, too, happy to have pleased him again.

"Come, let's walk the grounds before we go inside. Serafina wanted the inside of the house and the outside of the house to reflect each other. So to appreciate it, we have to see it in all its glory."

They walked through the front gardens and then to the left of the house, where the family cemetery stood protected under more live oaks, moss, ancient wisteria, and magnolia trees.

The back of the estate contained more gardens, low, swampy areas, wild meadows, and a half moon–shaped body of water with a strange little house built on an island at its center.

"What is that?" she asked.

"It's a lighthouse. See all the windows? It's lovely inside. We'll make love all day out there," said Edmond.

"People will see!"

"Who cares if they see?"

I do, she thought.

"Where are the cottages?" she asked.

"Cottages?"

"Well, on every plantation I've visited with Papa, there are these delightful little cottages. You know, the old slave quarters. And the people there use them as guesthouses for when they throw grand parties. I was thinking, Edmond, this place would be just perfect for an extended fête! A week of dancing and eating and drinking. It would be like we were back on the steamboat!"

Edmond's face turned serious again. "This land was *never* touched by slaves. On the contrary, Serafina used to buy slaves and free them. And all the people in our employ, for the most part, live in the east wing of the house. Yes, love. *With* us. But, there is plenty of room for guests as well. Plan your party, darling. It will be a first for us."

Helene picked up the note of disdain in his final words. Something had shifted between them, and they'd only just arrived.

"Let's go inside," he said. "I'm sure you'll be happy with what you see."

"But Edmond, I'm already happy with—"

"Follow me," he said, cutting her off.

Walking ahead of her, Edmond threw open the large, carved double doors. Then he swooped his arms under her and lifted her up. The hem of her dress was muddy, but he didn't seem to mind. He placed her lightly in the foyer of her new home. The staircase spiraled upward to the second floor and its wide, open porticoes. Light poured inside from all directions. And the rounded base of the staircase was painted with the most intricate mural depicting the bayou at sunset. Intoxicated just looking at it, Helene reached out to touch it but felt a shock when her fingers tried to glide along the glittering depictions of lightning bugs.

"Do you love it?" asked Edmond.

"I do," she said. And she did. Until they walked throughout the east portico on the first floor and entered the grand parlor.

Hanging above the marble fireplace was a portrait of a whore. Shocked, Helene needed a moment to gather her thoughts.

She'd held her tongue enough. That painting was an affront to her very soul.

"Who is that woman, and why do you have a portrait of her hanging in plain sight! It's *obscene,* Edmond," she spoke up force-fully.

The painting portrayed a woman with thick, dark, unruly hair that tumbled over tanned bare shoulders. She wore a simple white shirt, unlaced at the front, exposing her décolletage. A red—*red!*—vest secured midwaist both hid and pushed up her bosom. The painted woman stood in front of the Gulf, with one foot on a large chest and the other on the sand. Her long black boots went up to her thighs. Helene could clearly see the flesh of the woman's upper thigh, beneath a gathering of white skirts. A bright purple scarf was cinched around her waist just under the vest. Her torso was bare.

"I don't like this, Edmond, and I want it taken down immediately," she said.

"That, Helene Dupuis, is Serafina Sorrow. And besides what you think you already know about her, let me illuminate you further. She is my great-grandmother, a casket girl from France who came to the New World at thirteen years old and built a dynasty. And to answer your question, yes, she was thought to be a whore and a witch."

"A witch?"

"Yes. And in case you don't believe in such things, I believe she has just informed me, from beyond the grave and through your own mouth, that I've married an idiot."

He left the room, slamming through all kinds of doors.

"I hate you," she whispered to the painting.

Helene threw herself on one of the settees and cried.

They didn't stay angry with each other for long, but the seed of a cycle of fighting and trying to forgive had been planted in front of that painting. It was also the moment Helene began to believe in dark magic.

During her first week there, as she grew to know the staff and tried to become acquainted with a new set of boundaries, her canary, Goldie, began losing feathers. Little by little, day by day, one yellow feather would fall out, only to be replaced by a black one. And with each raven feather that grew, Helene Dupuis Sorrow lost pieces of her mind. By the end of her first year in Serafina's Bayou, Goldie had become Crow, and Helene set him free. She watched him fly high above her gilded prison and prayed that she, too, could fly far away someday.

Which was how she felt that morning, seventeen years later, as she looked out the window, waiting for the boat that would bring the sister-nurse and freedom back to her. A different kind of freedom than she desired, but still . . . freedom.

She finished saying her rosary, looking over the lawns at her family, who had gathered to wait for their new arrival. There was a collective excitement in the house, because after the first, disastrous party Helene hosted, she'd closed them up so tightly that even a simple nun inspired the kind of enthusiasm a grand fête would have given Helene when she was a little girl in New Orleans.

Edmond leaned against the stone pillar of the front gates and smoked a pipe. He'd railed against it when the walls and gates went up around the Sorrow Estate. But Helene had insisted after Suzy-Nell was born.

"Someone will try and steal her," said Helene, who'd read a newspaper story about babies being stolen from their families and held for ransom.

"You still don't understand it here, do you, *chérie*?" he'd asked. But he gave in to her demands, for much the same reason that Helene gave in to his physical advances.

Leaning there, against the walls, Helene surveyed the man she'd been bedding for all of her adult life. The years had been kinder to Edmond than to Helene. Still handsome, Edmond never seemed to age. He was like all the other Sorrows, with their signature dark hair, olive skin, and light eyes that ranged from blue to gray to green depending on whom they married. (Defying all sorts of genetic formulas, even a brown-eyed man or woman who helped a Sorrow make a baby couldn't seem to override the original characteristics.) The only thing different about Edmond now was the mustache he'd decided to grow a few years after they were married.

A "dapper," was what their oldest girl, SuzyNell, called him.

Helene, in contrast, was light and fragile. A little of the dewy, youthful beauty she'd had when they'd first met left, bit by bit, with the birth of each child. She was convinced she lost a little of her mind with each pregnancy as well, and she knew Edmond felt the same.

It was different with her first pregnancy and their firstborn. SuzyNell was a beautiful baby. The *première fête*—also the last party ever held on the estate—was held in her honor. And Helene had felt that same hope she had first setting eyes on the Sorrow Estate. But that night, Helene found Edmond making love to Rosella in the lighthouse, and as she stumbled away into the dense trees because she could not face her guests, she found the small shack that held the dark magic—jars, altars, candles, even bones—and knew it would be her undoing.

She sent all the guests home. She broke fine china. She slapped Rosella across the face. She demanded that the shack be burned to the ground and Rosella exiled out of their lives.

Her demands fell on deaf ears.

"You pray your way, she prays her way," said Edmond. "I will not exile her, I love her. I love you both."

After everything else failed, she tried to leave, but her father was too ill to take her in. For years she tried to fight off Edmond's charms as much as she could, moving to a separate bedroom, staving off his affections. But he'd wear her down eventually, and six more children followed. Each pregnancy was a reminder of her weakness and his betrayal. But all of the hate disappeared as she looked at the faces of her newborns. Her children were her salvation. Her hope was that whatever spell or curse Rosella placed on her was dispelled with each of her perfect children. Until her last child, the boy, was born.

Helene searched for him through the window, amid the rest. The older girls were playing lawn tennis, and their beauty made Helene misty-eyed. In her clearer moments, she felt a love for them that rivaled her love for Jesus, which terrified her.

SuzyNell and Edwina played against the twins, Lavinia and Grace. The youngest girls, Mae and Belinda, played a gentle game of croquet with . . . yes, there he was, Egg.

SuzyNell was wearing her hair up, and the high neck of her dress only emphasized her burgeoning womanhood. Her children were true Sorrows—all of them with thick, glossy curls and gleaming eyes. But something else as well. They all shared that mysterious heat pulsating in ripples around them. Helene, tortured by the idea of sin, made her children wear white at all times to counteract the seductive, Sorrow allure. "You are my vestal virgins," she'd tell her daughters.

Belinda B'Lovely—that whore Rosella gave her the nickname when she was a baby, and as Edmond refused to end his relations with her, it stuck—always found a way to get around it, though. She'd fasten a bit of red ribbon to her wrist, tuck a red rose behind her ear, anything to offset what she called "the hateful white." Helene took it in stride, gliding past her daughter in the hall or on the stairs, gracefully removing whatever item Bee had adorned herself with.

"Red is the color of sin, *ma chérie*," she'd say, and then kiss her youngest daughter on the top of her sweet head.

But that day, as the boat carrying her salvation found its

moorings, Helene was too far away from Bee to pull the red sash from her daughter's lovely white lace dress. And as Helene watched, her youngest daughter straightened that sash defiantly and looked up into Helene's bedroom window, right into her heart, before running down the covered path to meet their guest.

Helene didn't like to admit she favored any of her children, but she had a special place in her heart for Belinda because she was the one who needed the most saving.

She even favored her over the youngest. Edmond Seraphin Sorrow was his full name, after his father. But the girls all called him Egg. Not Egg because he was round. He wasn't round at all. He was very, very small, in fact. They called him Egg because he was fragile. Egg was always sick. Pale, drawn, *cher bébé Egg.*

He worried the family so intensely that Edmond ignored Helene's protests and asked Rosella's Maman, Patrice, a renowned *traiteuse,* to heal the boy using whatever bayou remedies she could conjure. "You invite the devil into our lives every day, Edmond," Helene would whisper icily.

Patrice visited Egg only once, because after the poultices of dried animal innards and duckweed were prepared in the kitchen, and their earthy odors filled the house, Helene became hysterical and went to her chapel, where she threatened to stay until a sister-nurse was employed.

"She will have to live with us, you know, and we tore down those rooms to build you your own kind of altar!" Edmond shouted throughout the heavy locked doors of the chapel.

"Then build her a cottage! If you'd run this estate properly from the start, there'd already be a place to put her. If I've said it once, I've said it a hundred times. No matter how far you put yourself out of society, Edmond, you will suffer the error of your ways in one way or another."

23

Albert Monroe

From The Sorrow Papers

My mind was working so fast. If what Sister Vesta said was true, and I simply could not believe such a detailed account to be false, then it meant Rosella had more of a motive than anyone else.

"So it was Rosella. Vesta, this will help me clear your name."

"No, Albert. It wasn't Rosella," she said, but I noted a hesitation in her voice. There was an accusation somewhere; I simply needed to find it.

"What makes you so sure it was not Rosella? Did she take you into her confidence as well? I can't imagine that with the close relationship between you and Helene, as evidenced by your intimate knowledge of her history, Rosella would have shared her deepest thoughts with you.

"It's late," she said, "and I'm tired. Come back soon, and I'll tell you more of their secrets. But I will not tell you anything that you can use against them, Albert. This is a documentation of sorts, a memorial so that they will not be forgotten. I am in no mood for redemption."

I left late that night more fascinated than confused. I was pleased that Rosella had sent a boy to come and escort me back to Trinity Bridge, even as I was building a case against her in my mind. My driver was asleep at the reins, and when I nudged him, he jumped.

"What is it, man? Why so startled? I've woken you from naps before."

"Do you see them, sir?"

"See what?"

"The *feux follets*. They be everywhere tonight. I've asked all who pass by for some salt, but no one wants to give any away. Seems everyone is sure those Sorrow souls are trapped in the bayou. And if we aren't careful, they may just get us. They angry we ain't got their killer yet. You sure you don't want to go on back over there and drag that nurse out by her habit?"

I reached into the cab and pulled him up by his collar. "Don't you ever let me hear you talk like that again. This is nonsense. Those people, that family of my dear friend, they suffered from a tragic set of circumstances. Nothing more, nothing less. Now, drive. I have rooms ready for us on Saint Sabine Isle."

"For me, too, sir?"

"Yes, of course. In the stables," I said.

I was glad to be at the Sorrow cottage at Saint Sabine Isle resort. It was late, but the staff had opened it during the day, and the gas lamps were lit. All the cottages were luxurious, but the Sorrows' was the most lovely of all. I fell asleep listening to the waves of the Gulf, thinking of better times. I'd been there before, of course. But one summer, the last summer they stayed, I believe, the summer before Egg was born, I was invited for the whole season. Helene kept to herself, reading and praying and doting on her girls, but Edmond and I had a riotous time. Belinda was just a little thing, but so different from her sisters. Determined to stay by her father's side, she followed us everywhere.

"She's the son I may never have," said Edmond.

"With such a lovely, healthy brood, why do you insist on having a son? Isn't it the Sorrow custom to lavish power and equality on their daughters?"

"I know the customs, Albert. And I know how I'm supposed to think and act and feel, but sometimes I wish . . . I just wish that things were a little more, I don't know. *Ordinary.* When Helene and I were first married, she was full of questions about slaves and poverty and social class. And I fought her on all of it, I did. But I've always wondered what things would have been like if we'd run our parish, our cane fields, our *lives,* like everyone else."

"Power can be a drug, Edmond. Think of all your family has acquired without the evil attached."

"No evil. That's funny, Albert!" He laughed at me, having a private joke, then cried out suddenly, "Race you to the ocean! Tonight, we'll make the journey into the *ville* and drink and whore and gamble. And stumble back here in the morning to sleep on the beach! How does that sound?" But his last word was muted and low because he was already halfway in the water. I ran after him, delighted as ever with my dear friend.

That night, Belinda made a fuss over her papa leaving. She

wrapped her arms around his leg and dirtied the bottom of her dress in the sand.

"Take me with you, Papa! I can wear a red dress and sit on your lap and play cards. I will put on lipstick, too! Like the ladies on Bourbon Street. Take me with you! I want to see the ladies dance. Please?"

If she'd been the daughter of any other Southern gentleman, she may have been sent off to be spanked by a servant and then have her mouth washed out with soap, only to be followed with a good dose of Bible reading as a bedtime story. But this was a Sorrow child, and Edmond, for all his protesting, was a Sorrow father. So he picked her up and held her close.

"Someday, my love, when you grow big, you can do anything you wish. Paint your face, or join the church, it is entirely up to you. But for now, you are still too little to stay up so late. And though I will miss you, I will be back when you wake in the morning. You can make me my coffee. Would you like that?"

"Oh yes!" she squealed, and skipped off clapping her hands.

The waves were like a metronome, and soon I was falling asleep deep inside the memories of that summer. But there was an overarching anxiety about Belinda. Could she still be out there, alive and all alone? I preferred to think of her in heaven with her family.

I really did.

The next morning, I woke to the sounds of the wealthy playing on the beaches. Little did we know, on that perfect morning, that in only two months' time, a hurricane would come and level the whole island. That no one would build it back up again. Those were the last, fading days of glory for so many of us.

I returned two days later to finish my session with Vesta. My time on the island had given me clarity. I could vindicate her.

As I saw it, there were only three possible things that could have occurred: It was as I believed, a terrible pairing of coincidence and accident facilitated (in some way) by Vesta, thus incurring her feelings of guilt; or it was Helene, a mother known to have mental instability and who died last; or it was Rosella.

Vesta had proven to me that it was not Helene. If I could get her to tell me what I already knew, but could not prove, she would be cleared. The accidental deaths needed to be explained, and the only witness left was Vesta.

I pleaded with her to simply tell me how all the events unfolded.

"Tell me, just tell me. I have ceased to care if you are guilty or not. Vesta . . . this was a horrible twist of fate. But I cannot create a fictional tale for you. You *must* tell me."

She put her finger to my lips and sent me away.

"Please don't come back," she said. "It will do my soul grave harm. I mean this, Albert."

And so I returned to New Orleans and began compiling my notes. It was clear to me that Rosella must have been at the heart of the issue. And then, after speaking with a historian visiting Tulane who specialized in toxins, I was equally sure that the rosary beads handed down to Edmond, which had stayed safe inside their boxes for so many generations, had slowly poisoned the family with mercury. I was also quite sure that Edmond himself had suffered from syphilis. All of this should have made me joyous, but it didn't. Because no matter how many notes I sent to Vesta that summer, her response was always the same.

"It does not matter. Stay away."

And I did, I stayed away until I could not. When the hurricane began to gain strength I knew I had very little time left to fetch Vesta. She couldn't turn down my offer of refuge from a terrible hurricane.

Or so I thought.

I went to her; there was no time to send a note. But though I pleaded with her, even tried to forcibly take her from the cottage, she would not come. And the officer, still out front, wouldn't allow me, either.

"You are killing her, letting her stay here locked in like this," I said.

"Serves her right. She killed all those babies."

"He speaks, finally," I growled at him.

I left that night in a dismal state. But I still had hope. I'd formulated a plan of sorts. That estate was the safest place to be on the bayou. Built high and with stone. If her strong will to survive began to set in, she could ride out the storm. I planned on riding it out myself at 13 Bourbon. Then, when the morning came, I would return. But before I went to her, I'd call a meeting. I'd go there under the pretense of helping with what I was sure would be a disaster, and then, when enough people were assembled for provisions, I'd tell them everything I knew. I'd explain about the metals and the syphilis. It was a good plan. Only I never got the chance to implement it because in the middle of the night, in the center of the raging storm, a drenched, mud-covered Vesta knocked on my door, holding a sleeping child with a dirty red sash hanging from her torn dress. Belinda.

"Help us," she said.

The Waning Moon

The Waning Moon

As the moon begins its journey from light back to dark,
We are allowed to shed any burdens we are no longer
required to carry.
Even if this means letting go of those we love the most.
Make no mistake, there will be times when we must carry
each other . . .
and times when we must set each other free.

—Serafina's Book of Sorrows

24

Frances and Sippie and

Nothing but Time

Frances

As we read Albert's narrative, the time passed in snapshots. Me reading aloud and making us tea. Us huddled on the floor, against the wall, heads bent down together. Sippie upside down on the couch, book in the air, as I picked up the mess we made.

"Help us," Sippie read.

I waited. "And then?"

"And then nothing." Sippie righted herself. "But look, Frances, there are missing pages."

"Of course there are." I sighed.

"Of course there are," echoed my Sippie. "Let me go see if Mr. Craven has the pages."

She ran downstairs. I could feel the wind pressing against the windows, like the pressure in my mind. The ache of Millie wanting to hurt me so bad. The crazy love bursting out of me for Danny. The fullness of finally knowing Sippie. And then Jack, who I somehow believed was safe. But the terror of waiting for an unseen twist made my heart into a mess of compressing parts. Like a machine with some parts working too hard while others were broken. But at least, after all those years, it was working.

"He's looking, but he doesn't think there's anything else," Sippie said, deflated, coming back inside the apartment.

"Let's not worry about what we don't know, Sippie girl. Let's worry about what we do know," I said, trying to lighten her a little. "Now, if the sister-nurse was alive and she didn't die in the storm and she has a child in her arms . . . and they are here, at Thirteen Bourbon, then . . . we know you were right, and he *is* here in the city."

"But not where . . . which is all we really need." She hung her head.

"Maybe if we read through it again," I said.

"Do you think Helene's Goldie is really our Crow?"

Sippie rubbed her head with exhaustion. I went to her and put my arms around her.

"Why not, right? What did you say that first morning: You don't try to explain what can't be explained? It's more interesting that way."

"Do you hear that?" she said, breaking free of my embrace.

"Hear what, Sippie?"

"I swear, I'm hearing blues," she said, and then sang, low and lovely, " 'Lover man, oh, where can you be . . .' Frances, I got to ask you something. I know you and me, we sort of, quietly agreed to skim over the top of this, and don't get me wrong, I'm not the needy sort of child, never was. And now, we got to find Jack, so I don't want you to think . . ."

"Sippie," I said, "you can ask me anything. We ain't got nothin' but time right now."

She glanced at me, then glanced down. And when she looked back up, there was a soft pleading in her eyes that made me want to wrap her back up in that little quilt and pull us both back in time. In that moment, I'd have given it all up, the life I lived with Danny . . . even Jack. In that one moment, I felt sure that if given the chance, I'd just turn back time and undo all the wrong. Because the Sippie I was looking at was the real one. Not the brave-faced girl who found all the exit signs. No, this was me, looking at myself in the mirror when I was her age. Terrified, broken, lost. *Hold it together, Frances. Whatever she asks you, you damn well better tell her the truth. That girl deserves that.*

"Okay, here goes . . . and you know you got to just tell me the truth, because I'll be able to tell by your eyes if you're lyin'."

Damn. This is going to be hard. "I'm ready, Sip. Hit me."

"Do you like my name?"

I have a terrible habit of laughing at the most inappropriate times. Sometimes it's shock. Sometimes it's the simple absurdity of the world. But that time, I'm pretty damn sure it was relief that she hadn't asked something bigger. All I know is she started laughing, too, with a small, tight smile that broke into a full-on *How much more ridiculous can this life get?* grinning, hysterical, rolling-on-the-floor sort of laugh.

"Yes," I gasped, breathless. "I love your name."

"I'm glad." Sippie beamed. "Well, now that we got that out of the way. . . . What should we do now?"

"Well, we can't go out, can't look for Jack, can't do nothin' but wait for Danny. Then I'll brave the streets with him."

"I don't like not being able to do anything, no exits . . . ," Sippie murmured.

"I know you don't, sugar. I spent far too long feeling the same way, and then I realized I'd walled myself completely in. My exit became a prison of sorts. Now, when I used to feel that way, Dida would tell me stories. How about I tell you a story?"

"Can you tell me something I don't know, something from when you were little?"

"Something good, or something bad?"

"Both." Sippie grinned.

"I like the way you think! Okay, so, once, when I was no more than five, when everyone still believed I could change all our futures, Dida and I were digging up roots and wild plants on the banks of the bayou when I saw a bird's nest on the ground with eggs in it all cracked and lonely. . . ."

"Can we pick it up and take it home, Dida? Maybe we can save them and bring them back to their mama. You got the healing touch. I bet you could do it."

"No, cha. We don't wanna mess wit nature. You see, nature takes care of itself just fine." *Juss fahn.* "Wish we were all a little bit more like that, don' you? Lettin' things be as they are, without fussin' ovah what could have or should have been. When we meddle wit fate, that's when things turn sour. It was all that meddlin' way back that caused dis sorry family to lose our way."

"But won't the mama bird be sad when she comes back? No nest, no babies, no nothin'?"

"I don't rightly know the workings of a mama bird's mind, Frankie girl. But I guarantee she won't be weepin' and carryin' on. She won't be jumpin' off no bridge or drownin' that grief in a bottle of whiskey. Nope. She'll be strong and brave. She'll have more babies someday. That's the thing about birds, about all living creatures who ain't us. They soldier on just fine. But people? We get turned all inside out until we can't remember what's what."

"Like my mama?"

"Like your mama and a bunch of Sorrow mamas before her. We can't remember that time when the world was ours and the sun felt good on our skin. All we know now is that deep ache you got right in your heart, the one that makes you downright miserable about those eggs. Sooner you learn you can't fix what's broke, the sooner you might help us out of this whole mess."

"But I thought that was my job to fix it? Make everything like it was?"

Dida stopped to take a hard look at me.

"It's important you understand the difference between the words *fix* and *heal*. You hear me, child? You can't fix anything, but you can heal it. Broken things are better when they're healed. But once a thing is broken, it never goes back to bein' all nice and new. The trick is to fix it up and make it useful again. You have the power to do all that. You'll be the one to find the cracks, glue the pieces back together, and heal us. Then those who come after you won't ever remember bein' anything other than happy and useful. And the beauty of it is the cracks will still be there, ever so light, so they know nothin's perfect and nothin's supposed to be perfect. What a day that will be." Dida got a far-off look in her eyes.

I sat on the grass in front of her, thinking.

"That would be sad. If my babies and their babies didn't remember the way it was . . . the way it is. Seems the remembering would be like a . . . um . . . a warning. Right? A warning to not be foolish like Edmond and Helene."

"You remember when I told you not to eat those molasses cookies right out of the oven last Christmas?"

I'd burned the roof of my mouth so bad, the skin peeled right off. "Yes, ma'am."

"Now, did that warning do you any good?"

"No, ma'am."

"You know why?"

I shook my head. The day was getting hotter, and the roots I carried had a strong scent that was making me dizzy. I was starting to feel sorry I'd ever mentioned that nest.

"I'll tell you why. See, if I warn you about something, it's human nature to want to see for ourselves. But if I'd just hid those damn cookies till they was cool enough to not burn you, I'd have saved you some pain and me that evil scolding your mama gave me."

"You think she loves me 'cause she loves me, Dida? Or you think she loves me 'cause she thinks I'll get strong enough to help her get to see for real?"

"You look here, child. Claudette loves you the best she knows how. And she loves you more than she ever loved anything. Why does it even matter? Love is love. Claudette is like that mama bird 'bout to come back and find that nest of yours. She's brave and strong and knows life hands out terror and pain. Nature is nature, cha. And the Sorrow women, well, maybe we've all become a little too much like Crow here."

Crow lit on her shoulder right then. He was always around.

"I don't mind bein' like Crow," I said.

"I know. But something's missin', don't you think? Crow flies and takes things as they come. He don't ask for anything else but a sunny day and a cool drink of water."

Wahtah.

I loved it when her speech got lazy. It meant she was relaxed.

"How that sound to you, Little Bit? Never having a real true feelin'. Just floatin' along from branch to petal to my shoulder here."

"It sounds . . . hollow," I said.

Dida laughed so hard then that Crow went flyin' off in a scattering of feathers.

"That is the truest thing I heard in a long time. Maybe you weren't born to fix anything at all, Frankie girl. Maybe you was just born to remind us what it's like to be less like Crow here and more like those wailin' people surprised when the world don't go their way. Maybe you are here"—*heah*—"to fill us up and take away some of that hollow. Dat sound bettah to you?"

"No. It don't. And I don't think Crow thinks like that. I think he feels a lot of things. I think he's different from all the other birds that ever were birds at all. Ever."

"And I think I was right about that, don't you, Sippie," I said, finishing. "Reading that history made me remember that conversation with Dida, and I can't quite believe I ever forgot it. I mean, I'd already somehow figured out what I would do. Only I didn't know it would be me that would be that mama bird."

"You aren't like that. You're not hollow," she said raspily.

"You don't know. I think I was, while I was all holed up."

"No . . . Let me tell you about *hollow*," she said through tears I wished so hard I could make go away.

"It was hot the night Simone . . . left . . . even for New Orleans," Sippie began. "She'd made dinner wearing her white slip and those shiny, red high heels she'd bought with the last of our small stash of cash she kept in a Crisco can. She had her hair wrapped tight and kept patting the back of her neck with a cool, damp cloth as she turned the chicken over in the skillet.

" 'Fried chicken on a night like tonight, I tell you I must be crazy,' she said, picking up a cigarette from the ashtray on the counter. I was standing on the kitchen chair, talking too much like usual. From the day I could talk, Simone told me I never shut up.

"I was the child who sucked the life right out of her.

"She'd make fun of me, repeating what I'd say in a baby voice. 'Where you goin', Mama, wit your heels on like dat? You goin' singin' again? You know Daddy don't like that. You should stay here. I got a funny feelin'. Daddy say, always trust your feelin's.'

"Then she'd say, 'Shut that rosebud maw of yours, girl. I'm here cookin' like a fool so you and that man can eat nice. I do what I want to do—hell, I do what I got to do to keep you fed and clothed and . . . Look at me, trying to explain myself to you. Go on, git out. I got to finish this. I'll burn it all up if you keep talking.'

"When the food was done, she practically threw it at me and Eight Track. 'Come on, y'all. Come and eat up. I got to go finish puttin' on my face.'

"The food was perfect . . . chicken, stewed okra, and tomatoes, grits. Simone could cook. And she could sing. And she could run. But that night, that night she decided to take me with her, and I still don't know why. All I know is that Eight Track was drunk, they had a fight, and she grabbed me. I was still in my nightgown, and her dress . . . it was so pretty, and her bangles were jingling. And she brought me here. And then . . ."

Sippie couldn't stop covering her ears, yelling, "I can't stop hearing her. All I want is for her to stop."

"Honey, maybe you keep hearing her sing because she has something to tell you."

"I don't want to hear it."

"If there's one thing I've learned recently, it's that you're gonna have to try and listen. *Really* listen."

"How?"

"You got some power when you sleep, Sippie. Some way to see things we both know are true. You saw Jack without Crow because you willed yourself there. Why not try that now? She's callin' you, sugar, you should answer."

Tears streamed down her face. She looked so lonesome.

"I think I have to do it now, get it over with. . . . I just go to sleep? Right? I don't want to hear it anymore," she said.

"Hush, love, come with me." I brought her into the room where she was born. "Open your mouth, baby . . . there," I said, placing a few drops of valerian honey under her tongue.

And then I lay down with her, my half-awake, lost-and-found-again Sippie Wallace Sorrow, who put her head in the crook of my arm and fell asleep, trying to shut out a world of memories that I knew, from far too much experience, she'd have to face sooner or later.

25

Jack Meets the

Sorrow Echoes

Belinda holds Jack's hand tightly as they skim through the fixed world. It looks too perfect, too still. She takes him past the Sorrow Estate—Jack can't believe he's seeing it in all its former grandeur—then over Sorrow Bay and around the lighthouse to Meager Swamp.

"I thought I knew this area better than anyone," he says, looking at the piece of land, obscured by bald cypress, just north of the swamp.

"This was a part of Tivoli Parish once, I think. Papa said he sold it when he found out there were people there years ago that had slaves. Papa doesn't believe in that. Neither do I. Do you?"

"Bee, I'm a Sorrow, like you. We don't think that way. Unless someone is downright stupid. Those people? Well . . . that's another story."

Bee laughs—beautiful chimes sounding—before growing serious again. "Well, I think stupid and evil walk hand in hand, Jack. And they walk here . . . right here. . . ."

They find themselves sitting in the center of a meadow full of violets. And shadows of time, come and gone, grow and fade as they sit, unmoving, and wait.

"What are we waiting here for?"

"I don't know. Do you hear your name?"

Jack listens. Then listens harder.

"Jack . . ."

He can't believe it, but he does. He hears his name.

"How do I go to it? How do I go to the voice?"

"Close your eyes, and let yourself go. That's all. And when you finish hearing what they have to say, you'll be back here with me. That's when it gets *très triste*."

"What?"

"Sad. That's what happens here. It's like a payment or something. I don't quite understand. But you go; I'll stay here and wait."

Jack closes his eyes and meets with his sister, Sippie.

Bee watches him smile, laugh. She hears the love growing. When he opens his eyes again, he is disappointed to be back.

"That was your sister, no?"

"It was. She's going to try and save us."

"Save you. No one can save me, Jack."

"Maybe I can."

"Are you ready?" asks Bee. "Best prepare yourself . . ." She trails off.

"Time to pay?"

"Yes, the sad things, the terrible things, have begun to take form." She squeezes his hand.

Jack looks across the field, seeing the shadows of so much evil. Native people dying, slaves being beaten and hung, plantation houses being built and then razed. Dark storms and sour land.

Then he watches as a small house is built and whitewashed, and a woman sits on the porch and cries.

"Who is she?"

"I don't know," says Bee. "She's stuck, too."

"Can we talk to her?"

"You can try. She can't see me. But that doesn't mean she can't see you."

Jack walks to the porch. The woman, her skin so black and her dress so white, is sitting on a faded, peeling rocking chair.

"Can I help you, ma'am?" he asks.

The woman looks up, startled.

"You Jack?"

Jack isn't surprised. Nothing is surprising him anymore.

She stands up, and with her hands shaking, she hands him something wrapped in a handkerchief.

"That be all I got. All I got for my whole life. And I gave it to my girl. Lord, I let that man . . . I let him . . . Jack . . ."

The woman falls to her knees, opening her mouth in a silent scream. He feels tears prick his eyes.

He unwraps the soft fabric and finds a pin, like a star, filled with opals.

"It's beautiful," he says, not knowing what to do.

"Give it back, you can't do nothin', no one can do nothin'! Git! Git out! Git out 'fore I make sure you stay in dis place forever!"

Jack runs back to Bee.

"Can we leave now?" he says, wiping tears away with his arm.

"Yes, Jack. I'm sorry. Yes, we can go. Let's see my family now, *ça va*?"

"Please," he says, and in a blink they are back on Sorrow land. "What is that all about, anyway?"

"Who knows. I don't have any answers . . . but just look, Jack! Sorrow Hall. Isn't it grand?" she says.

"I've seen it like this before, sort of. Not as real, or perfect, though."

"How? Do you have magic?"

"All Sorrows have magic."

"Really? Mother says it's a gift from the devil, and we don't have it because she's from God. I've never been able to do anything magical, and I've tried with Rosella."

Jack knows Rosella is the one history remembers as the voodoo witch. But he doesn't say it. "Well, you're here, ain't you? You got magic f'true."

"You speak like you don't read enough, *mon cher.*"

"And you talk like you read too much, little girl."

"There is no such thing as reading too much. And I'm only a little younger than you. And probably much older when you think on it."

They walk up onto the lawns.

"These are my sisters. Aren't they beautiful? SuzyNell is the prettiest, but she's planning on eloping. No one knows I know, but I do. And Mae, Lavinia, Grace . . . and Edwina, who looks mostly like Mama, though with dark hair. They can't see us. I love having sisters, do you have sisters?"

"I do. Only I just found out."

"How come you only just find out?"

"I don't know how to explain it."

"Was she the one who called to you?"

"Yes, she was."

"Does that make you sad that you don't know her very well?"

"Does it make you sad that your sisters can't see you here?"

"It used to. Oh! Look! There I am! I'm pretty, too."

"You are. But that's got to be strange, Bee. Seein' yourself like that."

"A little, but you get used to it." She sighs, gazing happily at her family. "Want to see what really makes me sad?" she asks, her face falling.

"If you want to show me, Bee," Jack agrees. He doesn't wish to feel sad, but he'd rather be here than stuck in that strange room looking at his sleeping body, unable to wake.

They walk into the house, and the world loses its fixed nature. All the walls seem hard and soft at the same time, like a sheer curtain tinted in blue. "This way . . . ," she says, climbing the stairs. "Stand here."

Jack and Belinda stand on one end of a long hallway flanked with open porticoes out to second-story porches.

"Here she comes," Bee says softly.

A woman, dressed in a beautiful yet prim gown, with light blond hair piled on her head, is opening and shutting each of the doors along the corridor. She's holding a set of silver rosary beads and kissing them as she worries down the hall. "That's my mother, Helene."

"I know," says Jack.

"Hush!" Bee whispers sharply.

Jack reaches out to hold Bee's hand. She lets him.

"It gets worse," she says.

The hall grows longer, and Helene begins her searching in and out of the doors with more speed; only the faster she goes, the more her image lingers, like the tail of a shooting star. She's crying, then weeping, now screaming, in slow motion through the hall.

"*Where are you?* Come to me, oh darlings! I've lost you!"

Bee is crying, too.

"Let's go," Jack says.

They are inside the lighthouse now.

"This is my favorite place of all." Bee smiles faintly.

"It's nice in here. Safe."

"I don't understand why Mother is so upset."

"Bee, do you know what happened? Everything that happened to your family?"

"No, I can only visit : . . see . . . whatever magic this may be, until the day Sister Vesta Grace arrives. That was us waiting for her on the lawn. Do you know, Jack? Is it terribly sad? If it is, don't say a word."

She reaches up and touches her finger to his lips.

Jack doesn't say a word.

26

Sippie Faces Her Past

She knew she wasn't awake because the rain wasn't touching her, even though she was out in front of 13 Bourbon and not in that strange little room with Jack. She wanted to scream, because she wasn't able to do what she came to do.

Then she saw him.

"Eight Track!" she called out. They went running toward each other, meeting up in a twirling dramatic sort of hug in the middle of the street.

"Sippie! What you doin' out in this mess? Those people you livin' wit crazy? Go on now, find somewhere's to go."

"No storm can hurt me, I been blown around by more than this."

"Wait, Sippie, how come the rain and wind don't touch us? Where we at?" he asked.

"I don't really know . . . inside a dream, or a memory. But I'm scared."

"Why, honey?"

"Because I think you're dead, Eight Track, and I don't want you to be."

"I think you right, Sippie girl. But if I am, I'm supposed to be. I'm a weak man."

"No, you ain't. You just lost."

"I thought I'd found my purpose when Frankie gave you to me, but I was wrong."

"Can't never find yourself in someone else . . . you taught me that. And you taught me to be strong. Because *you're* strong."

"No, I'm not. But I'm okay with knowin' that. And you gotta be on your way now, Sippie. And don't you worry 'bout me. You gave me more love than any temp daddy could've hoped for all these years. Go, be safe."

Sippie watched him shuffle away from her, as she had over and over again growing up. And finally, all that anger at watchin' him go broke through and she allowed herself to speak her mind.

"Wait! I need you! You come back here. Right now! *I need you.*"

He turned slowly, making his way back to her, smiling. "What you need?"

"I got to face something. And I think you got to bring me there."

"I think you right, honey." Eight Track pointed: 13 Bourbon was alive, overflowing with people and laughter.

Sippie had to find Simone, but somehow as she slept, she was small again, right back in that night, the last night Simone sang at 13 Bourbon. She found herself in Eight Track's arms, neither of them able to do much more than watch. It was like stepping inside of a movie.

"I didn't need to remember this," she whispered.

"She brought you here that night?"

"Yessir."

"Why didn't you never tell me?"

"Because I didn't want you to be mad."

"So you knew, somewhere deep inside, that these Sorrows were your people," Eight Track said quietly. "I think maybe I understand why we both here, baby girl."

"I've tried too hard to forget it. Wish I was with Crow, it was better being inside his eyes."

"You got me, and I ain't leavin' you till we done with this."

Simone was just finishing her set. Sippie watched her go into the office and fight with Millie. Then she went upstairs, those red heels of hers taking each step with certainty. Eight Track and Sippie followed slowly after.

"Give her some time in there, Sippie."

"This my dream or yours? I just want to fast-forward. I don't want to see her, Eight Track. Don't let me."

"There's got to be a reason, Sippie. Be brave."

They walked through the door and saw Simone already on the bed. Sippie tried to look away, wake herself up, tried to unsee what couldn't be unseen, Simone seizing up until she was still and her eyes blank.

"How old were you, six?" Eight Track asked.

"Yes."

"Too little to know what was what, I suppose. Frances send you here? She took a risk, could lose you, too, if what you see don't set right inside yo' heart."

"What else do I have to see?"

"I don't think that last bit was for you, I think that was for me. So I knew she tried to protect you at the end of it all, that she was tryin' to give us all a chance at somethin' better. I feel lighter, Sippie girl. But if you ready, I think I know what you need. And I feel good being able to give it to you. Come on now, you come hold my hands, I take you."

When she looked around, they were standing in a field of wild violets. Oceans of them. Across the field stood a shack with a small tin chimney and a woman hanging white linens on a line. She was humming a song, and she had a beautiful voice. A little girl, black as night and wearing nothing but a white nightgown, came running outside.

"Where are we?"

"Dis a bayou right by Meager Swamp near where you come from. So small it never got no name. And dat, Sippie, is our Simone. Not da grown-up woman—that be Simone's mama—da little girl all full of light right there is Simone. You didn't do nothin' to her. See, some of us are born strong, some are born weak. Dat's just the way it is. Claudette, she's a lot like Simone, can't be what she ain't. I'm weak, like I said. You and Frances, you be different. You got to know dat all the things people do, they start long before you ever came into the world. And dat's why you got to be careful with what you do, so you can change all this."

The little girl went up to the linens on the line and reached to touch the sunlight that came streaming through them. She was backhanded quick and fierce by her mama, who didn't even look when she fell down into the dirt.

A man came out of the house and chased the little girl into the violets. She kept crying out for her mama, but the woman just went back to humming and hanging clothes.

"I can't see anymore. I don't want to watch this. I want to go now," said Sippie.

"I love you, Sippie girl . . . but see . . . she didn't leave you, honey. She was never there at all. You got to know that. You ain't responsible for the way people hurt you. They hurt you 'cause they all hurt inside, too."

It was time to wake up and fix the future.

27

Rescue Me

Frances and Danny

When Danny burst onto the third floor, I had to hush him. "You be quiet, she's sleeping."

He looked at me. "What's the matter with her?"

"Danny, the whole world has gone crazy," I said, wrapping my arms around myself.

He went to the door of my room and walked in quietly. I followed. He double-checked the storm shutters on the window and put a lantern on the marble-topped dresser. "Lights will be off soon, I don't want her in the dark," he whispered.

Danny and I tiptoed out of the room, and before we closed the door, we looked in on her, just like when Jack was born and we'd stare at him for hours. We just couldn't believe he was ours.

"It doesn't change, as they get older. I still look at Jack like that when he's sleeping," said Danny, closing the door gently.

"Danny, I'm not sure . . . I don't know if . . ."

"I know. I know she's mine. I don't need a test or sixteen years of memories. She's as much mine as she is yours. And that's all the conversation we're gonna have about that. Now, sit your ass down and listen to me without talking for once because I had quite a ride here and I've been rethinking almost all the things I ever thought. And I don't know when I'll feel crazy enough to talk like this again, so hear me out. Now, look . . ." He began pacing. "I know things been good with us, and I know we are right in the middle of something that's too big to imagine, but I got to tell you—"

"So say it, Danny. Just say it," I interrupted.

He shook his head, smiling. "You never could just sit and listen, could you? All right, fine. Frances, the only thing I've ever wanted was you. Just you. You how you are. Not changed or normal or ordinary or wearing shoes. Just *you*."

"Danny, don't lie to me, not now," I said. My heart was beating so fast, I thought it might burst.

"Well, then what exactly is it you think I wanted? I'm not going to fight with you about this. You used to say I didn't hear you, but I heard every damn thing you ever said. I heard every eye roll and sigh. Only you don't believe me. So you tell me, what do you think I wanted?"

There wasn't any hate in his voice. He was serious, his words honest. So I put everything raw I had on the line.

"You wanted to play football. You wanted to travel the world and live in a great big city and be a lawyer. You wanted Bonnie Belmonte, the blond girl with the perfect clothes and padded bra. Danny, I was the worst thing to ever happen to you."

I looked up, expecting to see his expression cloud over with what he liked to call "the Frances effect" when he didn't think *I* was listening. But instead, that damn man was smiling.

"Bonnie Belmonte? You can't be serious." He started laughing.

"I'm dead serious. When kids, you came to that Christmas festival of lights on the bayou. I was there and you came up to me, asking me out. All your friends were laughing behind you. There you were, making a fool of me, and I hardly knew you, but man, did I have a crush on you! Who didn't? But whenever I tried to talk to you over the next year, you didn't talk to me at all. Next thing I know, Pete's telling Old Jim about how you're going out with the 'prettiest girl,' Bonnie Belmonte, while he was pumping gas and I almost threw up."

"Frances, I'm gonna say something right now and I don't want you to take it the wrong way. . . ."

"Go ahead."

"I was a thirteen-year-old boy. What in God's name did you think was goin' on in my mind? Besides, you turned me down that night."

"I don't care how young you were. You were careless with me, and you continued that mean-ass pattern for years. Thirteen, seventeen, twenty-two, thirty-five. It's all the same."

"I was careless with you? Damn, girl, you broke my heart. You broke it that night when you said no. You broke it when you shut me out before I left for college and all I wanted to do was go to school and keep my sweetheart. You broke it again when you tried so hard to be someone you weren't that I forgot who we both were. . . . What was I supposed to do?"

My mind went in a thousand different directions. I'd broken his heart? What was he talking about? He must be remembering incorrectly, because I couldn't have manufactured such an evil indifference. Could I?

But that's exactly what had happened. I'd been screaming so loud for love, I couldn't hear him whispering over the thousand years of days we had together. And by the time we were at the end, all that tight resentment was all our minds and mouths could taste.

"Frances . . . you want the whole truth? Here it is. All those things you used to say, the things I denied, they were true. Hell, I wish they weren't. Feeling that way made me ashamed. And now that I know the reason why you were all caught up inside, I'm even more ashamed. If I'd known . . . But it doesn't matter, we can't go back. So, yes, you embarrassed me sometimes. Yes, I blamed you for stealing away those things I thought I wanted. Yes, you frustrated me. Yes, I didn't want to understand you. But you are everything to me, Gypsy. My whole world. You and Jack and now Sippie. Nothing means anything without you. It's like food with no salt or somethin'."

He'd sat down on the sofa with his head in his hands. I went over, putting my arms around him, and he pulled me on his lap.

"Are we going to be able to fix this up, Dan? Make it right?" I asked.

"We can try. The worst thing that can happen if we try to piece it back together is that we can't make it just what we want it to be. You know, like new. But if we don't try at all, the worst thing already happened. Right?"

"Who likes things brand-new anyway?" I whispered, kissing him on the head. "Now—" A knock interrupted. "Probably Abe," I said, getting up to open the door. But instead: "Why, hello, Mr. Craven," I said. "I can't thank you enough for those journals, but there are pages missing. And, it seems, they are the ones we need the most."

"Oh, my!" he said, looking past me. "Is that the mirror? Why, yes . . . it is. I tell you," he said, walking past us, taking off his jacket, and rolling up his sleeves as if he were going to fix a car. "Stunning! Absolutely stunning!" Mr. Craven clapped his hands, aflutter with nervous energy. "And it's so nice to touch it. To run one's hands along the history of it, don't you think? Miss Frances, come here," he said. I walked forward, and he reached out, bringing my hands up to the mirror. He placed them on the frame so I was grasping it on both ends. "Can't you just *feel* the history pouring out of this mirror?" he asked.

I looked at him skeptically. I couldn't. But then the corner of a smile began because behind one hand I *could* feel a large raised bump on the mirror backing.

"The missing pages?"

"It could be, Frances. Let's find out, shall we? Help me here, Danny."

The two of them pried the back off the mirror just enough to take out what we already knew in our hearts were the lost pages of Monroe's journal.

"But why are they here?"

"It just so happens that I came across a little bill of sale while I was going through old Albert's things. It was for the refinishing of one large mirror. It was quite costly. So I thought, why would he do that? And I came here to you, in the hopes it was still among your many valuable possessions."

He put on his jacket and went for the door.

"Don't you want to read it with us?"

"Oh, my, no. I'll read it on my own later. What a treat. I think I'll have some dinner. The smells from downstairs are so entic-ing!" he called out as he flew out the door and down the stairs.

"Read it out loud, Frankie," said Danny after Mr. Craven was gone. "This is what you were talking about, right? That these pages will tell us where he is?"

"They should."

"Then read."

28

The Shell Seekers

Jack and Belinda

Jack looks out over the Gulf of Mexico with Belinda B'lovely at his side. They are on Saint Sabine Isle—he's explored it before, but it is not at all as he remembers.

In this world, it's a thriving luxury resort teeming with pretty little cottages and people milling about in old-fashioned bathing suits, sunning happily on the sand. He watches the Sorrows playing with one another, Helene resting under a tree.

"She's pregnant with Egg. This is before. I'm still little, see?"

He sees a chubby child with a red bow holding fast to her father's legs.

"I miss him and I miss my sisters and brother, but mostly I miss my mother. I didn't know how much I loved her until I couldn't smell her anymore. She smelled like moonflowers. I want to tell her I'm sorry for leaving her. And I want to find someone else . . . someone I . . ."

Belinda suddenly grows pale, transparent. Jack reaches out, his hand only barely able to touch her cheek.

"You're fading, Bee."

"I think . . . I think I am. I must be able to go to them now. What is this magic of yours, Jack? Must another child inhabit this place for me to be free? Are we making a switch?"

"I hope not." He really hopes not.

"Hold my hand," says Bee. "Think about where your body is. Think hard, Jack."

He grabs her hand as the scenery melts around them. They're back in New Orleans. It is night, and they are standing near a sad tomb that Millie once showed him on a trip into town.

The Lost Girl of August.

"I know it all now," says Bee looking at the stature. "I remember it all. It's so very sad . . . and still, I feel free."

They stand there, stuck in time, quiet together.

"What happened to me won't happen to you, Jack."

"Why not?"

"I was sick, Jack. So sick. Not sleeping at all. And I think, because of the fever, I was half on the other side already. I could watch and follow everyone around me while my body just lay there. You know how that feels, right?"

"It scares me, Bee."

"It scared me, too, at first, but then, when I'd lay back down inside that fevered soul, I felt like a hundred rocks were piled on me already. I missed my family. Even Mae. So I started to stay inside that place more and more. Then, one day, a naughty orphan ran away from the nuns and they found him standing at the foot of my bed."

"This won't do," said Sister Rose. *"We must make a secret door with a secret lock for protection."*

Sister Rose went down to Frenchman's Street and had a key fashioned in the shape of a mermaid tail.

"Isn't that fanciful, Sister. Wouldn't it be more appropriate to have one made with a crucifix?" asked the locksmith.

I wished so hard just then that I could give her a hug.

Bee's face grew long and sad. "Sister Rose . . . I wonder what happened to her? In the end, she was my best keeper."

"They locked you in?"

"I don't know if it was to keep me safe or to keep others away from my illness, but yes, they locked me in. And then, in time, I died."

"You died?" *Dida* . . . thinks Jack.

"I did. But not because I was sleeping for a long time, there is no magic as strong as that. It was because I caught ill from being in the water so long. It got into my lungs. The sisters buried me right here. It was the most beautiful thing. My father's lawyer, he came to the little funeral, and Sister Rose gave him that key that she'd made. She was crying, *mon Dieu,* so sad. Then I found my soul attached to that key, in Albert's hand as he made his way back onto Saint Sabine Isle, so broken and torn by the storm, like all of us. He tossed the key into the Gulf. I like to think that I am, perhaps, a mermaid."

Jack doesn't know what to say or do. He can feel the weight of her lonesomeness deep in his heart.

"Look, who's that?" asks Bee.

Jack sees Millie running against the wind, holding a shawl around her, her wild hair blowing every which way.

"That's Millie, she's the one who put me up there." He points to the little dark window nailed shut on the top floor.

"Looks like she's come to get you! Lucky, lucky boy. Let's see!"

Jack and Bee follow Millie up the stairs. She's crying and talking to herself. She even laughs a few times.

"Damn spell book, damn lies, damn witches! Please . . . please . . . please . . ."

She reaches a small bookcase, moves it aside, and then turns the knob. Back and forth and back again. The door holds fast.

"How is it locked? There was no key. Was there a latch?" Millie falls to her knees and feels inside the keyhole, then looks inside.

"It was open, the door was open. And I shut it . . . and there must be, oh . . . God, a spring lock?"

Setting down her lantern, she sits on the top of the marble staircase.

"Well, Millie, seems to me you got two options. Go back to Thirteen Bourbon and tell them what you've done, which includes stealing Jack, and a host of other things that are *most* unpleasant. Or you can leave. And quick."

She stands up, running a hand through her thick hair. "But if I leave, how can I be sure they'll find him in time? Oh, *puh-lease,* this is Danny and Frances we're talking about. They have everything they need. They'll figure it out. And Danny'll hatchet down that damn door."

Millie runs back down the stairs and out into the storm.

Jack and Bee watch her walk backward toward Bourbon. She gives a strange little salute and then . . . she was gone.

"*Mon Dieu,* she's leaving you here!"

"You got left here, too, remember?"

"Yes, Jack. And I am *still* here. There is no happy ending. Not yet."

They sit down together on the marble tomb of the Lost Girl of August, their chins resting in their palms, both wondering what to do next.

Time is strange and full of errors in the in-between. Soon, or perhaps much later, Jack looks up to see, through the rain that touched everything but them, tiny lights bouncing toward them.

"Bee? Are those the *feux follets*? I don't want to be caught up like that."

"Don't be such an idiot, Jack. Those aren't *feux follets,* those are lanterns. And I think . . . oh Jack, I think those are your parents. . . ."

"It's time to wake up, Jack. It's time," she says, walking away from him.

Jack is filled with a sudden, wrenching ache.

"Don't leave me, Bee,"

"Oh, Jack. Don't you see? Leaving is just another way to say moving on. We can never be afraid of moving on. I've been afraid, but you brought the brave back to me. Thank you."

"Wait! Bee!" yells Jack, reaching out for Belinda B'Lovely Sorrow. "Let me fix your bow."

29

Missing Pieces

Frances

The missing pages from the Journals of Albert Monroe:

"Help us," Sister Vesta cried out again, beginning to fall forward.

I rescued the child from her arms, and Sister Vesta fell against my body. Limp like a rag doll. "Mr. Solace, can you help me?" I shouted to the man who tends bar.

"Of course, sir," he said, and when he rounded the corner: "Oh, my dear, sweet Lord," as he picked up Vesta. We brought them both to the lounge, and I ran for blankets. Mr. Solace shooed out the late drinkers from the bar and went to make something hot for them to drink.

"Albert, we can't stay here. We need to keep her safe. Take me to the convent. The Ursuline Convent, a few blocks down. I swear, I wasn't going to involve you. I thought I could make it there, but after all the miles I walked, I could barely make it here."

She was feverish and stuttering.

Mr. Solace brought warm tea.

"The child, she wakes continually but can't seem to come out from the deep sleep she is in. She's under some sort of spell, I swear it. I told you, I've read their books, studied their ways. This is Rosella's doing. Please, for the love of God, take us to the Ursulines."

That's when I noticed that Vesta was wearing her nun's attire.

I wrapped Vesta up in a blanket and carried her, while Mr. Solace followed with Belinda.

"Tell them we need sanctuary," she implored as I climbed the steps, fighting back the rain, wondering how on earth she could have walked so far, so fast, in such conditions.

Two nuns answered the door, holding lanterns.

"She needs sanctuary for herself, this child, and their souls. Can you help us?"

They ushered us in, but when we tried to place them in the beds the sisters led us to, Vesta leaned forward from my arms, whispering in the ear of one of the nuns.

Understanding crossed her face, and she nodded, motioning for us all to follow.

We climbed what seemed like endless flights of steps, and then, on the very top floor of the building, they opened a small door.

It was a beautiful space, with beds covered in fine lace linens. We placed Vesta and Belinda down, watching as the nuns rang a bell and deftly got to work with basins of hot water and fresh, warm nightdresses.

"You must leave now, sir," said the sister to whom Vesta had whispered. "My name is Sister Rose and you can rest knowing you have left these two lost souls in God's loving arms."

"Will I be able to visit with her?"

She looked toward Vesta, who nodded.

"When she is well enough, we will send word."

The doors shut behind us, and all I could do was wait.

I tried to be patient, distracting myself by helping where I could with cleanup from the storm.

Finally, two days after we left them, Mr. Solace found a note slipped under the front door when he opened the bar.

Mr. Monroe,

Vesta is quite ill with fever. She will see you now. Come when you can, we fear there isn't much time.

Sister Rose

When I arrived, Sister Rose led me to the downstairs infirmary. Vesta was lying in a bed, very still, among victims of the storm.

"Where is the child?" I asked.

"We will not speak of her, Mr. Monroe. You did not find her. She does not exist," said Sister Rose sternly.

As I began to protest, Vesta called out to me weakly.

"Albert?"

I went and sat by her, holding her hand.

"It seems you will get your confession after all, Albert." She smiled faintly.

"Just rest, Vesta. You need say nothing. I do not doubt your innocence. I never did."

"Then you are wrong. Listen, so that we may keep her safe. . . .

"When I first arrived at the Sorrow Estate, Egg, *cher bébé Egg,* was in so much pain. Every little thing bruised or broke him. Every cut bled him until he could not draw air. He was loved, *so loved,* but he was also a very sick little boy. And his crying. Oh God, it still haunts me how he cried.

"I tried everything to ease his pain. But nothing seemed to work.

"I'd met Rosella and she seemed very kind during those first days. She pulled me aside in the kitchen and told me to go see her mother, Patrice, who lived deep in the bayou."

" 'But Helene was adamant that I only use standard healing practices,' I said, surprised.

" 'Sister Vesta, Helene is not well herself, deluded and worn thin. Egg is *suffering*. My mother can give you something to help. Why not try? For Egg? *C'est bon?*'

"The next day I took my basket and told Helene I would be going to the market in Tivoli Proper. Leon took me across the bayou. When I found Patrice, she gave me a small bag of powder.

" 'This will end his suffering, *ma chère*. He is bayou born and bred. He need a bayou cure.'

"I swear, Albert, it did not cross my mind, not for one second, that it was anything more than a folk remedy. I followed her instructions and gave it to him mixed inside warm milk.

"He did not wake up the next morning."

"But Vesta, you could not have . . ."

She brought her finger to her lips to hush me.

"The grieving was terrible, as you can imagine, and then, everyone seemed to get ill. I noticed after some time that Helene's hair was thinning and her teeth were soft. I noticed that all the girls, except Belinda, suffered from terrible stomach pains. I thought perhaps it was an allergy. I know, I would laugh at myself if I could. But so much was being written in the medical books about allergies. I wrote to my sister-nurses in Baltimore and they told me that a new article had been written about the curative effects of honey. Indigenous honey. I spoke with Edmond, and he agreed to pay for the hives and the equipment. He insisted Rosella, who knew more about nature than I, help with the placement of the hives. Soon, our honey was being given to them with breakfast and lunch.

"But much to my dismay, they all seemed to grow even more ill.

"Six months after Egg died, SuzyNell eloped. Her absence sparked only more grieving. Rosella, Edmond, and Helene had a terrible argument about it. Helene was convinced it was Rosella's doing. That she wanted to steal all her children away. And I was so ashamed, because Edmond called her crazy—only I knew the truth. Because Rosella had taken Egg's life, through my hands.

"Then, it all unraveled.

"I was the one who sent them out to play croquet, knowing Mae was in a sad and sorry state. She was angry at the world, missing SuzyNell, and she took it out on the croquet ball with her mallet. And that ball, a metal one, part of a set from France, hit Edwina in the head, in the temple. She was killed instantly. I told Mae no one had to know. When asked, I said we didn't know how Edwina got hit with the ball. But Mae was so full of guilt. She could barely look at Helene. And each time Helene reached for her, she ran. I should have let Mae confess, it was an accident, after all. Because shortly after, filled with guilt, Mae walked into Sorrow Bay and got caught up in the current beyond the lighthouse. Edmond didn't even wait for Mae's funeral. You found him, did you not, hanging in his study at Thirteen Bourbon?"

A chill ran through me as I nodded, remembering.

"After, the twins succumbed to the illness I was trying to cure in the first place, and Helene followed Edmond to the noose. I'd gone to get Rosella because Helene insisted. When we arrived,

Helene was hanging from the live oak on the front lawn, her face illuminated by a bonfire she'd set next to her. When Leon finally put out the fire, we realized Helene had her last moment of defiance. She'd set fire to the portrait of Serafina Sorrow."

Vesta leaned back, closing her eyes.

"This was a cursed coincidence, Vesta. None of this is your fault."

"Albert, I was the one who listened to Rosella about where to put the hives. And do you know where they were? Next to wild oleander. The honey I was feeding them to make them well was poisoning them. I killed them all. I was complicit—" Her voice broke.

"You did no such thing."

"Albert, there is one more sin on my conscience, one more thing you must help do. I must save at least one of them."

Vesta's face was damp with sweat, and her eyes had grown dazed.

"Anything," I said.

"Keep Belinda hidden. Tell no one. Not SuzyNell. No one. Rosella put a curse on her, some kind of fever dream. I'm sure she intends to kill her as well. Or worse. I found her in the lighthouse, Albert. You see . . .

"At first, I tried to be brave, staying all alone in my little cottage. But then, when the last candle burned out, I ran against the wind to the estate. Soon, though, the wind blew the windows out from the back gallery, and I looked and saw the reflection of rain on the windows of the lighthouse. I didn't want to die. And it seemed the safest place. The waters were raging, but something in me knew I had to get there. I let the current take me. The tiny island had not yet been swallowed up. So, relieved, I went in, and tried to wait out the storm. But not long after, I saw the water begin to pour into the foundation, and as that water rose up, I floated up with it. And when I got close to the ceiling, there was a small round handle. And when I pulled it, climbing up into the cramped top of that strange little house, there she was, Belinda. Sleeping.

"I broke a window, waiting for the waters to rise higher, and then put my arms around her waist and swam, as slow and steady as I could, against the storm. And I prayed, Albert. I prayed, and I do believe, for the first time in too long, God listened.

"When I was back on estate grounds, I saw Rosella struggling against the terrible confused currents at the mouth of Sorrow Bay. She was in a small boat, screaming into the wind, like a madwoman. *'Give her back to me!'* she yelled above the dying winds. *'Give her back!* She is mine. . . .'

"So I ran, Albert. I ran with this girl in my arms. And I steadied my own boat, and too afraid to take to the roads, I ran through the swamps. I fell, so many times. Finally, I gave up and went to the road. That is when God found me again. Leon was driving his horse through the rain. We'd hit the eye of the storm and he was trying to get to New Orleans.

"He lifted Belinda in the carriage, and I said, 'If you ever loved them, you will not speak of this. If you want to live, you will not speak of this.'

"I made him drop us off many blocks from you, Albert. And had you bring us here. I trusted the sisters and was sure they would know what to do. And now you must leave her. Leave me. Leave all of this."

"Vesta, we *must* make this known. Bring Rosella to justice."

"She will have her day. Before God. Sister Rose is caring for Belinda now and for as long as she stays cursed by that terrible woman. It will be your job to help me keep this quiet until we know Belinda is safe. Do you understand, Albert? I know you do. I see you taking notes in your head. You will document this; it's in your nature. Hide it, hide this, Albert. That way, someday, the world can know the truth, when they are ready to listen. That way, Rosella will be known for the villain that she is. And by then, we will all be gone in the arms of God. You will keep everything quiet; I see it in your eyes, Albert. You finally understand."

And so I hide this account, as she asked, in the hopes that the truth it reveals will help others see the truth as well,

Sincerely,

Albert Monroe.

"He's in the convent," I said. "Not two blocks away."

"Let's go," said Danny.

"Wait, let me tell her, I want to tell her," I said, quietly opening the door to my room. I leaned in and went to Sippie, kissing her forehead. "We found him, love. Safe, just like you said. I'll go get him right now. When you wake up from wherever you are, you know that I'll be right back, that I'm never leaving you again."

I came back out. "You ready?" I asked Danny. Then I saw the crowbar in his hands. The one we kept to prop open the windows in the atrium in the summer. I smiled.

"I am," he said.

Danny held his crowbar, and I held a lantern. Out in the storm, he walked and I ran beside him, two steps for each of his long strides.

"Wait," I said, a strange feeling washing over me.

"What?"

I turned around and looked up the street. Millie was standing there, watching us.

"*Give him back to me!*" I yelled, echoing the pages I'd just read.

"I don't have him, Frankie. But you know where he is. Just go get him. Leave me alone." Millie looked sadder than I'd ever seen her.

"What do you want to do?" asked Danny.

"You go on, I don't see him with her. I'll be right there."

"No police around, Gypsy. You gonna be okay?"

"She won't hurt me. Soon she'll be gone, and I won't see her again. And, I might never really know why she did all this. I *need* to know. I'll be right there, promise."

Danny pressed forward into the wind. I turned around, heading straight for her.

"*Millie!!*"

She looked up, unmoving. But when I got within half a block of her, she yelled, "You just stay right there, Frankie. I'm leaving. You don't have to bother with me. You figured it all out like I knew you would, and Jack is fine. In a few minutes you'll have everything you ever wanted."

"But I won't have you."

I thought she'd yell back something terrible. But she didn't, she just stood there, like she didn't know what to do at all. Suddenly I knew we'd arrived at that moment in time when the future would crack open and set multiple paths.

"Why?" I asked.

"I don't know if I really know the answer to that. Or maybe it's real simple. Maybe it's 'Why not?'"

"I don't believe that. This is what you do, try to evil your way out of everything," I shouted, exasperated.

"Maybe you just think I'm a better person than I really am. Maybe I wanted to be a mother, a wife, a daughter . . . or maybe I was just sick of taking care of you, of worrying about you. Or maybe I was scared I didn't have to worry anymore. Whatever it is, it doesn't matter anymore, I'm leavin'."

She opened the truck door and got inside. She tore off fast but skidded to a stop in front of me, banging the steering wheel.

"Damn! I wish you didn't bring out the nice inside me. I was all set to leave you, but I . . ."

"What?"

"There's a door behind a bookcase. I didn't mean to lock it, Frances, I swear it. I was trying to get him out but couldn't."

"To take him away? Or bring him back?"

"I don't know. Maybe I hadn't made up my mind. I just wanted you to know."

She skidded away again, only this time, she seemed to take the entire storm with her.

Danny was waiting for me at the wide front doors of the Ursuline Convent. "Who knew a hurricane could make things in this town convenient?" he said, throwing them open. "Don't have to worry about anybody getting in our way. You okay?"

"I am. I think. Let's get Jack. This storm just changed course, people'll be filling up these streets too soon."

Danny threw open those wide doors and we walked in, side by side.

"Now where?" he asked.

"Up," I said.

"What did Millie say to you?" he asked.

"I don't think we'll ever know why she did this or where she's going," I responded sadly. He gave my hand a squeeze as we went up the dark stairs.

We found the little bookcase on the top floor just like Millie said.

Danny walked straight to it, shoving it aside. And there was the hidden door. He went to turn the knob.

"Dan. Wait. It's locked."

I reached around my neck, lifting out the key I'd worn for ages on a bit of ribbon. The one he'd given me before the world fell to pieces. *"Of course,"* I thought . . . *"of course . . ."*

"She came from the sea," I said, handing it to him.

It fit perfectly, and the spring lock popped back, and there he was, our Lost Boy.

Jack looked so peaceful in that white wrought-iron bed, burrowed safely in pillows and quilts. Something inside of me thanked Millie for making him so comfortable.

Love is complicated.

Danny sat on one side and I on the other. We both kissed him, shaking him gently. "Jack, baby, time to wake up. . . . Jack?" we whispered softly.

It felt like forever before he stretched, yawned, looked around the room, and said, "You guys back together again? Damn, when I have an idea, it sure is a good one!"

"You are in a heap of trouble, boy," said Danny, burying us both in a hug so big and so tight, I thought we might get lost in it.

When we got back, the TV over the bar flickered on—like most things Sorrow, it had a mind of its own—and a news guy reported the storm had suddenly died down and shifted course entirely. That southern Louisiana would be spared.

"I trusted her, Mama. I really did. And I know I shouldn't have . . . ," said Jack, walking up the stairs. I felt dizzy with relief and guilty about Millie.

"Go easy on Millie, Jack. Sometimes it's real hard to be our best selves," I said.

"I guess so," Jack said thoughtfully.

We got to the apartment and walked in. "Because, Jack . . . see, your mama was not her best self for a long, long time. I . . . Jack, look at me, I have something to tell you."

"Jack, look at your mother," said Danny, trying to sound harsh, but still so damn happy to see him.

"Where's my—," he asked, ignoring us. That boy, I swear.

"I'm right here, Jack."

"Sippie!" he said, running to her. They held on to each other for a long time, while I told Danny about the dream Sippie had—the one that brought us all together—and grabbed extra quilts and pillows, making them a bed on the floor under a makeshift fort of sheets and blankets and old gowns.

Danny and I went to bed, listening to the sound of dying winds and stifled laughter. I couldn't help thinking about all the years they could have had together. Years I stole from them.

"Don't look backward, Frankie," Danny said, as if reading my mind. "We have right now."

Sometimes we lose things for a reason. We lose them because we wouldn't ever know their true value otherwise.

30

Rosella's Defense

Frances

A knocking sound coming from the mirror woke me up. I got up, slowly moving to stand in front of it, only it wasn't me looking back. It was another wild-haired woman, looking lost.

I began to place my hands against the mirror, but she shook her head. And then walked straight on through. It's one thing to question whether or not you walked through a mirror into another time. It's a heck of another thing altogether watching someone else do it. But, I suppose, *reality* on 13 Bourbon Street could be *skewed,* as Mr. Craven said. It made some sort of odd sense.

Besides, she was standing right in front of me!

Her face was bathed in a growing light—was it morning, was the storm over?—and she wasn't blurry at the edges or an echo of a feeling. She was as real as anything else around me. The room became bathed in sunlight. And though it looked unchanged, Jack and Danny and Sippie were nowhere to be seen, and the blanket fort had completely disappeared. The old furniture was a little newer, the carpet far less worn. And the smell, that was different, too, a perfume of figs and rain I remember inhaling from the trunks of clothes we used to play dress-up in at Sorrow Hall. Spicy and old-fashioned.

"This was my room," she said. She sat on a wingback chair next to the windows. They were no longer cracked or dirty, they sparkled. She smoothed back her thick, dark brown hair, attempting to refasten some hairpins in her easy bun.

"Rosella," I said.

"Don't fret, *ma chère*," she said, taking a hairpin from her mouth and trying once more to tame her curls. "Your children and your man are still safe and sleeping, you and I just need to have a little visit, *ça va*?"

She had a kind, clever face and wore a dress that was navy-blue satin with white lace at the cuffs and collar. She didn't look one bit like the voodoo mistress Albert had painted in his journals.

"It seems," she said, "that you have acquired some information about me, Frances."

"I have," I said.

"Well, if you don't mind, I'd like to be given the opportunity to clear up a few things. So maybe I can finally rest. It's not so bad, you know, being caught in time. But I think I'm ready to see what's on the other side. I'd always assumed that once our bones were found, mine and Bee's . . ." She paused, looking out the window. I could tell she was trying to stay the course, to clarify without muddying the water with some ghostly emotion. "I'd thought perhaps we'd be set free."

"That's the way it always happens in the stories."

"Yes, well, those stories are wrong. Or at least they're wrong when it comes to me. Because, as you can see, I've not gone anywhere. I am well aware of that wonderful thing called subjective truth, so I thought the only thing left to do was tell *my* side. Serafina was clear about truths in *The Book of Shadows,* was she not?"

"She was . . ."

We looked at each other, beginning in the same breath, "We must always be mindful of what we see, for how we feel is not the way others see and feel. Let us vow to be like the live oak trees, rooted in a constant, changing landscape, thriving on difference. Yet always knowing who we are and what our own truth is, as we grow ever skyward."

"One of my favorites." Rosella smiled.

"I'd forgotten how many passages I memorized from that book. It's been so long."

"I could reprimand you, as a proper Sorrow witch would, but as you know, I fell from grace long ago."

She stood up, smoothing the skirt of her dress.

"Come, let's retire to the parlor. It's lovely there, and this room holds too much pain for you. I can still feel it."

The door opened on its own as Rosella took my hand, guiding me into the front room. It was full of women dressed in beautiful gowns, practicing one form of fortune-telling or another. I heard one, a pretty little thing with a large bow in her hair, say, "No, Estella, you mustn't ever tell the truth if what you see is bad. That's not why they come to us! If we start telling the truth, we'll lose our business!"

"They were always so dedicated, so talented, our 'grove' of girls. Of all the sad things I watched happen from the other side, the most troubling was the death of our art," Rosella said wistfully. "And, Frances, if it is any consolation to you, you have been on the right side of history."

"How do you mean?" I asked, taking a liking to her.

"One moment," she said, stepping into the middle of the parlor. She clapped her hands twice. An almost incandescent light emerged. It could have been sunshine. "Serafinas! Please leave us. I must meet for a while with our future."

And they were gone.

"That's a nice skill, clapping and making people disappear. I could have used that one," I said.

"Oh, Frances, I'm sure I don't have to explain why we so often do the opposite of what we want. We come from a family . . . many families, no, a people, that have an overabundance of certain types of skills. Our minds, they can do magnificent and terrible things. But I don't want you to think there is any miracle involved. We are at our worst when we try to change things for ourselves. That's why we honed a few of them, the easiest to control. Herbal magic, root work. Talents that could help others and keep us away from the dark art of self-exploration. The reading of minds, the fortune-telling, even the prophecies . . . they only work with willing participants. The cards, runes, bones . . . crystal balls, those are translations of something larger, something we are not evolved enough yet to understand. Most of that is . . . how do you say . . . smoke and mirrors. And through the years, our people began to believe in the pageantry more than we believe in ourselves."

"I found that out the hard way," I said. "And then I shut it all down. I'm just now trying to relearn everything."

She'd sat down on the sofa, smoothing her skirt. "It isn't easy, *ma petite chère*. Telling ourselves the truth is the hardest thing of all."

"And you want me to know your truth, isn't that why I'm here?"

"Yes, I just don't know how to begin. I must admit, there is something delicious about the lies that have been told about me—something far more dark and lovely, more *memorable,* than the truth. A legacy is something I never thought I'd care about. But I don't think I understood what it would feel like to slip through time, watching the traditions you love the most fall to pieces. And then, to know that you are the one who is to blame? *Magnifique, non?*"

I went to her and sat down, breathing in the scent of roses coming from the small veranda as I sat. Topiaries. "It was so lovely then. I wish . . . I never knew it this way. It's dreary here now, like a half-forgotten thought."

"Not like a half-forgotten thought. You have all forgotten *completely.* But I will not judge you for that. Sometimes there are things we should all forget. Maybe you are supposed to let go of all of this. As I was supposed to let go of Edmond." Rosella gazed off into the distance. "Because that is where my story begins."

I curled up on the sofa, and Rosella turned to face me. I could feel the edges of that blue satin dress on my bare shins. It was crisp and new. She took my hand, and we sat like old friends as she told me her side of the story, set herself free. She laughed and cried, the edges of her fading until I could no longer feel the hem of her dress.

"The first thing you need to know is how beautiful he was. I know you must have seen photographs, or paintings, or even his ghost, but nothing . . . none of that could ever do him justice. Oh, Frances, the way he walked, so confident, and with humor, too. And when he left a room, he left a vibrant veil of constant summer in his wake.

"I loved him for my whole life. And he loved me.

"We were supposed to wed. It was determined before we knew what it would mean. When my family settled in Serafina's Bayou and my *maman,* Patrice, became the *traiteuse,* Edmond's family was thrilled because there'd been too many children born 'outside' our people, and we were going to save the family."

That's why Jack is the way he is; Sippie, too.

"I know how that must have felt," I said softly.

"I'm sure you do. And because of that, I'm sure you'll understand what I'm about to tell you next, though I'm still uncertain about my motivations back then.

"The wedding was to be in June of 1887. On the solstice, of course. And Edmond and I were madly in love. Not only in love, we were friends, the best of friends. I don't think a day went by that we didn't laugh about something, share a secret, or show our affection. Which is why he was so angry when I told him I wanted to postpone the wedding."

For a moment, I looked at her, confused. And then understood it perfectly.

"There was this heavy feeling inside me that I should explore, see the world, take advantage of the way the women of Tivoli Parish were unshackled by the rest of society. I never said I didn't want to marry him. I simply wanted to wait. I wanted to go to France and find out more about Serafina. I wanted to dance in the streets and touch all there was to touch in life.

"And I wanted him to come with me.

"I should have known he wouldn't understand. Sorrow or no Sorrow, men do have a peculiar way of hearing things completely false. He thought I was saying he suffocated me or held me back. He thought I wanted to explore the world to see if there was someone else I might love better. As if there were ever a chance of that." She laughed sadly.

"We had a terrible argument that ended with me on a ship

out of Port Orleans, and at the last moment, he'd come to apologize—or so he told me later—and waved to me when he saw me on the deck. But I was angry, so angry. I turned away from him. What a silly girl of a woman I was. If I'd known that he'd go to Thirteen Bourbon that night, get drunk, and decide to fall in love with Helene Dupuis, I would have jumped right off the boat.

"So, if you have heard that I am responsible for the death of that family, then it is true. Because if I'd listened to my heart and not my ego, I wouldn't have altered the course of so many futures."

"You don't know that, Rosella. Maybe you were supposed to go, and Helene was supposed to be his wife. Maybe . . . maybe they were *supposed* to die."

"I would agree with you, *ma chère. Mais non.*" She shook her head. "It was the feeling I had, queasy and straining, as if I'd taken too much of the loss tea. It felt as if I had a hot poison running through my veins. And when I returned, cutting my entire adventure short because my heart was aching, he was already married and on a honeymoon with Helene.

"I will never forget meeting her for the first time. How I hated her. And if you have heard that I seduced Edmond into my arms again . . . how could I not? And if you heard that I practiced the dark magic taught to me by the Cajun women living deep in the bayou, that is true as well. For the first few years of their marriage, I wanted her dead. Out of my life. A life I'd left behind. I was so selfish. I punished her for my decisions. And I punished Edmond, too, because he loved us both. Though I didn't want to admit it at the time. And for some reason, being torn between the two of us tore apart that thing inside of him that made him strong. Year by year, I watched him give in to all his weaknesses. Vices. That is when Helene and I banded together. You seem surprised, Frances. Was this part left out of the story? I thought it might be. But Helene came to me at my little cottage. I must have looked half-crazed that night, chanting and wandering around writing symbols on the walls. I was trying to learn new forms of magic to help him, but nothing was working.

"She asked me to come up to Sorrow Hall and have a drink.

"I believe I may have said, 'I don't drink tea, I spit it out and read your death in the leaves,' or something ridiculous like that.

"That is when she turned to me and smiled, the first real smile between us, and I saw the woman Edmond loved. 'I was going to offer you a glass of port. Come, Rosella, leave this hoodoo behind and have a drink with your enemy out on the back gallery, will you? *Ça va?*'

"I washed up a bit before I joined her. And we sat there, staring out over Sorrow Bay, getting to know each other, taking turns tending to the endless needs of the children. She'd had Mae by then.

"'What shall we do about Edmond?' she asked me.

"'He will not survive the life he is living, Helene. We must try to keep him here, with us. *Safe.*'"

"So, you lived together, the three of you, happily?" I asked, curious.

"For years, yes. *We* did. Until the poison in those Jesus beads ate into Helene's mind, and of course, there was the baby."

"Egg?"

"No, Frances. We have come to the end of my story, because as soon as I say this one piece, you will know the rest. I was Belinda B'Lovely's true mother."

"But why did Helene raise her?" I asked, trying to let the revelation settle inside me slowly. It was as if each word she said opened up new doors of understanding in my mind. *The past is nothing but a reflection in the mirror. It can't harm us, but it can teach us if we let it . . .* I thought.

"Because Edmond gave me no choice." Rosella continued. "Things had changed. Helene had fallen into a wild obsession with religion, and our docile—if odd—years of living together happily had ended. I'd been lucky not to be with child before, and thought maybe that was the true reason the fates had led him to Helene. She'd gone quite mad after the birth of the twins and was no longer letting Edmond in her rooms. Men, such fools. She told him she'd lie with him again only if I allowed her to raise Belinda. And he promised me it would only be for a short while, until he could get her back to some sort of sanity. I didn't know about the oleander. I swear it. *We* did not know about the mercury in those beads. *We* did not know that he was carrying a terrible disease. Belinda . . . well, she had my blood. Our blood. And we managed to stay safe from the madness. That nun, she was no help. Stuck in her beliefs and lying to herself about it. Right before the storm, Belinda came to me, begging me to help her. She was so scared. Scared of the storm, scared she'd die, too. Everyone she loved was gone. Everyone but me. So, I gave her a sleeping tonic and hid her in what I thought was the safest place, the lighthouse while I tried to help others from the remote reaches of the bayou escape the rising waters. But then, that storm, it came on so fast and fierce and sudden. I watched as the water rose higher and higher. I went to save her, I had to save her. I'd put her there. I can't . . ."

"Rosella," I begged her, "you have to know, you didn't do anything wrong, we know that now. But *you* have to know it."

"But I did. I never told her, Frances. She died thinking she was all alone. She didn't know I was her mother. She didn't know.

I've looked and looked for her here, in this place, but I can't find her. And it pains me to think of her, stuck in some other place. Darker. Full of fear and echoes."

That's when I learned that ghost tears glow when they glisten.

"She's right here," Jack spoke up quietly from behind me. I turned to see both my children, Sippie and Jack, on either side of a little girl who looked like a whole bunch of trouble, that crooked red bow in her hair, that gleam in her eye. There was no mistaking it, this was Rosella's child.

Belinda B'Lovely Sorrow let go of Sippie's hand first.

"Good-bye, Sippie, it was a pleasure to meet you. Be good to Jack, he's a nice boy. And boys need more attention than they say."

"Good-bye, Belinda," said Sippie, blinking back tears, trying not to be forced to feel something. I wanted to go to her, but it wasn't our moment. Not yet. We'd have a lifetime of moments.

Then Belinda turned to Jack. "I know we already said good-bye, but I think I need another kiss now that you know I'm not your great-grandma. I tried to tell you a thousand different ways. You are a stubborn person, Jack Amore Sorrow. But I'll miss you very much. *Bonne nuit.*"

My boy kissed her forehead. "Maybe we'll see each other again. You can never tell. I'd like to leave it that way, is that okay, Bee?"

"I know you, Jack. It doesn't matter if it is, as you say, a-okay with me. You will hope for it anyway." She took a deep breath, moving toward Rosella, who sat with her arms open to her daughter.

"I'm so sorry, my darling. *Je t'aime.* I'm so, so sorry." Her arms shook, her hands grasping at the air. Belinda B'Lovely walked into those waiting arms and sat, a perfect fit, in her mother's lap. "*Je suis ta maman,* Bee. I'm your mama." Rosella covered her with kisses. "I never told you. I should have told you. I should have never listened to them. That night, I tried. . . ."

Bee put her finger up to Rosella's lips.

"Shhh, Mama. I know. I always knew. I felt lucky having two mothers. Everyone should be so lucky. Helene smiled at me when she would yell at the others, so worried I would find out the truth that was so clear to me. Did you not know why I always wore the red ribbons? I wore them for you."

"Children always know the secrets parents keep," I said as I pulled my children close to me, wanting to hold them in a way that made them both know that I would never stop holding either of them again. And as they returned my embrace, I watched the room begin to grow worn as the worlds shifted and the smiling sunlight turned into the driving rain of our fleeting storm.

The three of us, along with Danny, and the rest of our family would have to become mapmakers of sorts. We'd be like Serafina, brave, and curious, and honest enough to know that we learn far more from Sorrow than from Bliss. It was the final compass point, allowing us to navigate the distance between who we were and who we could, or would, become with time.

Always time.

31

Renovation and Restitution

Jack and Sippie

Jack and Sippie Sorrow sat on the dock in front of Sorrow Hall, listening to the chaos of party preparations from a close but safe distance. Neither one of them had much interest in doing any more chores. Jack had taken Sippie to explore Rosella's voodoo cabin, which Sippie thought was the coolest thing she'd ever seen. She could almost hear the beats of trance-inducing drums and smell the burning of ancient roots. They'd walked along the thin strip of soggy earth that wound around the bay and ended up back at the front gates. Neither wanted to go back in just yet. Their parents had had them working too hard for too many moons.

Frances hadn't been able to give up the broken beauty of Sorrow Hall being half swallowed up by the natural world. She'd said, "If we're gonna reclaim this old whore of a hall, we better make sure we keep it pretty, like it is." So whoever wasn't working on structural things, roofs and ceilings and rotting beams, those lucky ones got paintbrushes and oils, and whenever a vine or a branch was ripped out of a window frame or crack in the wall, it was painted right back where it was, for eternity. And even though the house was almost the way she wanted it, there they were, touching up painted on cracks right down to the last few hours before Frances and Danny's "not-a-wedding."

Jack had urged Sippie to put down her brush and sneak out while Danny and Frances surveyed the work and got all lovesick with each other.

"I tell you what, Gypsy, the house is still weird," said Danny. "But pretty. Just like you."

As soon as the kissing started, Jack and Sippie made their escape.

Later, on their way back from Rosella's cabin, Jack reached into a deep pool of water in the cypress grove, trying to get some of the paint off his hands.

"So, it's over," he said.

"Or just starting," said Sippie.

"Oh, hey! Here comes the mail boat," he said, pointing down to the front docks. "Maybe that new comic I ordered came."

They raced each other through the maze of gardens to meet it.

"You planning on growing up anytime soon?" Sippie teased as they bounced a bit on the new storm-friendly dock.

"Nope," he answered, and turned to the mailman.

"Here you go, one package, one letter, same sender."

"Thank you, sir," said Jack. "Damn, not for me. One for you and one for Mama. Figures."

"For me?" asked Sippie.

"Just open it."

It was a small box wrapped in plain brown wrapping. Sippie opened it and caught her breath. "It's Simone's pin," she said, holding the opals up to the sun. "It's from Millie."

Understanding flashed across Jack's face.

"Sippie, I got to take you somewhere. Not far from here. Let's cut through the house."

"Where we going? We just got back. You okay, boy? They'll kill us if we miss this party."

"Just trust me."

They left the letter for Frances on the table in the front hall, and Jack dragged Sippie out back.

"And where do you two think you're going?" asked Danny, stopping them on the back lawns.

"Won't take but a short while, Dan," Frances said, coming up from behind. Sippie watched a look pass between Jack and their mother.

"You keeping secrets from me, Jack?" asked Sippie.

"I wouldn't be fool enough to try that. I'm just now figuring what Serafina wanted from me. I still don't know why, but at least I know what."

They took his pirogue from Sorrow Bay deep into Meager Swamp.

"You gonna talk to me at all, or are we on a secret mission?" asked Sippie.

"More like a quest," Jack said confidently.

"You and those games of yours," said Sippie.

"Think about it, Sip. It's like . . . everything's a level. And sometimes you get stuck on one for so long it makes you want to shoot the game. But then, you figure it out, get smarter and faster, and that's the win that makes you want to take over the world."

Then, when water met land, they walked out into the shallow mud that joined up to a large meadow.

"Wait, no . . . Jack, I've been here. Not really, but I don't want to be here. Jack, we got to go back, please."

"Sippie, take my hand. This place, it's sour. Something bad happened here. Worse even than what happened to our family back in 1901."

Sippie looked out over the field as it grew thick with violets before their eyes. The small house appeared through a subtle mist and the woman hanging clothes.

"What are we supposed to do?" asked Sippie. A cool breeze swept up and moved the tall grasses around their feet.

"Hell if I know."

"I bet you'd know the next move if we were in a video game."

"Bet you I would."

"Then tell me what to do next, O wise one. I mean, when you think about it, it's like we been on two lifelong quests that seemed different but are really the same."

Jack's eyes lit up. "You got to go to her. She has something to show you. At least, that's the way it would go in an adventure game. This place, it's stuck in time. Maybe you get to unstick it or something."

"I don't know if we're even allowed to mess with time, Jack."

"If you don't want to," said Jack, softening, "you don't have to."

"No," said Sippie. "You're right, I have to. And I think . . . I think I want to."

Jack watched her walk across the field and haltingly approach the woman. A small toddler in a white dress began to try to touch the clothes hanging in the sun. The woman didn't see Sippie. Slowly, gracefully, Sippie stepped next to and then into the woman. Jack could see both of them, somehow shadows of each other, blurred in their movements. The toddler ran over, raising her arms. Sippie picked up the little girl and held her close, walking onto the small porch, singing. Minutes later a man came rushing out of the house, and Jack watched Sippie put the child on her hip while reaching for a gun behind the rocking chair. She yelled something and pointed the gun, safely away from the child.

The man ran off.

Sippie put away the gun again and sat back down in the rocker, playing for just a short while with the child. Then she stepped back out into the meadow, leaving the woman and child right where they were, alone, uninjured, and full of love.

"You changed the past," said Jack.

"I think there are many different pasts, Jack. And presents, and futures, too."

"How come?"

"Because if I'd changed the only past there is, I wouldn't be here. Simone wouldn't have left me, and I wouldn't have ever got to know you. So I guess I'm trying to figure out what the whole point was."

"Maybe, if you're right, you changed something in some other past. And now all that good golden stuff can slide on over here to us."

Silently, they made their way back across the bay.

"You okay, Sip?"

"I'm better than okay . . . that was the most wonderful present," she said, holding the opal pin tightly.

Sorrow Hall lay before them, a flurry of last minute activity.

"Look at them," said Sippie.

Their family and a bunch of lost souls who'd come in dripping after the storm were on the back lawn of Sorrow Hall, setting up tables and other fancies for Frances and Danny's "not-a-wedding."

And those two were fighting. Again.

"Didn't we just leave them all happy?" asked Jack.

Sippie and Jack could hear every word echoing over the bay.

"You'll never change!" Frances yelled.

Danny hit a table with his fist so hard, its folding legs gave out underneath and a vase of flowers crashed to the ground.

"You are the most infuriating woman I ever met!" he yelled, and then Frances ran off.

"Should we go over there?" asked Jack, his voice tight with worry.

"No, cha, wait . . . I know you're worried about them, but things be different now. Watch."

"Are," said Jack.

"What?"

"Things *are* different."

Sippie laughed, punching Jack's arm. "Yes, they really *are*. Look."

Frances walked back onto the lawn and stood behind Danny, who hadn't moved an inch. She leaned her head against his back. He turned, held her tight, then picked her up and threw her over his shoulder. Their laughter became the music that would light up the entire world.

Sippie looked at her brother again. Tears were pricking the corners of his eyes, but she knew he didn't want her to see. "It'll stay good like this, right, Sippie?"

"It will, Jack. And if it don't . . . I'm here." She put out her arm, and Jack leaned into her, letting himself soften against his big sister. "You know what, Jack? I'm learning that I'm even better at finding my way into things than out, entrances instead of exits. That make sense?"

"Sure it does, like levels in a game."

So maybe, we just need to figure out what new level we're on now. What's our new quest, Jack?"

"Well," said Jack, calming down, "quests should be about something you need, or something you lost in the last part. Usually the whole point to a new level is finding another piece of something you won after a battle. And in our case, we lost family, money, *and* power during that last level of *The Game of Sorrows,* right?" Jack grew more and more animated.

"So, what's the missing thing we need for this new quest?"

Jack stood still, thinking. Then his eyes lit up, happy and excited. "Magic!" And then, knowing what she'd done . . . how she'd distracted him, he paused. "You're a good sister, Sip."

"I'm trying . . . so, now . . . what level should this be?"

"Since we haven't been counting, let's make it level thirteen!" he said excitedly.

"Perfect . . . Welcome to level thirteen of *The Game of Sorrows:* 'Recapturing the Magic.'"

"Hell, Sip, that sounds like a romance novel. Don't ruin it. Such a *girl* sometimes. . . ."

"Got a better idea?"

"Of course I do. It's called 'There Ain't No Names to Levels.' You really got to play more."

"Let's not lose focus, we're on to something. I *know* you have an idea."

"Well, each time you win, most games give you a new set of tasks. So, how about this—" Jack took a damp, well-worn notebook out of the back of his cut-off Levi's jeans. "No, let's go back to the house and write it all down there. I hate it when the words get all messed up 'cause I'm not writing on a table or something."

"You are such a *girl,* Jack Sorrow."

"Am not."

"Are, too."

They playfully pushed each other as they got out of the boat and, teeming with excitement, ran up the back lawn through the maze of tables and people and waiters who were beginning to arrive from Tivoli.

"Watch yourself, kids!" Danny yelled.

They sat in the newly painted back gallery, and Jack pulled up a side table by the porch swing. He turned to a new, limp page and wrote:

"Level thirteen of *The Game of Sorrows:* 'You Must—'"

Then he stopped.

"It's harder than it seems," he said.

"Let's brainstorm, you know . . . think it through out loud."

"Okay, so we got to figure out the full extent of our 'powers.' Some may be hidden. And some need to be practiced. Like this—" Jack stared hard at the candle centerpiece lined with roses. It didn't go out.

"Or maybe, like this," said Frances, walking out of the house and onto the porch, and neither of her children could believe what they saw. She was ethereal, like a medieval bride with her curls tamed and pinned up in different places, lavender wound in her hair; a simple white cotton dress clinging to her.

Barefoot and shining, Frances Sorrow looked like what love feels like.

Then she glanced at the candle and it went out. "Now light it back up, and go get dressed, the both of you. You haven't been a bit of help today. I got lazy children. Who knew?"

"Yeah," said Jack, lighting a match and reigniting the candle. "We should start with that." He wrote down:

1.   *Reclaim the magic.*

"Go get ready! *Now!*" Dida yelled from the lawn chair she'd occupied all day just so she could yell at everyone. Old Jim kept checking on her, covering her tenderly with their very own "not-a-wedding" quilt, because she was always chilled lately. But her lungs were still strong enough to cast fear deep inside her great-grandchildren.

"How about we leave it at that, Jack? Maybe we won't know the rest of what we need to beat this level until we accomplish that first step . . . right?"

"Right. Now we better go get ready."

"I thought we *were* ready."

"We got mud everywhere, Sip."

They walked into the house and upstairs to their bedrooms, which were next to each other, sliding open the huge double doors connecting the rooms so that they could get ready and keep planning at the same time.

"First thing we gotta learn is all the root stuff," said Sippie, washing her face in a basin of water Frances left for her. Flowers floated on the surface.

"Dida will teach us," said Jack. "Should I wear long pants? It's hot."

"Just wear those khaki shorts," said Sippie.

"Look at this," he said, coming into Sippie's room. "Mama wants me to wear this white shirt, it's all pressed and everything. Got a note pinned on it that says, 'Wear Me.'"

Finally, all cleaned up and ready, Sippie and Jack stood at the top of the wide staircase. They looked at each other.

"Should we?" Sippie asked.

"Do you have to ask?" said Jack, and he slid down the curving banister to the foyer.

Old Jim stood at the front doors, greeting guests. When Jack made it to the black-and-white-checkered floor, he slipped, sliding right into a girl about his age who was walking into the house. Sippie slid down fast to try to help him save face.

"I dared him to do that," she said to the young beauty standing in front of her.

"No, you didn't. But it's nice of you to try and make him feel better."

"Well now, that's a fine way to say hello," said Old Jim. "Grant, Wyn, Byrd Whalen . . . meet Jack and Sippie Sorrow. My wild, godforsaken, poor-mannered great-grandbabies."

"Nice to meet you!" said everyone in one way or another, and then Old Jim ushered the grown-up people inside and through the house to out back, where the not-a-wedding was going to start.

The girl named Byrd sat on the bottom step of the staircase and put her chin in her hands. Sippie looked at Jack, who seemed, lost . . . under a spell. "What's gotten into you, Jack?" she whispered, trying not to laugh.

"Don't pay him no mind," said Byrd. "He just done gone and fell in love with me. And honestly? I'm sittin' right here just thinkin' on how I looked at him and felt all sorts of crazy rise up in me. I guess we just gotta grow all the way up and see. What you think, Jack?"

Jack just nodded, gazing at her. Sippie laughed.

Byrd stood up. "To tell you the truth, I didn't even want to come to this shindig. But with Grant and Danny old pals, and that other layer of distant Amore relations, I got curious. Now, I'm glad I came. You two got strange ways, don't you? And this house? It's got spirits. Too damn many of them. Seems like a lot of work. I like the saint garden, though. That your idea, Sippie, makin' those roses come right out of Mary's eyes?"

"I can't remember . . . maybe. It was a long, short time ago. A lot of things have changed."

"I know," Byrd said as if she were one hundred years old and knew everything there was to know about everyone. And by the end of the night, Jack and Sippie thought maybe she did.

The house and gardens were bathed in the bayou sunset as Danny and Frances made their unvows. And as night fell, the lightning bugs sparked in and around the paper lanterns and candles set out all over the Sorrow Estate. Danny had taken down the gnarled, overgrown wisteria trees that blocked the view from Sorrow Hall to the cottage where Frances lived. Now the saint garden and family cemetery could also be seen, and everything the eyes could look upon had some sort of decoration, lamp, or lantern, making the entire property glow with warmth and deep, rich colors.

The party went late into the night, and when everyone was finally gone, Sippie and Jack climbed out onto the roof of the back gallery and looked out over the moonlit night.

"I'll never forget that girl, Byrd. I swear, Sip. I think I fell in love. Don't tease me; I'm mad at myself enough. Weak. I'm gonna be a weak man. . . ."

"I once knew a weak man, Jack. And he was one of the best men I'll ever know. But, it's no matter. You're not gonna be weak. And you shouldn't forget her; this family has to stop forgetting everything. You remember her, Jack, and when you're older, we'll go find her. See, we just found ourselves number two on our list of quests."

Jack pulled out the notebook again.

2. *Find Byrd.*

"Hey, little brother, look!"

Danny and Frances were out on the small island in the middle of

Sorrow Bay, inside the lighthouse. The golden light from candles lit inside created silhouettes of the newly unweds.

They were dancing. And down on the lawn, under the moon, the Sorrow sisters, and Egg, Edmond and Helene and Rosella, they were dancing, too.

And in the shadows, off on the banks of the cypress grove, they both thought they saw Mr. Craven . . . who straightened his tie and crouched down low, drinking water from the bay, and as he stood up, he flew away, high into the sky. As crows so often do.

Epilogue

Millie Bliss's Confession
To: Frances Green Sorrow
Sorrow Hall, Serafina's Bayou
Tivoli Parish, Louisiana
From: Millie Bliss
Somewhere off the Coast of Ridiculously Freezing Massachusetts
and . . . very, very drunk.

Dear Frances,

I thought long and hard about writing to you. I thought maybe it'd be easier if I left things messy, like a nice juicy question mark. Do you remember when we were little and I used to tell you about how life should always remain a question? Well, I guess I'm breaking that rule. I'll never understand how it's somehow infinitely more painful to find what was lost than to live thinking it would never be found. I've decided to stay safely ignorant of that pain. I'm sorry for the suffering I caused you. But I'm glad that it brought you home to your magic, your son, and the love you'd thought was gone but was simply too hard to feel. I suppose it would be selfish of me to take credit for that, but I'm selfish, so I do. I never meant to hurt Jack or to steal away your life. I only wanted to borrow it for a little while and got caught up. If things had turned out different, and I'd had my way, I wouldn't have been brave enough to hold on to that kind of joy. You are the brave one. You've always been the bravest girl I know. And if it makes me feel a little less evil, convincing myself that what I did was some kind of backwards way of leading you home, well then . . . that's what I'll do.

Dance, Frances. Dance through the rest of your days. Love loud and cry, too. Kiss Danny in the rain. And when you get scared, trust the shelter offered to you. I never did, and look how well that went.

And on the off chance you ever want to throw it all away, there's this lovely little cottage on a remote island off the coast of Fairview, Massachusetts. The place Old Jim grew up, the place I was born. There's plenty of whiskey, and magic, too . . . a stuffy sort of magic, though. All controlled. I'm teaching them a little voodoo. What the hell, right?

All my love,
Your soul sister forever,
Even if I did try to steal your life. Love is love.
Millie Bliss

1. Throughout the book there are two narrative lines, that of the Sorrows of 1902 and of those living under their shadow in the present. In what ways do the plot lines and/or characters mirror one another? Do you think the present-day Sorrows fixed the mistakes of their ancestors in some way? If so, how?

2. This novel and Palmieri's first novel, *The Witch of Little Italy*, both use memory and family history and lineage to unravel the lives of her main characters, allowing them to find and understand themselves. Why do you think the author uses this storytelling technique?

3. All of Palmieri's novels have a narrative thread that focuses on interracial relationships in the present and, sometimes, in the past. How does this add to the complexity of her work? Do you think she is making a social statement? If so, how?

4. The author holds a master's degree in sociology, the study of human behavior. How do you think this aspect of her background informs her character development?

5. A major theme in the book is forgiveness of oneself. Could Frances have ever been able to truly forgive herself if Sippie had not returned? Why?

6. Frances and Danny have an intense but less than perfect relationship. How do you feel their relationship evolved over the course of the book? Do you feel like this was directly related to the return of Sippie? Why?

7. How do you think the evocative setting of New Orleans and the bayou contributed to the narrative? Could the story have been different if the Sorrows lived elsewhere?

8. Much like the Big House in *The Witch of Belladonna Bay*, the Sorrow Estate is very much a character of its own. In what ways do you think the "life" of the estate mirrored the journey of the Sorrow family?

St. Martin's
Griffin

9. In *A Farewell to Arms*, Hemingway wrote: "The world breaks everyone and afterward many are strong at the broken places." How is this reflected in Palmieri's characters and the things and people they love? Do you think being broken and then put back together made them more interesting, more beautiful somehow? Why?

10. As a woman of the church, Sister Vesta Grace is devout in her beliefs of what is right or wrong. However, when tragedy befalls the Sorrows of 1902 she is forced to confront life's ambiguities. Was she right to think what she did regarding her role in the Sorrow murders? Why or why not?